ESTATES LARGE AND SMALL

ALSO BY RAY ROBERTSON

Home Movies

Heroes

Moody Food

Mental Hygiene: Essays on Writers and Writing

Gently Down the Stream

What Happened Later

David

Why Not? Fifteen Reasons to Live

I Was There the Night He Died

Lives of the Poets (with Guitars)

1979

How to Die: A Book About Being Alive

The Old Man in the Mirror Isn't Me: Last Call Haiku

ESTATES LARGE AND SMALL

RAY ROBERTSON

BIBLIOASIS
WINDSOR, ONTARIO

FIRST EDITION

Library and Archives Canada Cataloguing in Publication

Title: Estates large and small / Ray Robertson.
Names: Robertson, Ray, 1966- author.
Identifiers: Canadiana (print) 20220144095 | Canadiana (ebook) 20220144184 | ISBN 9781771964623 (softcover) | ISBN 9781771964630 (ebook)
Classification: LCC PS8585.O3219 E88 2022 | DDC C813/.54—dc23

Edited by Daniel Wells
Copyedited by Chandra Wohleber
Text and cover designed by Ingrid Paulson

Canada Council for the Arts
Conseil des Arts du Canada

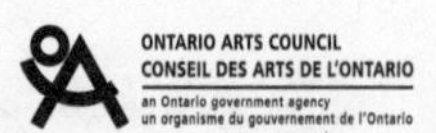

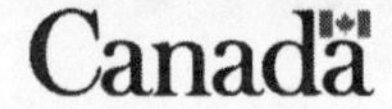

Published with the generous assistance of the Canada Council for the Arts, which last year invested $153 million to bring the arts to Canadians throughout the country, and the financial support of the Government of Canada. Biblioasis also acknowledges the support of the Ontario Arts Council (OAC), an agency of the Government of Ontario, which last year funded 1,709 individual artists and 1,078 organizations in 204 communities across Ontario, for a total of $52.1 million, and the contribution of the Government of Ontario through the Ontario Book Publishing Tax Credit and Ontario Creates.

PRINTED AND BOUND IN CANADA

To Randy Harnett and Tim Hanna

And all the other true believers at She Said Boom!
The City & The City, Pandemonium and Zoinks!

And Sister Patti McCabe and Eddy Webster

And Mara Korkola and the Ums

Til things we've never seen
Will seem familiar
—Garcia/Hunter, "Terrapin Station"

ONE

Brick and mortar, horse and buggy, say hello to tomorrow today. But I'm down, I'm not out. Not yet anyway. If readers won't come to the bookstore, then the bookstore will have to come to them. A virtual bookstore, with 10,000 or so more-than-virtual books, as well as full-on, full-time partnership with abebooks.com, the very sort of e-commerce marketplace that's one of several reasons why I'm in the position I'm in now. I miss having somewhere to go every day and people to talk to once in a while, but on the other hand it's nice to not have to wear pants to work if you don't feel like it. Or a mask. You win some, you lose some, it's how you keep score that counts.

But even if head office and the warehouse do happen to share the same mailing address as your house, that doesn't mean you always get to do whatever you want. Until every one of those 10,000 books that used to fill the shelves of the Queen Street West bookstore I owned for twenty-one years is inputted and eventually put online, every Tuesday, Wednesday, and Friday means my nephew Benjamin, and having to be up and fully dressed by 11:00 a.m. It's difficult to inspire loyalty and dedication in your staff while attired in a housecoat and flip-flops.

And today there's someone else too, Cameron, from something called Toronto West Social Media Solutions. The world, it seems, is increasingly populated with Benjamins and Camerons. At what point did parents come to believe that bestowing their children with three-syllable names increases their offspring's chances of being private-school worthy? My own childhood was full of Davids and Donnas, Julies and Jims, names remarkable only for their ordinariness. Of course, I wouldn't trust a nature writer who had never stepped outside, so my offspring-free opinions about contemporary child-rearing are likely equally suspect. Doesn't stop me from having them though.

The only child in my life is my mother, and that's not cruel, that's the truth. Or maybe it's both. Either way, it's not my fault, just like it's not hers. Besides, it's not so bad. Oh, it's bad—retirement-home, borderline-dementia bad—but it could be worse. Much worse. Mum isn't Alzheimer's-losing it—doesn't forget any of the really important stuff, least of all the name of somebody she knew sixty years ago, and the rheumatoid arthritis in her hands and feet and knees excepted, for an eighty-one-year-old woman she's ship-shape physically—she's just losing it. And seems as if she's having a pretty good time doing so. Forty years ago, she'd just be called dotty. What we call things matters. Words matter. My mother is just dotty.

Another hour until the doorbell and Benjamin, and an hour after that the person from the social media company, but I can't complain, I've been my own boss for a long time, haven't had to endure chattering co-workers or team-building exercises or casual Fridays for just as long. The mass of men *wish* they led lives of quiet desperation. You meet someone and they ask you how you got into the used books business and you say something about always wanting to be a writer or an English professor and neither being in the cards and always loving books and it just making sense and that's all true, but it's not the truth. Not the entire truth. I like sleeping in and I don't enjoy chit-chat and I could never listen to someone else's music all day at work, so I had to run my own business.

Not that every hour is my own until all of the books are online; I still need to periodically replenish the store's stock, the healthy red corpuscles of any respectable used bookstore, which is why I need widows. The wives of dead collectors are my bibliophilic blood supply. Not that there aren't women who are collectors themselves who die and leave behind houses full of suddenly superfluous books. There are—I've bought a few of their collections—but it's mostly men and they usually die before their wives and it's the widows I ordinarily deal with. Women, I've found, tend to be the better, more knowledgeable readers; men, the more conspicuous collectors. The widows call me on the telephone and invite me into their homes and I spend an hour or so sorting through a lifetime of fervent collecting before eventually making them a cash offer for their recently deceased dear one's lifelong labour of love. I don't buy textbooks, musical scores, or encyclopedias, and what I'm most interested in is literature (all genres, including criticism), history, philosophy, and biography, and, no, I can't give you a rough idea of how much I think your collection is worth without first looking at it in person. But I do buy entire estates, large and small.

Before any of that, though: a shit (hopefully), a shower and a shave (probably), breakfast (almost certainly). At fifty-two years old, you learn not to take anything for granted. Visit enough widows, you discover the same thing.

•

I used to be in a relationship—for nearly ten years—but then I met Jerry Garcia's guitar and good weed. That's my theory anyway. Debbie might have a different answer if you ask her, but you'd have to call long distance to get it. And she's a busy woman, be prepared to leave a message.

We both liked being busy. It's probably why we lasted as a couple as long as we did. We liked to work hard and enjoyed what we did for a living and appreciated that the other one felt the same way. We even met because of work. Debbie was employed as a paralegal near Osgoode Hall, which wasn't too far of a walk to my store on Queen Street, and she came into the shop one day and said she had to buy a gift for the head of the law firm she worked for who'd decided to run for Parliament on the Conservative ticket. I succeeded in suppressing the desire to suggest *The Idiot* and instead recommended an expensive first edition of Robert Penn Warren's excoriation of political power, *All the King's Men*. She'd seen the movie it was based on and got the joke and we shared a conspiratorial smile while I rang up her purchase, which led to an afternoon cup of coffee and then to a late dinner and then to sharing the same bed. The sex was good and she didn't seem to mind that I had books on the brain the majority of the time and it was easier to keep my toothbrush in one place instead of two.

We were born in the same year, but entering our late forties and intimations of holy-shit-I'm-going-to-be-fifty-soon meant something very different for each of us. Debbie grew up in Northern Ontario, on the north shore of Lake Superior, and was always after me to visit where she was from and to sample its bucolic delights. I went once—her parents still lived up there—and it's sublimely beautiful, I get it, but when she took up hard-core hiking in the shadow of the big five-0, however, she was on her own. She never made me feel as if I wasn't welcome to join her and her growing circle of hiking buddies—just like she'd always encouraged me to emulate her daily hour-and-a-half workout at the gym or to join her whenever she'd run or walk or climb for one good cause or another—but driving several hours somewhere just to be able to spend several more hours slogging across the Canadian Shield while swatting away mosquitoes and keeping an eye out for bears isn't my idea of R&R. Sounds more like punishment than pleasure.

Around the same time, I began to feel that, staring down my own half century, I'd earned the occasional timeout from human interaction as well, and discovered an unexpectedly effective way of simultaneously shutting out the outside noise while turning up the volume inside. Turning it *way* up. Headphones and red wine and the right record album had always been a favourite means of washing away a busy day of words, words, words, whether buying them or selling them or reading them, but marijuana took the cerebral cleansing of a full-bodied Chardonnay to a whole other level of psychic relief. It was as if I'd never really heard music before; or, I'd heard it, it was the same sounds, but it was like listening to them in stereo for the first time, each instrument clearly, magnificently audible in isolation as well as a participating piece of the greater musical whole. It was like learning a new language. And the best music to get the best value for your doobie was music made by Jerry Garcia.

Garcia's guitar tone, his instrumental DNA, was, like pot, a late-in-life revelation, was delicately, powerfully, swoop-and-soar sinewy and inimitably his, his ceaseless musical curiosity compelling him to eschew guitar-solo clichés and squeeze out the full emotional range of almost every note he played. I'd listened to rock and blues and hard country most of my life, and could appreciate a tasteful, economical guitar or keyboard solo as much as the next person, but the prolonged exhibition of instrumental virtuosity had always been something you waited to be over with until you got back to the song and the words. But Garcia's guitar had a personality; Garcia's guitar *talked*—was alternately thoughtful, playful, melancholy, anguished, ethereal, obstinate, joyful, bewildered, blissful, and oftentimes all of these things over the course of the same ten- or fifteen-minute song. They couldn't be any shorter. It would be like asking Monet to paint a pond full of water lilies on the inside cover of a book of matches.

Debbie thought I'd regressed to being a Grateful Dead–besotted teenage pothead. I thought she was mindlessly marching her life away. Maybe we were both right. You'd think, though, that it was the kind of impasse that two people who cared about each other should have been able to overcome by listening to each other and jointly seeing the bigger picture and by working out a mutually satisfactory compromise. You'd think.

They say that if you could correct an author's weaknesses, you'd also eliminate their strengths. I could have been more understanding of her need to reconnect with her woodsy upbringing. I could have cut back on the weed and the Dead and bought some OFF! and roughed it with her in the great outdoors once in a while. When she found a job in BC that would allow her access to mountains and ocean and miles and miles of unknown hiking trails, I could have packed up shop and gone along. But it's hard not to be who you are.

As far as these things go, the breakup was amicable. She took the job and moved west, I bought out her half of the house and had room for more books and music, and two thousand miles between us meant a fresh start for us both. The saddest part is that I don't think we missed each other.

•

After we split, I'd work all day, eat whatever takeout I'd picked up on the way home, and get stoned and listen to the Dead before falling asleep in bed watching YouTube videos on my laptop. It's easy to get lost when you haven't got anywhere else to go.

When there wasn't any her and me any longer—only me—I realized I really didn't have anyone to talk to anymore. Life is mostly just a bunch of things that happen, or don't, but a good story makes up for it. Reality is just the rough draft, and a story needs not only a teller, but a listener. Not that I noticed much. Aided by just enough red wine and a great big fatty and one of Jerry's winding, probing, silky guitar solos circa, say, 1973—sweet-and-sour satori with a wah-wah pedal thrown in to seal the deal—being able to actually experience what you'd previously only been able to read about in mystical poetry made up for not having somebody to share a pizza with or to sit beside at the movies. Warm oneness with the coldly indifferent universe; individual consciousness solemnly merged with a great big cosmic belly laugh; maybe not quite William Blake's world in a grain of sand, but certainly a decent-sized portion of that same shimmering world contained in a sustained E chord: in comparison, being by myself a lot didn't seem like such a big deal. Even when the world was in full-on COVID-19 lockdown, except for a chronic shortage of toilet paper and having to stand in line at the liquor store or at Loblaws, I can't say it made that much of a difference to my day-to-day life. It turned out I'd been practising social distancing long before the government told us it was a good idea.

I didn't do much dating after Debbie and I broke up. Or any, actually. I wasn't celibate, but what few next-mornings there were never turned into anything more. And then there weren't even any more next-mornings. Sometimes I felt like even though, all things considered, I had a pretty nice life, it might be even nicer if I had someone to share it with, but then you get busy at the store, or when you're not busy working you're dealing with sundry this-and-that connected to selling your mother's house and easing her into her new retirement community, or Canada Revenue decides to audit your already-struggling business, or...Like a lot of things, being alone wasn't a decision, it just happened.

When I had to shut down the shop because, even before COVID, sales had been declining for years (digital books, online-buying sites, the decline in interest in reading in general) and I couldn't afford another Toronto retail rent hike, that was something else that happened. Thankfully, the house is mortgage-free and the wine I drink is cheap and I can't recall having bought a new shirt or a pair of shoes since mullets were the haircut du jour. Between having to close down and box up and move several thousand books and needing to think about things I'd never had to think about before, like venturing into the world of virtual retail, I didn't have as much time to puff away the night and ponder the infinite.

And what do you know? Not only was I reminded that there wasn't anyone in my life I could have a conversation with, other than people I was biologically related to or ex-customers or a handful of neighbourhood merchants, it also turned out I was tired of listening to all Jerry, all the time. Jerry was still Jerry, the Dead were still the Dead, but even the sublime can become samey. I also suspected I might be smoking too much pot. I even drew up a list of pros and cons. As might be expected, the cons side of the page filled up rather quickly. The pros side of the page was slight by comparison: *I like to get high.*

So I've made a decision: less pot and less Dead; more red wine and more reading. More specifically, I've decided to teach myself

2,500 years of Western philosophy, all of the most important thinkers, the greatest hits of intellectual history. Like a lot of people on the other side of middle age, I've come to realize relatively late in the game that I've been so busy living, I've tended to neglect my life. I went to work immediately after high school, a stock boy at Coles bookstore, partly because I never enjoyed sitting in a classroom all day listening to someone else talk, partly because having a full-time job meant I could move out of my parents' house in Etobicoke and into my own place in Toronto. It worked out, I don't have any regrets—went from stock boy to sales staff to my first job working for an antiquarian bookseller to one second-hand bookstore to another until my own shop and *que sera sera* where did all the decades go?

But if seventy-something is my approximate expiration midnight—thanks for being born, Phil, and goodnight and please turn out the lights on the way out—my metaphorical mortality clock is coming up fast on 10:00 p.m. I figured I'm overdue when it comes to getting a better idea of who I am and what I'm doing here and where we're all going. Or at least finding out what philosophy's biggest and best-known brains believed it all means. Why not? I've got the time.

TWO

This, I wasn't expecting.

"So how are we going to do this?" the young woman in the wheelchair says. I'm standing on the front porch of my house with my phone still at my ear; she's at the bottom of the steps doing the same thing with hers. We both lower our phones and look at each other. She's wearing a white mask and black sunglasses.

"I didn't, uh…" I say. "I mean, the house isn't really…"

"Don't worry about it," she says, removing her knapsack from the back of the wheelchair and tucking her phone inside. "My bad. I remember now, you told me on the phone, but I guess I forgot that Queen West Books is a house, not a store." Zipping her bag back up, "Let's see what we can do about that," she says. "If you can just grab my knapsack and my chair and bring them inside, that would be great. I'm hoping your computer is on the main floor."

"It's in the back, in the mudroom."

"What's a mudroom?" she says. She takes off her sunglasses and sticks them inside the knapsack too. Her hair is naturally wavy and dirty blond and falls well past her shoulders. She's wearing black gloves without fingers on both hands, presumably to aid her in wheeling herself around.

"I'm not sure," I say. "These old houses, that's what they called the back rooms back then."

"How long have you lived here?"

Christ, I don't look *that* old, do I?

"We moved here in '07. No, '08. February 2008."

"I got the impression from when we talked on the phone that you're the only person who lives here," she says. "Because you said you only have the one computer in the house."

"Right. I mean, my ex and I bought the place, but I'm the only one who lives here now."

She nods a couple of times, as if it's best if we put the entire subject behind us, and pushes herself up from her wheelchair, her hands on its armrests delivering her to her feet where she manages to stand up by holding on to the back of the chair. Without the slightest self-consciousness that I can see, she uses the wheelchair as a makeshift walker to get to the wooden handrail at the bottom of the steps which she uses for support.

"Do you think you can lift my chair into the house?" she says.

Again: How old does this girl think I am?

"No problem. But what about the steps?"

"Just get my bag and chair and I'll be right behind you."

I place the bag on the seat of the wheelchair and give it a heave-ho and start up the stairs. I can hear slow, thuddy, but steady steps behind me and want to turn around to see how she's managing, but by the time I get to the porch and set down the chair, she's there too. I lift her bag from the seat and she sits back down and we wheel and walk, respectively, inside.

Where Benjamin is ostensibly entering the title, author, publisher, year of publication, and condition of book into his tablet to aid in getting the store's inventory online. As he's reminded me more than once, newer books can be catalogued simply by scanning their ISBN, but as I've just as often reminded him, older books, the more valuable ones, still need to be manually catalogued. By the smirk on his face before he sees me and the look of feigned concentration after he does, it's obvious he's been texting someone instead of doing his job. Just when you thought people couldn't possibly get any dumber, duller, or more distracted, along comes sage technology to bestow upon humanity the ability to effortlessly engage with one another over such timeless questions as *what 4?* and *what r u doing?* and *is she there2?* That I managed to avoid owning a cell phone for as long as I did is my single proudest act of civil disobedience.

Benjamin looks up from the screen like it physically pains him to be interrupted from his weighty labours, and I introduce him to Cameron and her to him.

"Hey," he says.

"Hey," she says.

And that's all it takes—to be approximately the same age. I can walk into a coffee shop, and if there's a geezer at a table sipping his espresso, we might not have a single thing in common—or, even if we did, might not like each other—but there's an undeniable ease of understanding between us merely because we were born in the same decade. The same songs, the same television programs, the same I-remember-where-I-was-when-that-happened stories: who we are isn't just us.

"The computer's back here," I say, leading the way to the small office at the back of the house. Over my shoulder, in my best long-suffering-yet-nonetheless-benevolent boss tone I can manage, "We'll be out back, Benjamin."

A U of T undergraduate who can't decide whether he wants to be a postmodernist poet, a discipline-shattering academic, or perhaps a beguiling blend of both *has* to have a name like Benjamin.

I get it, I was young and existentially amorphous once too: until we turn into ourselves, it's necessary to impersonate who we want to be. And Benjamin's okay. Really. It's just that it's the generational obligation of every twenty-two-year-old to be insufferable to anyone over the age of fifty. I'm actually a little jealous of him, and not just because he's got me as an uncle. He's young. He's finishing up one university degree and planning to go to graduate school and get another. His parents are rich. No wonder he gets on my nerves sometimes.

Almost everything to do with my actual computer we could have done over the phone, but it's Toronto West Social Media Solutions policy to discuss with each of its clients in person their various web-based needs, and to do it, of course, in as safe and hygienically responsible a manner as possible.

"You don't have to wear your mask if you don't want to," I say.

"Great," she says, taking it off. "I never know if somebody..."

"It's fine."

Her face is thin and her nose is the same and long, and she has what looks like a permanently furrowed brow, like she's been pondering some impenetrable riddle her entire short life.

Eventually, "I want to sell people books," I say. "My books. Over the web. Like I used to do over the counter."

"Right," she says, tapping away at her tablet resting on her thigh. I wait for more questions; she continues to tap. Looking up, "Have you given any thought to what URL you'd like to use for your new e-business?"

"You mean the name you type into Google?"

"Among other things, yes." She says this with a slight, tight smile, the kind patience of the younger for the endearing cluelessness of her elders.

"Queen West Books," I say. "That's the name of my store."

"The one that closed."

"That's right."

"Hmm..."

Hmm is the polite version of *Are you sure you wouldn't like to reconsider your answer*?

"Why would I want to use a different name?" I say. "I was in business for twenty-one years. That's nearly a quarter century of brand identification and customer loyalty." I impress myself with this unexpected burst of business speak.

"Customers who in large part don't exist anymore. Or at least not enough of them to keep your doors open."

What I need is a website; what I don't need is a Twitter-literate Millennial's—or is it Gen Z's?—cursory dismissal of the last two decades of my life. "I'm keeping the name," I say. "Whatever this"—I gesture toward the computer sitting in the middle of my desk—"is, I want it to be called Queen West Books."

Another partial smile. "No problem," she says, attacking the keys again, only neglecting to say aloud, *It's your money—if you want to waste it, that's your business.*

"And what about your social media presence?" she says.

I know what she means—Facebook, Instagram, Snapchat, Twitter, plus whatever other modern miracle I'm too old or indifferent to know about—but even if I'm destined to be only a virtual bookseller, I prefer the idea of spending my days primarily with paper and ink and the smell of old books, and not online chattering and posting and doing whatever else is cyber *au courant*.

"I just want to sell books," I say.

"Right. Which is why it's important to utilize every means possible to help you do just that. And social media is one of those means. We had a client—she sold imported glassware, so it's not directly comparable to what you're doing—but within just a month of putting together a fabulous Instagram page and a fairly active Facebook and Twitter—"

"I just want to sell books."

"And I want to help you do that. That's what you're paying us for. Let us help."

We're sitting at opposite ends of the desk in what's been my home office for years, but now is the store's small office. It might feel good to spew and spit about pandemic bad luck and philistine landlords who would rather rent out their buildings to child-labour-powered multinational clothing stores and to chic restaurants whose bills are as large as their portions are small, but it won't reduce your monthly rent cheque a nickel. Better to be honest and admit that the world doesn't really want the things it really needs and to just get on with the job at hand. Which, in my case, seems to mean playing squeezed-out roommate to a house crammed full of book-filled cardboard boxes and getting used to the idea of being a cyberspace salesman.

"I guess I could get my nephew to look into handling that part of things," I say. Isn't everyone under the age of thirty ipso facto a social media authority?

"Great. Maybe he and I can have a quick chat before I go."

Once we're done discussing for the day design alternatives and online payment options and what kind of "traffic" I can initially expect once queenwestbooks.ca is eventually up and "live" and linked up with abebooks.com, Cameron deposits her tablet in her knapsack and wheels herself into what used to be my living room but is now just one more room full of more and more books that need to be computer catalogued. Benjamin is on his knees pulling several volumes of the English Men of Letters series out of a cardboard box. They're hardback and uniform blue, and although none was published earlier than 1892 and there's some foxing to their fore-edges and ends and tanning to the pages and slight damp staining to a few of the covers, considering their age they're in overall very good condition. It's an incomplete set—the Sterne and Hume volumes are missing—but it's books like these that remind me why I do what I do and want to continue doing it.

Benjamin thumb-flips through the book in his hands, beginning to end, a long, page-fluttering fart. Although he's a skinny kid from the suburbs of Calgary who's never been out of school longer than summer vacation, with his black beard and the Mason jar he insists upon drinking his water out of, he could pass for a turn-of-the-twentieth-century Virginia coal miner. I suppose I should just be thankful he doesn't vape.

To Cameron, and still on his knees, "Can I interest you in a rare first edition of the White, Heterosexual, Land-Owning English Men—and I do mean men only—of Letters series? Did I mention it's very rare?"

For the first time today Cameron laughs. "Not nearly rare enough," she says.

"You've got that right," Benjamin says, snapping shut the book, and then he laughs too.

JUNE 19

—All of the history of philosophy books begin with the pre-Socratics, so here we go, Thales, sixth-century BC, *resident of Miletus, a Cretan colony on the coast of Asia Minor.*

—Aristotle said that Thales was the first real Greek philosopher because he was the first person in Western civilization to attempt to understand

the world not by reference to mythology but via theories and hypotheses and the search for first principles.

—Impressive: the guy who created science. Too bad nobody knows where he's buried. That would make for a humdinger of a tombstone epitaph. Everybody wants to be remembered for something—procreate a kid or two, get your name engraved on a plaque, sweat your way into the record books—and to be known as the person who created the primary means by which human beings have been conscious of existence for the last 2,500 years is a pretty good way to do it.

—My old store was a neighbourhood fixture for twenty-one years. Now it's a Gap Kids.

•

Zoran is my Serbian friend. He appeared in the shop one day and asked me if I had any books "about the famous author and poet W.H. Auden—full name Wystan Hugh Auden—the English writer, you see, who moved to United States of America at beginning of Second World War." He wasn't my most lucrative customer, but he was definitely the store's most frequent visitor. Every couple of weeks he would unfailingly buy a book—likely history or something political—but it was always as if he was paying for a parking space rather than purchasing something he was actually going to take home and read. He *is* a reader, but of newspapers; every morning, accompanied by his pug Tesla, walks to the corner store and buys all four Toronto dailies as well as the previous day's *New York Times*. Thales wrote that "A multitude of words is no proof of a prudent mind," but I don't think I'll tell Zoran. Wisdom shouldn't get in the way of friendship. Which just might be wisdom, but, being a bookseller and not a philosopher, I wouldn't know.

Besides, now that the bookstore is closed for good and the entire operation has been relocated to my home, Zoran is my sole in-house customer. I wasn't expecting him and Tesla to show up at my front door a week after the store went out of business, but I wasn't especially surprised either. He knocked, I let them in, and I went back to unpacking boxes and he went back to doing what he's always done, filling me in on what the world has been up to lately.

"This, I think, will interest you," he says, as he always does before proceeding to tell me anyway. I go to the kitchen to get the clear glass bowl I keep for water for Tesla, and Zoran doesn't wait for me to return. "This, you see," he says, "is the situation. Nine people in lady beauty parlour in United States of America shot with gun and killed—*killed*—by man who is one time married to woman who work there, and this is only one little article"—he squeezes the thumb and forefinger of his right hand together until they're almost touching to illustrate just how little—"at back of newspaper. Like man killing nine people with gun in lady beauty parlour in middle of day is..." He shrugs a so-what shrug and curls his lower lip and raises his upturned palms in front of him. Then he folds his arms across his chest and glares at me as if I'm personally responsible for laying out the foreign news section of the world's newspapers and the consequent media diminishment of American gun violence. The grey fedora and dark blue suit jacket he always wears only add to the severity of his expression.

I respond the same way as I always do, regardless of the specifics he supplies me with—"You're right, you're right"—with eyes on the floor, hands on my hips, and a few slow head shakes to complete the troika of concern. Satisfied that I've understood, Zoran drops his hands to his sides and shakes his own head.

"So," he says, clapping his hands—once, hard, loudly—"what is the new thing with you?" Tesla is used to these periodic explosions of sound and doesn't lift his chin from the floor, just looks at me with his bulbous pug eyes like he's also awaiting my answer.

"Not much," I say, using the exacto knife to slice open another box of books. "Not much at all, actually." It sounds like an evasion or an attempt at humility, but unfortunately it's the truth. I consider telling him about my crash course in 2,500 years of Western philosophy, but decide against it. What if I get lazy or bored or overwhelmed and never make it past Plato? Ignorance is bad enough; advertising it only makes it worse.

Zoran purses his lips and nods a couple of times, as if I've just told him I've been busy helping to develop a cure for cancer. Like most Europeans, Zoran believes that what I do is important—that I'm important. A seller of rare and good books is almost as impressive to a European as being an actual writer, the North American equivalent of being a successful defence attorney or a surgeon. I try not to blow my cover by saying anything that might lead him to discover that I'm not a cultural ambassador but, in fact, only just another struggling salesman. Too many days of just me, my exacto knife, and Benjamin, and it's difficult to escape the impression that your life's work has essentially consisted in locating, acquiring, and making available for resale a product that society would really rather not have. In Economics 101 terms: plenty of supply, not so much demand. But Zoran doesn't see me or what I do for a living this way, views my occupation not as an unsound commercial enterprise but as a venerable vocation. What the people around you think about you makes a difference.

Like the first time he came into the shop asking for a book about Auden. He'd read or heard somewhere that Auden had immigrated from Britain to the United States just as war was declared between his native land and Germany and the Blitz was about to begin, and Zoran thought that his conflicting feelings about leaving home around the time of the NATO bombing of Serbia (relief and guilt; excitement and apprehension) might be clarified by learning how Auden dealt with his own bemused move. I'm not sure they ever were—he's lived in Canada now for over twenty years, and I think he's slightly surprised to find himself still here and an old man—but he returned to the bookstore the next week and the week after that, so the biography I pulled off the shelf must have meant something.

When NATO bombs began to fall on Belgrade soon after Serbian troops were ordered into Kosovo to quell the independence-seeking uprising there, Zoran's son, whose business interests often took him to North America (what those interests were Zoran has never volunteered and I never pry, although I suspect the black market), decided it was time for his father to join him on an extended holiday in Canada. Zoran was a night porter at a hotel that catered to rich Westerners, so it wasn't as if he was leaving behind a lucrative vocation. One of the reasons I enjoy Zoran's company is because he has a strong natural antipathy to bullshit, which speaks every language and knows no borders. "Understand," he told me, soon after we met, "what Milosevic and those other murderous swine were up to—that, and the bombing of Belgrade, our city, our home—weren't the only reason my son want to move us here. Civil war and international sanctions, these are not so good for business, you see. Middle of decade of 1990s, Serbia has highest inflation rate in history. In *history*. There is time during these years when inflation is 3 percent per hour. Per *hour*. Everyone who get paid for job, he run—*run*—to turn pay into American dollars. Hard for you to believe, I understand, but believe me, at worst of it, my pay at end of week is worth newspaper and cup of coffee. My son, he may not be this, he may not be that, but he is good businessman." Zoran tapped a forefinger to his head. "Smart," he said. "In business-making way, you see. Very smart."

I didn't need italics for Zoran's words to register. As with most Canadians, aside from the occasional interruption to our culture of cozy consumption, like during a worldwide pandemic, history is something I've learned in school or read about in books, not something I've actually lived through. Picking up a copy of V.S. Pritchett's mammoth *Collected Essays* from a pile on the floor, "Now this, this is a serious book," Zoran says. He opens the cover slowly, reverently, like if he goes too fast all of the power and perception inside will evaporate. He turns each page just as carefully, not so much reading the words as inhaling their import. "This man," he says, "he is well-respected writer, yes?"

I get up from my knees and massage my lower back, retract the blade of the exacto knife and stick it in my rear pocket. "He was commonly regarded as Britain's best living critic while he was alive, but he was also"—I reach into the same pile and pull out Pritchett's equally gargantuan *Collected Short Stories*—"well-known for his short fiction." I pass the book to Zoran who stands there with a thousand-page door-stopper in each hand. He feigns weighing each collection and nods his frowning approval, the scales of literary justice in his ten stubby fingers.

"Dobro, dobro," he says, the Serbian word, I've come to know, meaning "good." Zoran may own a Canadian passport, but when he's especially impressed or upset or otherwise excited, it's Serbian words that are first out of his mouth.

"This is a good life," he says, and at first I misunderstand him, think he's referring to himself or to me or maybe both of us. "This," he says, arms extended now, holding each volume in front of him like a preacher intent on spreading the Word, "is excellent use of lifetime. You *feel* what you have done with this life, yes?"

"Yes," I say, because what else can I say?

Although he's recently turned seventy and there are chairs to be had if he bothered to clear them of books, Zoran sits cross-legged on the floor beside Tesla with both Pritchett volumes resting on his lap. He opens the collection on top, the essays, and begins reading where it falls open, one hand keeping the book in place, the other hand stroking the sleeping Tesla between the ears. I retrieve my knife from my pocket and get back to work. I try not to be too loud. I don't want to disturb them.

THREE

First the widow, then my mother.

Three o'clock, four o'clock, before, during, or after dinner—Mum is way beyond worrying about anything as trifling as time. Whenever I get there she'll be glad to have a visitor—as long as I've tested negative for COVID-19 within fourteen days of any planned visit—and she either will or won't recognize me, and either way it'll be okay, it'll all be exactly as it's supposed to be. A happy flotsam on a seemingly endless jetsam, and with three prepared meals a day and your very own fifty-two-inch high-def smart TV. People spend decades studying Zen or sitting for hours in the lotus position and don't feel nearly as cosmically content. Maybe the Buddha had incipient dementia. Perhaps the five paths of enlightenment are paved with progressive brain cell death.

Technically, Mum's a widow, but Dad's been gone for so long now, I don't think of her that way. I'd just moved into my first apartment of my own downtown—a tiny basement bachelor (naturally) on Bathurst near Dupont, $165 a month, utilities included, wall-to-wall mildewy rugs and perpetually gurgling toilet complimentary—when Dad dropped dead of a heart attack in the backyard while manning his prized gas barbecue, the tongs lying in the grass still gleaming with chicken grease when my mother came outside to see what was taking so long with the meat. My brother, Fred, three years older than me and Benjamin's father and an engineer working for the oil and gas industry, flew in from Calgary, and most of the people Dad worked with at Ontario Hydro showed up for the funeral along with the usual array of aunts and uncles and cousins whose names you have difficulty remembering. There was a reception at the house afterward and everyone ate macaroni salad and devilled eggs and bite-sized ham sandwiches, but the gas barbecue remained unlit and unused. I thought it would have been fitting to have a big final cook-up—liberate the freezer of every frozen, carefully labeled piece of pig, cow, and chicken—but I knew Mum wouldn't have approved. Too showy, too much of a production, too—although she never would have called it this—symbolic. She was right, of course, but so was I. I suppose it's no surprise why I always preferred books to life. Actual people tend to get in the way of the dramatic gestures and subtle insinuations and narrative arc that life so clearly requires.

Before Mum, though, 437 Wilson Park Boulevard and a recent widow, one who wants me to appraise and hopefully purchase her deceased husband's personal library. I don't make house calls without vetting the person who makes the phone call or emails me—How big is the collection? What kind of books predominate? Ratio of hardcover to softcover and what kind of condition is the collection in?—but once I decide that it's worth a trip, I get the address and directions and pack my notepad and pen and a wad of cash. And when I arrive, after inquiring whether they prefer I keep my mask on, I always ask if I should take off my shoes. It's everyday etiquette, but it's something else as well. This isn't just someone else's home, it's also—for the time being, at least—a newly opened museum of the recently departed, a glue-and-paper monument to who the suddenly, inexplicably missing person in question is. *Was.* As much as any emergency room doctor or extra-attentive mortician, an estate-appraising bookseller understands the tragedy of continuing to think in the past while attempting to live in its awful opposite. The person whose foot has been amputated can still feel the phantom limb underneath the sheet. Being dead takes time, for everyone. A visit from the second-hand-bookstore owner helps nudge forward the big hand on the clock.

I knock, I ring the bell, I wait. The widow pulls aside the curtain in the door and I say my name and she unlocks something then unlocks something else then turns the handle and lets me in. After establishing that a mask-free visit is okay, "Shall I take these off?" I say, lifting a shoe.

"If you wouldn't mind. It's just that I just—"

"No problem." I can smell the lemony fresh mopping testament to her recent widowhood, a mind at rest a mind distressed.

She waits for me to remove my shoes then says, "They're in the basement. Harold's books, I mean."

"Okay. Let's take a look." The widow nods and smiles but doesn't move, continues to merely nod and smile. As casually as I can, "And how do we get down to the basement?"

"Oh, I'm sorry," she says. "It's this way. The door downstairs is just off the kitchen."

"Great," I say, and I let her lead the way to the kitchen, to the door downstairs, to her late husband's books.

Where it's not any less impressive for being so entirely typical of some many of my house calls. Relegated underground, Harold—over a number of years, obviously—had slowly, carefully constructed a personal library in the truest, best sense, the cheap IKEA shelves and cut-rate parquet floor belying the singularity of the several hundred books almost filling up what could have been but isn't a rec room or storage space or a man cave equipped with an unnecessarily large television and electrically massaging easy chair. It doesn't take me long to determine that I haven't done my vetting duty and that I'm not going to discover anything special here—no rare first editions, no authors or subjects out of the ordinary—but one man's pennies-on-the-dollar ho-hum paperback Penguin Classics are another man's lifetime of spiritual life support, the best that has been thought and said as best as Harold Murray could acquire and consume. If I still had my store—my real store—I'd offer her a couple of hundred bucks just to fatten up my meat-and-potatoes paperback section, but not too many people are scouring the internet for a five-dollar copy of *War and Peace*. But I'm not ready to leave, I want to know more about the library's former sole compiler and custodian. Benign nosiness is an occupational hazard for a book buyer.

"So what did your husband do for a living?" I say, pretending to check the copyright page of a two-volume edition of H.G. Wells's *Experiment in Autobiography*, about as unsalable a used book as there is.

"He was a fireman," she says. "For thirty-six years."

"Wow." Given the circumstances, it's the kind of thing I'm supposed to say, but wow, it *is* impressive. Cops can get drunk and disorderly on power, civil servants frequently forget who they're supposed to serve, most schoolteachers' favourite subject is summer vacation, but all firefighters do is risk their lives in order to save other people's lives. The people who put out our fires deserve our *Wows*. Particularly if they also happen to have copies of *Ulysses*, *Mrs. Dalloway*, and *Remembrance of Things Past* in their libraries.

"He must have been quite a reader, too," I say, putting the H.G. Wells book back where I found it.

"Oh, he was, he was." Now she takes a paperback down from the shelf, but without bothering to open it, just stares at the cover. "He did a lot of his reading at the station, when he was on duty, but he always made time for it when he was at home too. He usually didn't even mind if I had the television on while he was reading."

Further indication that Mr. Murray was a fellow sufferer of TB—True Believer disease. He "made" time to read; he didn't "find" it. Also, the only other sound in the basement besides our voices is the steady hum of a dehumidifier, the basement-exiled book collector's best friend. Wit and wisdom and elegantly constructed sentences might not age, but the old books that contain them do and need our assistance to keep them dry and upright and out of direct sunlight.

The widow slides the book back into place on the shelf and runs the fingertips of her right hand over a long row of spines. "It'll be strange not to have these down here anymore," she says.

"You'll have more room now," I offer.

She readjusts a book that's slightly out of line with the others. She doesn't say anything.

Back upstairs I pull the roll of bills I'd brought with me out of my pants pocket. I don't need these books. I don't have room for these books. These books need a new home. "How about two hundred and fifty dollars?" I say.

"For everything?"

"Everything. All of them."

She looks at the cash in my hand. "I suppose that's why I called you," she says.

"Take the money," I say. "I'll have my nephew come by and pick them up tomorrow if that's okay."

"Tomorrow is fine," she says. "Any day—anytime—is fine."

•

A good start: even with my mask on, Mum knows who I am.

"Do you remember when I used to take you and your brother to the park and let you sit on the old cannon by the river and the two of you would split a cold-cut combo from Mr. Sub and I'd just get a coffee and it used to make you so upset that I didn't get a submarine sandwich too because that's what you were supposed to do when you went to Mr. Sub?"

"I remember," I say. And I do, too, for the most part. The park that was a short bus ride from our house in Etobicoke; the cannon with the plaque that was so old and weather-worn it was impossible to read; it being summertime and Dad being at work and the three of us eating our lunches by the river underneath the trees, and when we were done, when all our garbage was put in the metal garbage can, waiting for the bus by the busy road to take us home again.

I *don't* remember being agitated by my mother's choice of a hot liquid lunch, but it does sound like something that would have probably bothered me. I know that I didn't like it when all four of us would go to dinner at A&W on Friday night and Dad would get the Papa Burger and a root beer and Fred and I would order Teen Burgers and root beers (although neither of us had joined the teen fraternity yet) and Mum would get a coffee and a hot dog. *Phil, I don't like hamburgers and I don't care for root beer*, she'd say when I would complain that she wasn't doing it right, she was supposed to get a Mama Burger and a mug of A&W's world-famous root beer. My brother, with almost identical DNA to mine, couldn't have given a shit what Mum ate or didn't eat for dinner, so there you go, nature versus nurture and whatever else goes into making a human being making me the sibling who was distraught by the lack of fast-food consistency in the Cooper family. Presto, you are who are.

"Don't play with your food, Fred," Mum says, through her own mask. "There are plenty of starving children in Africa who don't have enough to eat who would be happy to have what's left on your plate."

I'm not Fred and I'm not playing with my food—the sugar cookie Mum insisted I take along with my cup of tea lies untouched on my saucer—but I don't bother to correct her. When she first began to mix us up and I would say, "I'm not Fred, I'm Phil, Mum," she'd immediately snap, "Of course you are," accompanied by a look that said I might want to look into visiting a mental health care professional as soon as possible. At this point, at her age, it's necessary to perform a cost/benefit analysis before attempting to set her straight on matters factual. Is it worth potentially embarrassing her merely to confirm which of her sons is which? Sometimes, maybe, but the majority of the time, no. One of her sons is here sitting with her in the residence's dining room and he loves her and she knows it and what's a little mental confusion between loved ones?

Lifting the bottom of her mask, then her teacup, "They say they're going to take away another one of my teeth," she says.

"Really? Which one?"

"Which one what?"

Edgecroft Retirement Village is A-1, top-shelf, grade A—hasn't had a single COVID-19 case yet—and doesn't lack for doctors, physical therapists, a nutritionist, a psychologist, or a dentist, everything the aged need to stay as healthy as they can and above ground for as long as possible. I know that whatever the dentist has decided is best for her is what's best for her, but just because my mother is eighty-one doesn't mean I'm not fifty-two and I don't resent my own traitorously decaying teeth. Crying when your chompers arrive as a baby, sweating and grousing and sighing when they yank them out when you're old: appearances to the contrary, the beginning and the end don't seem all that much different. You're in pain, you wonder *Why me?*, you get over it and get ready for what's next. Five minutes in the dentist's chair is long enough to remind you that we're all only minutes away from being scared, sedated, and sliced open. Safety and security are only popular superstitions.

"You're missing a button," Mum says.

"I am?"

She lifts an arthritis-gnarled finger and points at my shirt.

I look down. Where, yep, I sure am, the second button from the bottom, the fact of which only your life partner or your mother would notice and care enough to alert you to. "Oh."

"You need to ask Debbie to sew it back on for you," she says.

"Okay. I will."

"And don't just say you will. I know you, Phil. You're an expert at saying okay and then doing whatever you want to do anyway."

This is Mum's disease, this is who Mum is now: oblivious to the fact that Debbie and I broke up a few years ago and haven't spoken in almost as long, yet spot-on about what a lazy, scheming procrastinator I can be. She tends to forget the facts, she's rarely wrong about what's true. There are far worse illnesses to suffer from.

"See that one over there?" Mum says.

Not being an octogenarian and thereby exonerated from observing such social niceties as not turning around in your chair to stare at strangers, I move around enough in my seat to see the old woman that Mum must be referring to. Lunchtime is long over—coffee and tea and cookie time too—and there's only Mum and me and a few others left scattered around the dining room.

"Yeah, okay," I say, swiveling back around as nonchalantly as possible.

"She bakes her letters in the oven and wears gloves when she mails them because she doesn't want her daughter to catch a cold because of germs."

The old woman looks like an old woman—carefully coiffed grey hair; too much red lipstick; stooped, time-pummelled shoulders—not like someone who oven-bakes her letters to her offspring. But that's the point, I suppose: just because all of us look exactly like who we're supposed to look like doesn't mean we're not also capable of wearing oven mitts to the mailbox.

"I should let you get back to your room so you can take your nap, Mum," I say.

Mum smiles; raises, finishes, her cup of tea. "You mean you want to get going so you can go home and take *your* nap."

It's pointless for a fifty-something-year-old man to lie to his eighty-something-year-old mother—makes about as much sense as cheating at solitaire—so I just drink what's left of my own tea and stand up and stretch, wait for Mum to take my arm. She doesn't need my help, can get wherever she needs to go without me, but she slowly rises from her chair and entwines her arm with mine and we begin the stroll back to her room.

"What's it like out today?" she says.

"Nice. A little humid. They say it might rain later."

"I don't like the humidity."

"I know. You never did."

An old man in a motorized wheelchair chugs past us down the hallway far more quickly than he needs to, faster than he ever walked. We all exchange silent smiling hellos.

"It's nice to take a little nap in the afternoon when it's raining out, though," Mum says.

"It sure is," I say.

Mum squeezes my hand, and then we've arrived at her room.

JUNE 24

—Not everybody gets their own separate billing in the history books or in other people's memories. Even the pre-Socratics are lumped together as pre-someone and something they're not. Someone had to be first and that was Thales and then there are all the rest. Most of us are all the rest.

—Anaximander, also of Miletus, thought that Thales was on to something in claiming that underlying everything there's got to be something else, but instead of water he posited "the Indefinite," an embryonic substance from which all the elements came into being.

—Two philosophers in and already ho-hum, maybe he's right, maybe he's wrong, maybe it really doesn't make any difference.

—Next up is Anaximenes, the third Milesian, and at first glance he's just watered-down Thales (actually, he declared that, contra Thales, it was mist, not water, that was the fundamental element), but he made his own contribution to the discussion by suggesting that one element could change into another element.

—Good for him, good for the link of continued logical thinking, but man cannot live by scientific rationalism alone. This man can't anyway. Love, sex, loneliness, death: what's logic ever had to say about them?

•

"Well, in that case, if you want to do that, then you just click—excuse me." Cameron leans across me and taps the appropriate keys on my computer keyboard.

"Right," I say, leaning back in my rolling wooden desk chair.

"So," she says. "Do you think you've got the hang of it? I can write it down for you if you want."

"No, no, I'm good," I say.

"Great. You're a fast learner. And like I said, when we're eventually live the website will pretty much tell you what to do. It's designed that way. It's very user friendly."

"Right, you were saying."

"Okay then, then I guess I'm going to get going," Cameron says. Since her last time here, I've installed a makeshift ramp for the front steps. It's the first home renovation project I've undertaken since Debbie was around to guilt me into action. We probably could have done my little tutorial today over the phone, but Cameron insisted upon stopping by and doing it in person. She's a professional. I like that. She packs up her knapsack and slings it over the back of her chair and maneuvers through the obstacle course of boxes full of books into the front room, where I follow.

"Ready?" Benjamin says, looking up from his phone.

"For what?" I say. I'm surprised he's still here. He's usually out the door the moment his shift is over.

"Just a second," Cameron says, and I realize she's speaking to him. Meaning he was speaking to her.

Turning to me, "Like we were saying before," she says, "feel free to play around on the site, just until you're comfortable. Remember, it looks like the real thing, but it's not live yet. You can't do any damage." She smiles.

"I will," I say, smiling back. "Thanks."

Benjamin taps his phone a couple of last taps before sliding it into his pocket. "We should get going," he says.

"Okay," Cameron says.

"We're going to watch a doc at Cameron's place about the Belleville Three," Benjamin offers.

I nod. Almost convincingly, I think. Wrong.

Perhaps taking pity on my old-guy incomprehension, "It's about Detroit techno," Cameron adds.

"Oh," I say. "Right."

"Okay, see you next week," she says.

"Later," Benjamin says.

After they're gone, I briefly consider Googling what the hell they're talking about, but instead decide that I'm better off with my philosophy books and a bottle of wine. Twenty-five hundred years ago doesn't sound like such a bad place to be right now.

JUNE 29

—The bigger the buildup, the larger the letdown, that's the way it usually works. The parade of pre-Socratics continues, but the prefix-inspiring man himself is still a hundred years away from strutting his philosophical stuff. Whatever life advice the poster boy of ancient Greek philosophy has got to offer, I could use it now, not later, but later is where it's located, if it exists at all, so I guess I'll have to wait. I've put off being wise for fifty-two years, what's another century or so?

—Xenophanes is the first thinker so far who doesn't sound so ancient. He not only didn't buy into the officially sanctioned Greek pantheon of deities, he claimed that if lions had gods, they'd look like lions, and that it was no coincidence that Ethiopian gods were black and had snub noses. Xenophanes's skepticism didn't stop with religion—according to him, not only could we never know the "true" god, human beings could never possess real knowledge of the external world, and if someone did happen to express an actual truth about it, it was only accidental and there was no way of verifying it.

—Pythagoras is a big deal too, apparently, but in a way he's the anti-Xenophanes. According to him, not only can human beings possess absolute truths, we don't need to rely upon our eyes and ears to learn them. Basically, Pythagoras invented mathematics. How's that for a line on your resume?

—With his belief in the struggle between opposites which leads to perpetual change, Heraclitus took his proto-scientific conviction to some pretty far out metaphysical places. Most famously, he posited that this struggle never ceases and that you can't step into the same river twice, the only permanence in life is perpetual flux. That sure sounds like life.

—Hitting the home stretch now, there's also Parmenides (contra Heraclitus, there's no such thing as change or motion, only unchanging Being) and Empedocles (earth, water, fire, and air are four distinct elements, not aspects of a single substance, and "love" and "strife" are what make other elements possible) and Anaxagoras (each of Empedocles's four elements is present in all material substances) and Democritus (material objects are composed of "atoms" that are unchanging and cannot be destroyed, only reorganized), and by this point it's hard to separate the pre-Socratic forest from the trees.

—Protagoras is last on the list, and with him we're back to Xenophanes-style skepticism, Protagoras famously claiming that "Man is the measure of all things."

—Of course. But wait a minute: Really? Maybe. I don't know. Hey, I thought this philosophy stuff was supposed to make you feel good. Or contented. Or something.

FOUR

Experience would seem to indicate otherwise, but sometimes it's a good idea to go outside. When the sole email you've received all day is a notification from a bank with which you've never banked that your account has been frozen and a credit card number is necessary to reactivate it; when the only letters in your mailbox are pleas for money you don't have for foreign children with cleft palates, for the fight against abused circus animals and puppy mills, for the need for freshwater conservation; when your phone has had the audacity not to ring, not once, since yesterday: maybe a stroll around the neighbourhood isn't such a bad idea. It's either that or get started on Socrates and I've had my fill of wisdom for awhile. Isn't Aristotle famous for saying something about all things in moderation? I'll have to remember to check that when I get to him. *If* I get to him. All things in moderation, even optimism.

I'd always lived in the Annex or right around the university—it was Debbie's idea to head west once we were looking for a house. Roncesvalles had never really registered to me—and I couldn't pronounce it properly for years—but moving out here was a good idea. An older, mostly Polish neighbourhood, it was just starting to shed its new-immigrant skin, and properties were still cheap and four hundred acres of High Park were within a short walking distance and the businesses and restaurants and bars and fruit markets were inexpensive and unpretentious and there wasn't a single Starbucks or Future Shop or Burger King among them.

Gentrification is a bad urban word, but it's worked out okay for Roncesvalles. Undoubtedly you could find someone who was disappointed to see the disappearance of the twenty-four-hour coffee shop with the twenty-four-seven cigarette-smoke smog, the filthy laundromat with the KILLING A CHILD IS NOT A CHOICE poster (complete with accompanying picture of thumb-sucking fetus) hanging in its front window, or the Blue Flame Grill and its invariably intoxicated owner who, spewing his warm, sour-boozy breath, would usually ask, "How about I cook you up a nice steak with that whadayousay?" when all you wanted was to be left alone with your pint and the last couple innings of the Jays game, but you rarely hear anyone complain about the fair-trade coffee shop or the locally owned microbrewery or the specialty cheese shop that have taken their places, nor the fact that it's safer to walk the streets at night and everyone's property values have increased by about 300 percent.

Diversity is a good urban word, and there's a good reason why—I wish that the majority of my neighbours weren't so lily-white liberal and upwardly professional and not quite such obedient virtue signallers while remaining so entirely devoted to the twin grown-up gods of churning out children and endlessly renovating their already exquisitely up-to-date homes—but if you're going to get stuck with cultural homogeneity, it might as well include an above-average used record store, a made-from-scratch-on-the-premises bakery, and a health food store that has that wheat-free bread you like that they don't stock at Loblaws. Besides, there's the Lazy Rooster. Heraclitus said that the only constant in life is change, but Heraclitus never drank at the Lazy Rooster.

On the weekends (which are to be avoided) the clientele is younger, hipper, and better off than it used to be, and there's even a menu now that includes things like Cajun bacon caramel corn and Liptauer with Wasa crisps (whatever that is), but even after COVID-19 made it an outdoor patio–only proposition, at the right time of the night on the right day of the week it's still the Lazy Rooster, a sort of Polish redneck bar where its customers' tendency toward paralytic drunkenness and talking aggressively loud about things they don't understand are among its principal charms. I hadn't planned on dropping by, but it's the perfect recipe for a quick cold one (or two): a warm night, nothing to do, no one waiting for me at home.

"Well, well," Angie says, her usual greeting if she hasn't seen you for awhile, sliding a cardboard coaster underneath my bottle of Zywiec on the metal patio tabletop. Zywiec is the Budweiser of Polish beer, and is the beverage of choice for most Rooster regulars. You begin by wanting to fit in, you end up being an example of what to do if you want to fit in. I've been a Zywiec man for nearly fifteen years.

"Thanks, Angie," I say. Angie is as old as me or older, but is doing as well as anyone our age can—isn't overweight, isn't too wrinkled, isn't dead in the eyes from too many too-long days. She even wears the same no-fuss pixie cut she had two decades ago. It's streaked white now, but it looks more like a hairstyle decision than time's silvered reprimand.

"I don't feel so good. I feel like shit."

"I told you. That stuff is terrible for you. It's poison."

"You're supposed to take it when you're sick, how can it be poison?"

"Yeah, and now you feel twice as bad as you did before, am I right?"

Pause.

"I don't feel so good. I really don't feel so good. I feel like shit."

"That's what I'm talking about. *Poison.*"

I'm tempted to turn around and take a peek at who's talking, but I lift my bottle and have a drink of beer instead. The first swallow is always the best—so cold and clean and portending genial refreshment, both physical and psychic, like when you were a kid and it was the first day of school and your virginal notebooks were still unsullied by messy mistakes and sloppy handwriting and bored doodles. I set the bottle down on the patio table. Inside the Rooster, where we're temporarily pandemic-prohibited, the walls, the wood trim—even the ceiling—are shiny, real maple. Because Angie keeps the place so polished clean, if you're not careful, at the right angle, and if the lighting is just so, you can almost make out your reflection on the bar top. It's one of her few flaws as a tavern proprietor.

"Give me one of those things."

"What?"

"One of those."

"Why?"

"Just give me one."

"Why?"

"Just give me one."

Pause, presumably for *him* to give *him* one of *those*. I wouldn't care about the identity of any of the aforementioned mysterious pronouns if I was ensconced in my usual wooden booth inside and listening to my music, but the jukebox, which Angie has wheeled to the backyard patio and keeps at an acceptable outside level, is playing Bon Jovi, the second such aural assault in a row. Somebody's loaded it up with loonies, so all I can do is wait it out.

"Now watch."

Plop, hiss, hisssssssssss.

"Jesus Christ."

"I told you. That's what's going on in your stomach."

"Jesus H. Christ."

Now I *have* to turn around. In the middle of a small table identical to mine, where two men are sitting across from each other practically knees-to-knees, there's a highball glass full of a bubbling purple liquid. One of the men—judging by the pleased smile on his face, presumably not the sick one—looks up at me looking at the fizzing, smoking glass.

"Alka-Seltzer and straight vodka," he says. "And they pass this stuff off as medicine."

"Right," I say, without adding that you might want to double-check the instructions for usage, they probably don't suggest taking it with four ounces of straight Finlandia.

Right on time, "Do you want change for the jukebox?" Angie says.

"That would be great," I say, turning back around and pulling a five out of my pocket and smoothing it out flat on the table. I get my loonies and toonies, but before I can say thanks, the same man says, "Put on some kick-ass music, brother. I've only got another six or seven tunes left."

"You got it," I say.

I wonder what Socrates would do.

•

One for the road one more time, another chance for another last call, this time of the herbal variety. I'm down to a single pot cookie and less than a quarter ounce of weed, and I'm committed to not replenishing my stock at least until I'm done with my amateur amble through two and a half millenniums of Western philosophy. After a few drinks, though, I feel the need to slow things down and lower the lights and soften the music. Booze is good for yakking and screwing and saying and doing all sorts of invigorating things you'd never imagine yourself ordinarily saying or doing, but the pull of the unpredictable and the indecorous isn't nearly as strong after age fifty as just chilling the fuck out with some good weed. Fortunately, at times like these, I don't need to exhaust my private stash any further, I can always drop by Hidden Rec Room Records on the way home from the Lazy Rooster.

As expected, Alex—owner, overseer, and sole employee, in fact, of Hidden Rec Room Records—is still up and at it at 2ish a.m., fighting the good fight for personal irresponsibility and corporeal debasement in the name of record-spinning, scotch-guzzling, dope-smoking nirvana. He's in his mid-thirties, his only friends are a few other vinyl obsessives whose idea of a good time is all-day used record conventions and the local appearance of whatever geriatric post-punk band is coming through town to plump up their retirement fund, I've never heard him mention a girlfriend (or boyfriend), he lives illegally in the back of his shop and sleeps on a foldout cot he hides away in the closet in the morning, and it's a small miracle he's able to pay the rent every month. Naturally, I'm fond of the fool.

I knock on the glass door, he sees who it is and grins and lets me in, and I've got a drink (cheap red wine for me—the scotch he's drinking packs more punch, but I've never been able to stand the taste) and we're sharing a sneaky joint and he has to be in a good mood because he's let me select the next LP for the turntable. I don't want to take advantage of his rare magnanimity—it's his store and his weed, and you don't become an authority like he is without being more than a bit of a proselytizing fanatic—so I try not to stray too far from what's Alex-acceptable, which isn't difficult to do because his musical catholicity encompasses everything I enjoy (rock, country, blues) as well as everything that I either don't like or don't understand enough to intelligently dislike (metal, rap, electronica). I'm tempted to put on a copy of the Dead's *American Beauty*—it's only a cheap reissue from the mid-seventies, but no one's an audiophile at this hour—but I know that if enough of that sweet smoke gets into my lungs it'll likely be goodbye Alex and hello Jerry Garcia's guitar and what kind of guest is that?

I flip through the new arrivals section and almost instantly find the perfect late-night, well-lubricated solution. Carefully removing the disc from its inner sleeve—it only seems like it's part of Alex's fabulously large and eclectic personal record collection; in reality, it's just raw material waiting to be turned into rent money and grocery money and, most importantly, money to be turned into more used records that will wait to be turned into...Like a shark that can't stop moving, once a second-hand seller stops buying fresh stock, they start dying. I place the record on the turntable and lower the needle and take my place on the customer side of the counter.

"Jimmy Smith," he says, sitting up a little straighter on his stool behind the cash register once the music begins, the same place he's ensconced every day from eleven until seven, a wise and benevolent little musical prince perched on his throne. Alex is of below-average height with longer-than-average blond hair that I don't think he's ever bothered to comb, and he must purchase his clothes from the children's department of Value Village. It's obvious, though, that he's very proud of his thick mutton-chop sideburns. I only worry sometimes that his pencil neck will snap in two one day from having to support them. "The king of the Hammond B-3 organ," he says. "Great choice." He takes a satisfied sip of scotch. The entire storefront is glass-encased to better display the vinyl wares, and no one walking by is going to be fooled by our dirty, chipped coffee cups, but it's surprising how often if you pretend to be a responsible adult people tend to treat you like one.

"How'd you do today?" I say. I wouldn't ask if I didn't suspect well. Alex doesn't do what he does in the hopes of one day turning his shop into a national chain or retiring early so he can spend the rest of his life playing golf, but an especially profitable eight hours today is money in the bank for tomorrow's rainy retail day. When your occupation is selling good music to a world that is so often content with what is bad—or, worse, mediocre—it tends to rains a lot.

Alex takes a toke and passes me the joint; holds the smoke in and smiles a fellow peddler's conspiratorial smile. "I've had stuff in my two-dollar bins for years—years—that I wished someone would just take away. I mean, if anybody would have asked nicely, I probably would have just *given* them to them." I pass back the spliff and he takes another, if smaller, toke. "But it's the weirdest thing. Lately, like all day today, people have been coming into the shop and actually *asking* for this crap."

"What kind of crap?"

"You know, the usual two-dollar-bin stuff: Tears for Fears, Culture Club, Simple Minds."

"Eighties stuff."

"Eighties stuff, right. It's like it's been around long enough now, it's . . . I don't know . . ."

"Classic."

"That's right! Culture Club is now classic rock!"

He laughs, I laugh, but I can't find it as funny as he does. How could I? I actually remember Boy George and the other Culture Clubbers. Never liked the music, didn't buy the records, but I was almost a grown-up when the songs were inescapable and His Boyness's face was as ubiquitous as leg warmers and mullets. It seems that I'm now old enough to have lived through a pop band's rise, fall, obsolescence, and eventual resurrection.

"Is there any more of that joint left?" I say.

FIVE

Yes, yes, a hangover, yes, but that's the way the deal goes down. You receive emotional contentment and mild euphoria and a general sense of physical and psychological well-being; you pay for them all the next day with free-floating anxiety and generalized despondency and a variety of bodily discomforts. It's the free enterprise system of getting fucked up. I *didn't* fire up a fresh joint and dig out some Dead when I got home, though, so there's that at least.

There's nothing that can be done about dues that have to be paid, but you can control when the transaction takes place, and I could have chosen better. I've got to meet a widow in the east end at eleven forty-five and it's almost eleven now and Benjamin should be here any minute and a shower isn't a good idea, it's a civic responsibility. My spin-cycle stomach means eating isn't an option for the foreseeable future, so that'll save some time, there's that to be thankful for. Always look on the bright side.

By the time I'm out of the shower and dressed and have called the widow to apologize and say I'm running a little bit late and it'll be more like noon when I get there, Benjamin is on his knees in the living room slicing open a box of books. He's on time, he's doing his job without me having to ask him to, his phone is nowhere in sight. There's zero chance I'm still drunk and imagining it all, so good for him, the children are our future, it takes a village, any cliché will do. Speaking of which, he's also whistling. While he works. Is that a cliché or a song from *Snow White and the Seven Dwarfs*? Regardless: *he's whistling while he works.*

"Hey," he says.

I nod and continue to towel-dry my hair. "You're in a good mood," I say.

He smiles, shrugs, and goes back to work.

I continue to watch him unpack the box with enthusiasm, not only because of the relative novelty, but because I feel as if I'm missing something. I don't have time for this, not today, but I try to recall the last time I saw him and what's different now. The last time I saw him was when he was leaving here to watch a movie with Cameron. *Bingo*. He's either in love or got laid or both.

Still working the towel over my head even though the little hair I have left is as dry as it's going to get, "How was the documentary?" I say.

"What documentary?"

"The one you and Cameron were off to see the other night."

"It was okay."

"Did Cameron like it?"

"I guess."

"You guess?"

"I don't know. I suppose she did. She didn't say she didn't like it."

"Did you talk about it afterward?"

"What, the documentary?"

And he's in university. On a scholarship. What's it like to talk to a community college student, I wonder. One hundred forty tweetable characters and 127 to spare. "Yeah, the documentary," I say.

"Did you discuss it? That's what people who watch movies together frequently do."

"I've never done it."

"Well, believe me, they do."

"I guess."

Benjamin stands up, puts his hands on his lower back, and leans back to stretch; yawns, says, "What's your point?"

"I've got to be in Cabbagetown in half an hour," I say. "And don't forget to break down the boxes when you're done with them, okay? They won't pick them up if we don't flatten them out and tie them up."

And it's true. Every word of it.

•

The streetcar clanks to a stop and I get off. The street I'm looking for is where Google Maps said it would be, and I follow the rising numbers until I find the house I'm looking for. The house looks like mine—a century-old, semi-detached, two-story brown-brick job, but squat and undistinguished in spite of its relative antiquity, and virtually indistinguishable from its neighbours, a whole row of other turn-of-the-twentieth-century factory workers' lodgings built by some long-defunct company for its equally extinct employees. Old yet lacking distinction: I know the feeling.

I knock, the widow answers, I ask if I should take off my shoes. She's wearing a mask, so I don't ask if I should take mine off.

"Not unless you want to get your feet dirty," she says.

The house isn't actually dirty—no dirtier than mine—so it's a shame about the light blue headscarf she's wearing. Quick witted self-deprecation is as good an indication of intelligence and unpretentiousness as any, but headscarves on women elicit the same question as do men with goatees: Why? This likely means she's also an ardent amateur lover of the arts: an apprentice flautist, perhaps, or a long-time member of a local poetry-writing workshop, the kind of person who believes that films with subtitles are intrinsically superior to domestic movies because they have subtitles, you see, and aren't made domestically. Double shame: she's around my age, but tall, trim, and remarkably toned, especially her legs. She must play tennis or jog. And with eyes that actually look at you when you're looking back at them, if with a smudge of sleep-deprived dark underneath each.

I don't need to ask where the books are because they're everywhere. Two feet indoors and you'd be forgiven for thinking you weren't inside someone's home but had entered a small bookshop. There's an old red leather couch in front of the window and a matching reading chair on the other side of the room with good-quality reading lamps attending each, but otherwise it's hardwood floors and built-in, floor-to-ceiling bookshelves. Whoever he was, the widow's husband didn't believe in relegating art and ideas to the basement. I can see through to the kitchen, and there are bookshelves covering the walls in there too that I'd be willing to bet aren't filled with cookbooks. It's a sunny July day outside, but inside it's curtain-drawn dim and the air is rich with the familiar fragrance of old book dust. I could easily lay down my hangover on the cool couch and not get up again until the fall.

"So," she—Caroline—says. "How does this work?"

A motivated seller, time is money, let's get this show on the road: I like the way this woman goes about her business. Maybe she's just having a bad hair day, maybe sometimes a headscarf is just a headscarf.

"Basically, I just snoop around your house and eyeball your books and see what I can use. Then once I've got that part figured out, I'll try to work up a figure that makes sense for both of us."

"Okay, well, snoop away."

While I pull down books from the shelves to check their publication dates and editions and condition—many of them hardcover firsts and all of them in excellent shape, mostly history and biography with a smattering of literature, and all of them online-bookseller ideal—Caroline is busy in the kitchen washing a sink full of Mason jars. Some people are lingerers, like to watch you while you work. To them what you're doing isn't really work, you're just perusing their personal belongings which they're happy to tell you all about—where they purchased this particular volume, how much that one cost, the funny story that this one reminds them of that you might find interesting. Caroline doesn't do any of that—doesn't inquire every ten minutes "How's it going?" either—just continues to fill up the drying rack with more Mason jars. I'm surprised to realize that if anybody's keeping tabs on anybody, it's me on her. Then I hear myself say, "It's a bit early for canning, isn't it? Although I guess technically you're not canning. 'Jarring'?"

"Hmm... 'Preserving,' maybe?"

"'Preserve.' That's the word I was looking for."

Satisfied with our mutually arrived-at verb, we return to our respective labours, although Caroline hasn't forgotten my initial question.

"I suppose I am jumping the gun a little," she says. "It's just that the less I have to do when the time comes, the easier it'll be to get the job done."

"What do you usually..."

"Preserve?"

"Yeah," I say. "What do you usually preserve?"

"It depends. Whatever manages to survive the bugs and the squirrels and the raccoons and global warming."

"You grow your own vegetables? The ones you preserve?"

"That's the plan. If I bought them from the grocery store it wouldn't feels as... I don't know..."

"Complete?"

"Complete. That's it. Thanks."

"Just returning the favour."

I continue itemizing and calculating, and after Caroline finishes washing the jars she turns her attention to several piles of newspapers and magazines stacked high on the kitchen table. She's slid her mask down around her throat and smokes a cigarette while she sits and flips pages, presumably deciding which periodicals to keep and which ones to discard. Each time she brings the cigarette to her mouth and inhales, her eyes close and it's like watching someone swallow a cool drink of water on a hot afternoon. She sees me watching her.

"Do you want one?" she says.

"No thanks. I don't smoke."

"Me neither."

She takes another long pull.

"You don't see too many people smoking in the house anymore," I say. "Even their own."

"What's the point of owning your own house if you don't do what you enjoy doing in it?"

Good point, I think. "Good point," I say.

I usually bring five hundred dollars or so with me when making house calls, but after less than an hour it's obvious I've hit the jackpot and need more money. She's got what I need and wants to unload almost the entire collection, so I'll have to come back with more funds. I could send them along with Benjamin when he comes to pick up the books, but it's probably better if I deliver the cash in person.

After she immediately accepts my initial offer—a little low, but that's part of the game, she was supposed to come back with a counteroffer a little high—we work out when the books can be picked up and when I'll come by with the rest of her money. We're standing where we started, at the front door, when I notice the rejected newspapers and magazines on the kitchen floor and offer to help move them to where she wants.

"You don't have to do that," she says. "I can manage."

I sneak a peek at her long, muscled legs and don't doubt it. "It's not a problem," I say. "Besides, it'll feel, you know, more complete this way."

"Complete."

"Right," I say, and by now the two of us could win a synchronized smiling event.

"Okay, well, it's recycling tonight, so if you grab those piles on the floor I'll get the blue bin out of the mudroom."

"You've got a mudroom too? So do I. My house does, I mean."

"Most of these old houses do."

"Why do you think they called them that?"

"I don't know," she says. "Because they get muddy?"

"Makes sense to me."

I carry the newspapers and magazines—old copies of the *Times Literary Supplement* and *Harpers*—to the curb in two trips, and Caroline meets me there with the recycling bin. It's her name, not her husband's, on the periodicals' mailing strips, so I have to ask. "Your husband," I say. "He wasn't the only reader in the family."

"Husband?" Caroline says. "I've never been married." We've filled up the bin and then some, but she's come prepared and brought a ball of string and a pair of scissors with her. On one knee and binding the leftover TLSs, "Put your finger here, would you?" she says, and I do.

"Sorry," I say. "Partner, I mean."

"No partner either. Not for awhile." She pulls the two ends of string and I yank my finger away just as the string tightens and the job is done. It's a perfect knot.

"So why are you selling all of your books then?"

Caroline stands up and sets the newspapers beside the recycling bin. "Because I'm dying," she says.

"Oh."

"That's what I said when I found out."

JULY 3

—As a child it was easy to get confused about where God ended and where Jesus began, and now it's Plato and Socrates who need untangling.

—Socrates never committed a word of his philosophy to paper—apparently just hung around early-fourth-century Athens and gabbed with whomever was game—but one of his pupils, Plato, was inspired enough by his golden patter to make the recreation of it in his Dialogues *a big part of his life's work. Jesus had Matthew, Mark, Luke, and John and all the rest of them; Socrates had Plato.*

—Plato inherited his idea of a supra-sensible reality from Pythagoras, the concept of perpetual change from Heraclitus, the dichotomy between appearance and reality and the untrustworthiness of the senses from Parmenides, but his originality as the first philosopher to systematically

investigate the ethical and political realms of human experience he owed, at least in part, to listening to Socrates.

—Thank Christ, thank Socrates, thank whoever needs to be thanked. One more Greek with epistemological paradoxes on the brain and I might not have made it any further down wisdom's winding path. The answers most of us are looking for are bigger than the universe's innumerable hows *and* whats. *All of my questions are human being* hows *and* whys. *Like how much Dead and dope and delightfully brain-foggy solitary evenings are compatible with a well-lived life. Like why bad things happen to good people named Caroline who you happened to meet just the other day.*

—Pythagoras was on to the idea of universals a century or so earlier, but Plato's contribution to the theory was that there are definite ethical universals, which he called 'Forms.' According to him, there's a Form of courage, magnanimity, justice, et cetera, which here-and-now, in-the-flesh instances merely emulate. In other words, there's right and there's wrong and it's right or wrong for all people, at all times, everywhere. It's the thinking person's task to discover the nature of the various Forms of Goodness which will make him or her not only wise but virtuous because knowledge of the Good also leads to acting Good. When someone acts immorally, it's because they're ignorant. Makes sense.

—Then there's the cave. Everybody's heard of Plato's Allegory of the Cave. In The Republic, *Socrates describes a group of people who've been chained to the wall of a cave and facing a blank wall their entire lives. What they see on the wall of the cave are just shadows of things passing in front of a fire, but which the people chained to the wall believe to be reality, going so far as to give all these illusions names as if they're existent things.*

—This makes a lot of sense, a variation on the time-honoured belief that the majority of people have their heads stuck so far up their asses that they can't see what's really going on. Then Plato goes on to explain how the philosopher is like someone who has been freed from his chains and can see that the shadows aren't actually reality.

—This part's a little harder to swallow. Who believes that they're the ones chained to the wall? Who doesn't believe that they're that rarest of things, the one who sees things as they really are? Maybe everybody is free, maybe everybody only sees what they alone see, maybe nothing is ever really real.

—Maybe *is a big word.*

SIX

I've got a date. I *think* I've got a date. I'd talked Caroline into holding on to her books, but only after consenting to hand over half the amount we agreed upon for her entire library as proof of my commitment to paying the full amount once she... doesn't need it anymore. After we'd settled on a day and a time for me to deliver the money, she said, "That's dinnertime. Why don't you plan on staying for dinner?" A dinner date is just dinner, but it's still a date, right? Right. Maybe.

I'm shaving when my phone rings. I pick it up and see that it's my brother calling from Calgary. I don't feel like talking to anyone right now—it's been a long time since I've attempted to look presentable for anyone but book browsers—but if I don't answer I'll have to call him back and it'll just be something I'll have to remember to do later. And this way it's on his dime, of which he has considerably more than me.

"Fred. How are you?"

"I didn't catch you with a customer, did I?"

"No, I'm free. What's up?" He must know from talking to Benjamin that the only interactions I have with clients these days are of the virtual variety—or will be, once I'm cyber-certified—but Fred is a man of simple piety, and Thou Shalt Not Impede Free

Enterprise is his number one commandment. Fred already had two paper routes (before and after school) when I was still busy concocting excuses to keep our parents off my back because I'd rather lie in bed and listen to the radio and read Kurt Vonnegut than get a part-time job. He's also the family high achiever when it comes to domestic matters—is on his third marriage, this time to a woman almost half his age who's given him twin daughters.

"Not much. How's things? How's business?"

"Pretty good," I say. "Anytime you to try to reorganize things to this degree it can get kind of stressful, but it's coming along."

"Oh, for sure, for sure. And like I said the last time we talked, I was sorry to hear about your having to shut down the shop. I can't tell you how much I hate to see another small business go down the tubes because of high taxes and all the rest of it."

Actually, he can, and has, told me. Many, many times. My brother rarely fails to see the despotic hand of big government lurking behind the majority of society's ills, including the shutting down of his brother's second-hand bookstore.

"It was actually mostly because the landlord kept raising the rent," I say.

"Oh, you know, it's all related, it's all related. It's a damn shame, that's all I'm saying."

"Hey, how about you?" I say.

"Oh, same old, same old."

Same old escalated devastation of the air, earth, and water for the convenience of SUV owners everywhere and the swinish delight of oil refinery stockholders both foreign and domestic. But we had this argument decades ago when Fred moved out West and took his first job with Suncor. *I'm just an employee, I'm just an engineer, I don't make the rules, you can't believe everything you read about the petrochemical industry, would you rather we go back to travelling by horses and heating our homes with timber?* A quarter of a century later, only the details of the delusion are different: *Global warming is just a theory, without a strong oil industry the Canadian economy as we know it would collapse, that's just another part of the eastern Canada elitist agenda meant to...* The only argument he doesn't trot out is the only one that matters. Fred's my brother, and this is what he does and who he is, and he's my brother. The tautology of blood.

"I hear you," I say. And Fred hears me and I hear him hearing me and there isn't a whole lot else to say. Loving your family doesn't always mean having anything to say to each other.

"Anyway, look," Fred says, "the reason I called is to see how Mum's doing."

"Why don't you call her and see for yourself? You know she'd love to hear from you."

I can hear him frown three provinces away. "Because the last time I talked to her she thought I was you for the first ten minutes," he says. "And once we got that straightened out she spent the rest of the time trying to convince me that the staff was hiding her dentures on her."

"Maybe they were."

"C'mon, Phil, I'm being serious here."

Theoretically, whether in person or over the phone, Mum's conspiracy theories and occasional bouts of confusion should be things we jointly endure, but Fred pulls his weight in other ways, ways in which I, with my ninety-eight-pound-weakling bank account, can't. Dad's Ontario Hydro pension and the pittance the government chips in would never be enough to earn Mum a place in Edgecroft Retirement Village. For that she needs Fred's generous monthly top-up, and for that I'm grateful. Fading eyesight and diminished hearing and decreased mobility and steadily enveloping dementia aren't going to go away just because Mum's got a large, airy room with plenty of natural light and the food is actually quite decent and her TV has five hundred channels and the people who look after her are plentiful and well-qualified and resolutely cheery, but being comfortable while the ship goes down isn't a luxury every octogenarian passenger on planet Earth enjoys, and Mum does, and all thanks to Fred and the oil sands and the attendant environmental and health horror show fallout. In philosophical terms, I believe this is what is referred to as an ethical dilemma. Maybe whoever comes after Plato can help me figure it out. Maybe he had a rich brother too.

"She's fine, Fred," I say. "You just have to be patient when you talk to her."

There's a pause. "You were always better at that than me."

"You mean I was always lazier than you."

We both laugh. "That's not what I mean and you know it. And I appreciate you looking after her, Phil, I really do."

"Believe me, it's not me, it's the folks at Edgecroft. They're the ones who take good care of her. I just drop in once in a while and shoot the breeze."

"I know, but it's good that she has family there. I keep telling Benjamin he should visit her more often, but you know kids at that age, he's always got something going on, and it's not like I can force him, he's an adult."

"Growing up out West, he never knew her. Not really."

"She's still his grandmother. Julie and I have been talking about us coming out for a visit for awhile, but even leaving aside what a shit show it is to jump on a plane these days, we're finally getting the twins to sleep through the night, and work right now, geez, we're working on this new—"

"You'll come when you come," I say, saving him from having to tell me about whatever new environmental torture technique his company has come up with and me from having to listen. "Just call her and let her talk about whatever she wants to talk about. And don't try to correct her. She's eighty-one years old."

"Yeah."

"I mean, what's the point?"

"Yeah."

I look in the bathroom mirror. I've got a face full of white foam. Why is it that every time I shave—every time—I always use too much shaving cream? "I should let you go," I say. Fred laughs because it's the same thing Mum would say whenever she wanted to get off the phone with somebody when we were kids.

"No, I should let *you* go," he says.

"I'll talk to you later, Fred."

"I'll talk to you, Phil."

•

Elephant in the room, hell—this is Tyrannosaurus rex on steroids. But I'm doing my part to pretend that the person I'm breaking bread with isn't going to be dead soon. I tell myself that *everyone* is going to be dead soon. But everyone isn't anyone. *Caroline* is going to be dead soon.

Not that you'd know it by her appetite or her conversation or how she looks. Hearty, witty, and beautiful aren't adjectives normally associated with the terminally ill. When she answered the front door, she was maskless, and told me I could put mine away if I felt like it. She also wasn't wearing her headscarf, the light stubble covering her scalp a sexy surprise. Her lips weren't bee-stung plump, her nose wasn't beguilingly Roman, her neck wasn't swanlike long. There was nothing about her that was beautiful—she just was.

We're done dinner—a simple but delicious pasta made with tomatoes and basil from her own garden; crisp green beans; a tray of sliced fruit and good, ripe cheeses; a couple of bottles of Domaine les Yeuses—when Caroline asks me if I mind if she smokes the one cigarette she allows herself after dinner. I hesitate, but not for the reason she thinks.

"Don't worry about it," she says, getting up and grabbing her cigarette pack and lighter from the counter. "I'll just clear these away and step out back."

"No, let me get these," I say, standing up too. "And I really don't mind, really. I just..." I begin gathering up plates and utensils. "Just nothing. C'mon, sit down. It's the least I can do. This is the first meal I've had in I don't know how long that didn't require a can opener."

Caroline takes her chair while I clear the table, and I'm pleased we don't have to do the usual civilization dance for the next five minutes (*No, no, please sit down. Oh, no, you sit down. Not at all, please, please, you sit down.*). Instead, she lights up and watches me work through a cloud of smoke. "Let me guess," she says. "You're worried that smoking might be bad for my health."

I hesitate only long enough for her to laugh first. "Something like that, yeah," I say.

Caroline takes another long drag on her cigarette; holds it in, savours the smoke, slowly releases it through her nostrils. "I guess you could say that tobacco and I have a complicated relationship."

"Maybe you two need to see a therapist."

Caroline smiles. "I think a separation is more likely." She takes a last, hard pull before stubbing out the cigarette in the middle of a large glass ashtray. There's more than half of it left and it looks lonely, all dressed up in red lipstick and nowhere to go. "A permanent separation."

I rinse and rack the dishes while the jazz station on the radio plays. I'm glad to have something to do and that we've got something to pay attention to because for the first time tonight I don't know what to say next and Caroline doesn't appear inclined to pick up the conversational slack. The song on the radio sounds like it was made by a trio—just piano, bass, drums—and isn't jumpy jittery like a lot of jazz, which is one of the reasons I've never been much of a fan. Jumpy jittery is the human condition—who needs their very own nervous soundtrack? But this is lively without being frenzied, energizing without being overpowering, open-ended but not anarchic. "Who is this?" I say.

"No idea," Caroline says. "Do you like it?"

"Yeah, I do, actually."

"Then what more do you need to know?"

I could disagree—there is an argument to be made—but that would mean talking over the music. We both listen in silence until the tune is over and the announcer informs us that it's the Bill Evans Trio that we were hearing, that the drummer was Paul Motian and the bassist Scott LaFaro, and that the album is called *Sunday at the Village Vanguard*.

"And now you know," Caroline says.

"And now I know."

"Feel better?"

"A little, yeah."

"Why?"

I wipe my hands on the dishtowel hanging from the oven door handle and sit back down at the table. "I don't know," I say. "Maybe it's a bookseller thing. Maybe because if I know who it is and what it's called, it's more real. More permanent. I'm not sure."

Caroline looks at the extinguished cigarette in the ashtray. "'Permanence' isn't a word that carries a whole lot of weight with me these days."

"Sorry, I was just—"

She puts her hand on top of mine. "Don't apologize. *Please.* One of the reasons I seem to be spending even more time alone these days than usual is because I can't stand people being so careful around me. If *I* can deal with it, everybody else should too. It's not my favourite topic, but I'm not going to stop living the way I've always lived just because I'm going to die." Caroline picks the cigarette out of the ashtray and relights it.

"I was taking a taxi once," she says, inhaling, "and I had one of those cab drivers who just lives to talk to his passengers. You know the type: the kind of guy who no matter what he ended up doing for a living would need to talk to people all day. I don't remember how we got on the subject, but he started talking about his children—he was born in Syria, I think, but all his kids were born and raised here—and he was crazy proud of all of them, but the one he talked about the most was his oldest daughter. He said that when she graduated from medical school he wanted to get her a graduation gift that was worthy of what she accomplished, but what she wanted most, he said, was for him to quit smoking. What a kid, he said, like he still couldn't believe it. Here she was, on top of the world, it was supposed to be all about her, and all she could think about was her old man's health."

The radio is playing music again, solo piano this time—tinkling, shimmering notes—soft but distinct. "He got me," she says. "I was all warm and fuzzy. Immigrant success story, a child's love for her parent, the whole shebang. So I asked him, "Did you stop smoking?" And he says yeah, he hadn't touched a cigarette in six years. But he didn't sound like most people do when they manage to finally quit cigarettes or booze or drugs or whatever. You know—proud and kind of born-again, sort of in-your-face about it. He did what his kid asked him to do, but when I asked him if he ever missed it, he said that no matter what else had been going on in his life, no matter how bad or boring or however things were, part of him knew that every twenty minutes something good was going to happen, something he knew he was going to enjoy."

"A fresh cigarette."

"A fresh cigarette. Every twenty minutes you're awake, you're guaranteed a little piece of happiness."

It was still light out when we sat down to dinner, but the room has grown dim. Someone should get up and turn on a light.

"There isn't any dessert," she says.

"That's okay. I never eat it."

"I do. I love it. I mean, I did. Sweet stuff doesn't seem to agree with me anymore. It just started to be like that one day, and now I can't. My doctor says the disease and the drugs I take affect everybody differently."

"Maybe you'll be able to just as suddenly as you couldn't."

Caroline stands up and clicks on a small lamp on the top of the refrigerator, next to the radio. With her back to me, "Maybe," she says.

•

I come home and pour myself a glass of wine I don't need and take it into the living room, where I turn off all of the lights except for a dim single floor lamp standing next to my easy chair. With books stacked on almost every available surface, there's not a lot of room for living anymore, but so far I've managed to keep the stereo and my small record collection from being entirely entombed with store stock. First pressings of LPs are original artifacts and exert some of the same coveting and collecting charms as books (which is why I've asked Alex, if he comes across any original Grateful Dead pressings up to and including the *Blues for Allah* album, to please not sell them but to save them for me), but a lack of space and disposable income aren't the only reasons I've managed to keep my vinyl collection down to a perfectly reasonable hundred or so records.

To listen to the Dead, the real Dead, you have to listen to them live, and at twenty minutes, tops, to an LP side, that's usually not a big-enough canvas for Jerry to paint his pictures. To properly appreciate Jerry Garcia, you have to either go the bootleg route or stock up on Dick's Picks or Dave's Picks or Road Trips or Pure Jerrys or any of the other posthumously released, officially sanctioned band and solo concert recordings. Upstairs in my bedroom, where I used to do the majority of my Jerry-gorging in a comfortable chair by the window overlooking the front yard, I've got a lot of them.

I don't feel like listening to the Dead tonight, though—I don't know *what* I feel like listening to—but their *Wake of the Flood* album is already on the turntable, so I blow on the needle and place the toner arm on the record. I pull on the headphones and sit in my chair and take a drink. By the time the last track on side one, "Stella Blue," spins around, I'm ready for glass number two and the record's other side. Because I'm being, by my definition, a reasonably responsible human being, however, and only getting drunk and not stoned, and am downstairs and not upstairs disappearing inside something appropriately lively lovely live, time has not, unfortunately, become a highly contestable human-made construct, and living and dying do not appear as simply different sides of the same cosmic coin flip we like to call life.

More wine, more Dead, and then side two is over and it's time to change records. I decide to go to bed and try to read instead. It's nearly midnight. Too bad. I'm not the texting type and it's too late to call Caroline and tell her I had a good time tonight.

SEVEN

What else to do when you like a girl but tell your mother about it? Actually, I never have before and I wouldn't be doing it now except that, given the state of Mum's mind, even if it does compute that her fifty-two-year-old son is gabbing away about his somnambulistic love life, chances are the data will be wiped clean the next time I come to visit. Queenwestbooks.ca officially goes online tomorrow and I'll have abebooks.com up and ready to go as well, so I've got computers on the brain. That, and the first woman whose company I've enjoyed and who I'm physically attracted to in a long time. A woman who apparently isn't going to be around for a long time. I could go to the Lazy Rooster and tell the stranger sitting at the patio table next to me about it, but Mum needs the company and it's not as if we share an abundance of mutual interests.

"She grew up and went to university in Halifax," I say, "but she moved to Toronto about ten years ago because she said she got tired of looking at the same people and at the same buildings. How neat is that, right? She was a mailwoman. Before she got sick."

"You can't be a mailman and be sick," Mum says. "Neither rain nor shine nor..." She stares at the red-lit EXIT sign at the other end of the lounge where we're sitting. Neither of us is in a hurry to complete the motto of the United States Postal Service. These days, fragments are just fine, the episodic is perfectly all right, the incomplete is entirely sufficient. If we were his students, Aristotle would probably fail us, but we manage to say what we have to say anyhow.

"A government job," Mum says, back from wherever she was. "Government workers get good pensions. You don't have a pension. You never worked for the government."

"Hey, take it easy on your kid, okay? And if you recall, you never had a government job either."

"Don't be ridiculous," she says. "I was married to your father. I was you and your brother's mother." If I didn't know any better I'd say she looked just like a sad old lady remembering who she used to be before she was a sad old lady remembering who she used to be. I lean over in my chair and give her a hug.

"You were a good mum," I say. Wincing at my use of the past tense, I linger, hug her harder, say, "You're the best mum anybody could ask for."

"You're hurting me, Phil," she says, pulling away.

I sit there watching my mother massage her left shoulder. "Sorry, Mum."

"You've got to be more careful," she says. "You forget, I'm fifty-two years old."

"I know. I'm sorry." I lay my hand, carefully, on her knee.

"It's all right," she says, patting my hand. "When you get to be my age, you'll see, nothing is like it used to be."

•

The bus that takes me from Mum's place to the subway station that will take me home passes by what used to be fields but is now something called Russell Estates, the numbing architectural effrontery of which is thankfully mostly obscured by a very tall grey metal fence bearing an enormous sign providing the usual enticement: IF YOU LIVED HERE, YOU'D BE HOME BY NOW. If I lived here, I'd be dead by now, either of a self-inflicted gunshot wound or from a prolonged, withering depression. I grew up in the suburbs and it was okay, it was fine, when I was a kid. Safe, abundant backyards and bright plastic toys, plenty of other kids to play with. But unless your idea of civilization is an extra-large garage where there's plenty of room for not only two cars, but also a riding lawnmower, a leaf blower, *and* a snow blower, as well as a treadmill or an exercise bike that's doomed to spend the majority of its existence as an expensive coat rack, suburbia is something best remembered dimly. Real men don't mow.

There were three million people living in Toronto when I moved here thirty-three years ago. Now there are over six million and the number is expected to rise to eight million by the time I'm Mum's age. It's better now (greater diversity, more things to do and places to go, more and more varied opportunities), it's worse now (louder, denser, more expensive), it is what it is. You can't beat city hall and you can't stop people from procreating, even if the planet plainly doesn't need them to. Every year, tens of thousands of wretched refugees are desperate for somewhere, anywhere, merely livable to call home, and for all the indifference and irritation, for all the honest concern and concerted action, no one mentions the most obvious solution: stop making more people. I doubt if Aristotle had anything to say about birth control and sane social planning. Too bad.

Besides, a bigger, better city doesn't mean a whole lot once you've reached my age. There's a new cider bar opening up on Roncesvalles where there used to be a Polish deli—evidence, I suppose, that the neighbourhood is condo-growing enough that someone believes they can make a go of it selling nothing but something I've never had before—but I'm not about to become a late-in-life cider connoisseur any more than I'm likely to turn into a regular at the new skateboard shop or the graphic novel store. New Toronto is for new people. And that's okay. I was them once, just like one day they'll be me now.

The bus pulls into the Royal York subway station. Twenty more minutes and I'll be home.

JULY 11

—Act 3 of the big three: Aristotle. Socrates said it, Plato wrote it, Aristotle read it and said, "Yes, but . . ."

—Just like Plato was Socrates's pupil, Aristotle studied with Plato. After his teacher's death in 347 BC, he left Athens and was Alexander the Great's tutor for awhile, which goes to show that sometimes everyone has to do what they've got to do to pay the bills and put olive oil on the table. A few years later he was back in Athens setting up his own university, the Lyceum, and it's basically his lecture notes that constitute his surviving writings. Plato's Dialogues *are lively and witty and surprisingly entertaining; Aristotle's prose reads like lecture notes.*

—Aristotle had a lot to say about, among other things, the difference between form and matter, actuality and potential, and the causes of existence, and some of it actually means something even if you're not cramming for a philosophy exam. Like his contention that the soul can't exist independent from the body any more than the form of a table can exist independently from the actual table, meaning that when your body is dead, so is your soul, your personality, you.

—Aristotle didn't just deviate from Plato metaphysically, he also rejected the latter's ethical belief in the concept of "Good" as something supra-sensibly real. Instead, "Good" must be defined with reference to the function of the thing called good. Just as a good bucket is a bucket which performs the proper function of a bucket (i.e., hold water), a good person is someone who performs the proper function of human beings—the thing it can do best and which distinguishes it from the rest of the animals—namely, think. Therefore, the good life is the life consisting of actions which involve thought.

—When you're dead you're dead and the purpose of life is to use your inimitable reasoning ability to conclude that, among things, when you're dead you're dead.

—I don't like it. Aristotle might be right, but I don't like it. Which isn't a reasoned critique, I understand. But I still don't like it.

•

"That's it?" I say.

"That's it," Cameron says.

"You mean we're good?"

"You're good."

I continue to stare at the computer screen. "So . . . now I just . . . ?"

"You got it," Cameron says. "Now you just wait. For either a notification from abebooks.com that someone wants to buy something or from someone who's interested in something they've found on your website. Plus whatever inquiries or action you get in response to what Benjamin's been up to on social media."

"I feel nervous. I feel really nervous."

"C'mon, you've been doing this your whole life."

"Not like this I haven't." We're both staring at my new homepage. Is this the beginning of my new life? I'll have to buy a porta-potty and a mini-fridge and sleep at my desk, existing only for cyber notification that my human packing-and-posting services are required.

"You used to wait around your shop for somebody to come in, right?" she says. "It's no different. And now you don't have to vacuum up after them or put up with any windbag time wasters."

"In the shop I could at least keep busy," I say. "I didn't just sit and stare at the door waiting for it to open."

"This—your house—*is* your shop now. Be as busy as you want to be. Your virtual store's not going anywhere. And now you know how easy it is to check if there's an inquiry or an order. A watched website doesn't boil."

"Mixed metaphors never helped anybody."

"Put your computer to sleep and go do whatever you need to do. Or whatever you just feel like doing. Anyway, walk away from the computer. That's the kind of sound professional advice you're paying us for, so listen to me: walk away. That's an order." She places her hands on the wheels of her chair. "Or roll away."

Speaking of paying, I owe Cameron money, so I grab the chequebook out of the desk's middle drawer and follow her into the living room. Which, for the first time since the store shut down and its books were relocated here, somewhat resembles somewhere where someone might actually live, as opposed to an obscenely chaotic stockroom where they try not to get lost. The basement is large enough that a lot of the books can go down there, so the goal has been to fill every room of the house with the overflow without walling me in and making it impossible to locate a door or a window. There's more cataloguing and organizing to do—you think you're done, you're never done—but this is the new Queen West

Books. Although it's not on Queen Street West. Although it's not really anywhere. Although there aren't any customers.

"Who do I make this out to again?" I've got the chequebook balanced on top of a stack of sturdy hardcovers, a complete set of the ninth edition of the *Encyclopedia Britannica*, the one that has Thomas Huxley writing on Darwin, Swinburne discussing Keats, and William Morris laying out the history of mural decoration. There's not much chance anyone will ever buy it, but it's the rarest and well over a hundred years old and I'm using it as makeshift office equipment in order to pay my website designer. If there's such a thing as bibliophilic sin, I've just committed it.

"Toronto West Social Media Solutions," Cameron says. "Or TWSMS. Either one."

"Right, right," I say, scribbling down the name. I fill in the rest of the cheque and sign it and date it and eyeball it one last time before handing it over. "I guess this is the last one," I say.

She slips it into her knapsack without bothering to look at it. "Yep, you're all paid up. Assuming your cheque doesn't bounce."

"Oh, I plan on being long gone by the time the truth gets out."

"Any place in particular you're thinking of hiding?"

"Can't decide. Either Hawaii or Tahiti."

"I don't think so," Cameron says, shaking her head.

"You don't think I have it in me?"

"To sneak off and hide from the world? Absolutely. I just can't picture you someplace really hot. You don't seem like the beach type."

"That's true," I say. "I'd be more likely to hide in my own basement, right under everyone's noses."

"Except you can't. You don't have room anymore."

"Hey, not cool," I say. "Once you start fantasizing, you can't switch back to reality."

"Oh, right, sorry. We'll put you back living in your basement then."

"No, that wouldn't work either."

"Why not?"

"I'd be my own landlord. And everyone has a responsibility to dislike their landlord. It's in the standard landlord-tenant contract. I know what kind of asshole I can be. I just couldn't take all that hostility."

Cameron manages to simultaneously laugh and check her phone. Then she's tapping away and I know I've lost her. The call of the wireless. She laughs again, but this time it's got nothing to do with me. She looks at me like she's surprised to find me standing there. Quickly recovering, "I've said this before," she says, "but I mean it: if anything comes along that you need help with, don't hesitate, just give us a call. Whatever it is, somebody will be able to figure it out."

"Can I call you if it turns out no one wants to buy books anymore?"

"You can call, but unfortunately there's not a whole lot we can do about that."

"I thought you advertised yourself as a full-service business."

"Not quite that full-service."

"Whatever happened to truth in advertising?"

"You mean there was such a thing?"

Holding the front door open for her, "Probably not," I say. "If there was, it was before my time."

We're on the porch when Cameron says, "At least you'll be able to put away the ramp now."

"Yeah, but..." But what about Benjamin? I almost say, before remembering that well-meaning uncles inquiring into the state of their nephews' burgeoning romantic relationships isn't a good idea.

But the thought *is* well-intentioned. Cameron is exactly the sort of level-headed person who could rub some of the prig out of Benjamin if they hung around each other long enough. "Maybe I'll leave it," I say. "You know: old dogs and new tricks, time to get on the train of social progress, that sort of thing."

Strapping her knapsack onto the back of her wheelchair, "Get rid of it," Cameron says. "It looks like you've got a moat or something. Or serious sewer problems."

A Canpar delivery truck stops in front of the house. A man pokes his head out of the driver's-side window. "Queen West Books?" he says. "One twelve Golden Avenue?"

"That's me," I say. The man nods and disappears into the back of his truck.

"Let me guess," Cameron says. "More books?"

"I know, I know, but I couldn't resist. An old customer of mine who moved into an apartment in Sarnia offered to sell me back the complete Riverside editions of Emerson's and Whitman's collected works."

"Are they valuable?"

"Probably not to anyone but me. But hey, if you're not growing, you're dying."

"Maybe we should have used that as a banner on the website."

"It doesn't exactly scream, 'Welcome, shoppers!' though, does it?"

"Good point. You know, your ability to translate your potential customers' needs and desires into a fully satisfactory virtual retail experience has really improved since we've been working with you."

"If for no other reason than that, it's been worth every penny."

And here comes the masked delivery man pushing a dolly stacked with two boxes of books up the ramp.

"Maybe you should keep it," Cameron says.

"I was just thinking the same thing."

•

Bertrand Russell's *A History of Western Philosophy* on my knee, a freshly made cup of Earl Grey tea steaming on the side table, my mind should be on "Ancient Philosophy After Aristotle," but my mind has a mind of its own this evening, would much rather worry over whether anyone will ever buy another book from me. It's about being able to pay the bills—when isn't it?—but it's also about being able to feel like a useful human being again. I haven't accomplished a lot in my life—no children, no lasting long-term relationship, no significant contribution to culture or society—but I've been a good bookseller. People's lives have been changed because of the books they've bought from my shop. It was the books themselves that made the magic happen, but it was Queen West Books that put the abracadabra into people's eager hands. Some people make music, other people are metronomes. But even a mere timekeeper like me needs to hear that reassuring *tick tick tick* once in a while to know that it's doing what it was put here to do.

I get up for the third time since I sat down to read and check my website for a sale, an inquiry, even a complaint would be preferable to this smothering cyber silence. Zero for three. I put the computer back to sleep and sit back down and wish that my tea was too hot to drink, so I could blow on it and have something to do, when my phone rings. Saved by the bell. Or at least by the chirp of my phone.

"Hello," I say. Although *Queen West Books* is what I want to say.

"Hey. It's Caroline. You know, the woman whose library you absconded with."

"You mean the woman whose library I gallantly refused to abscond with."

"Right. Until a date to be determined later."

I attempt to laugh, but it sounds more like a muffled cough.

"Just say 'Right,'" Caroline says.

"Right."

"Right. So. What are you up to tonight?"

"I thought I'd blow up my computer."

"It's not working?"

"No, it's working. That's why I want to blow it up."

Caroline laughs.

"After you finish destroying your computer," she says, "do you think you'll feel like coming over?"

"Sure. Should I bring anything?"

"Not a thing. Unless you drink coffee. I'm off it. For what that's worth."

"That's okay, I try not to drink caffeine after dinnertime."

"The coffee would be for the morning."

"Oh, right. *Right.*"

"Phil, I really don't have enough time left for too much subtlety anymore. Unless I'm reading this wrong—and if I am, please, tell me—I think we get along pretty well and I'd like to get to know you better."

"You're not reading it wrong. I feel the same way."

"Good. See you in about an hour?"

"Or less than that."

"Don't rush," she says. "I'm not going anywhere."

EIGHT

I remember this: a woman lying asleep in bed beside me, her head on the pillow next to mine, her eyes closed and my eyes open and what to do, say, think, next? Until then: Caroline asleep in bed beside me, her head on the pillow next to mine, her eyes closed and my eyes open. Except for her bra, she's naked, and the room is central-A/C cool and she's got the blankets pulled up to her chin. She's wearing red fingernail polish I don't think she had on the last time I saw her. She couldn't have painted her nails just for me, could she? *Could* she? Even if she didn't, she might have, it's possible, it's the kind of thing people who are seeing each other do. Are Caroline and I seeing each other? I blush, therefore we might be.

Caroline opens an eye, sees me seeing her, shuts it. "Tell the truth," she says. "You were just about to strangle me, weren't you?" She pulls the blankets almost up to her nose, but keeps both eyes closed. The smile lines on her face betray the smirk hiding underneath the blankets. Who knew wrinkles could be so sexy?

"It sounds like you've been out of the relationship game longer than I have," I say. "You don't start thinking about strangling the other person until you've been dating for at least six months."

Her eyes still shut, "Is that what we're doing?" she says. "Dating?"

I roll over onto my back and put my hands behind my head, stare at the ceiling of Caroline's bedroom. "Dating," I say, trying the word out. "It sounds kind of..."

"Weird."

"Juvenile."

"Antiquated."

"All of the above."

I can't see her face, but I know she's wearing a grin just as wide as mine. "So when was the last time you did something as weird and juvenile and antiquated as dating someone?" I say. I hadn't planned on broaching the whole relationship-history subject, but I suppose the question was inevitable. And just as to be expected, it had to happen in bed, after sex. The mating and dating habits of the human species haven't changed that much since the last time I had any personal experience with either.

"Oh, my God, we're not really going to do this, are we?"

I know what she means, but, "What do you mean?"

"You know: so-and-so and I were together until X years ago, and before that there was another so-and-so, and that lasted for Y years, and before them there was..." She opens her mouth and sticks her finger halfway in and makes a surprisingly convincing retching sound.

"It's no big deal if you don't feel comfortable talking about it," I say. "I was just—"

"I don't find the subject uncomfortable. I just find it boring."

"That's interesting."

"You find it interesting that I don't find the subject interesting?"

"I find it interesting because most people would be thrilled by an invitation to talk about themselves. Most people's own life is usually their favourite subject."

"Is it yours?"

"I don't know. I don't think so. I think I always preferred the idea of reading a good book to writing in a journal about what I was feeling or anything like that."

"Well, that's pretty much the way I've always felt about relationships. I mean, I've had the average number, I suppose. The serious. The not-so serious. The out-and-out mistakes."

"Careful, I'm lying right here."

"Before I got sick, I mean. Thankfully, I wasn't seeing anybody when I was diagnosed, so no one but me has had to deal with that. But even before then, I usually enjoyed my own company enough that I didn't relish having to put up with all the usual relationship BS."

"Relationship BS. Please be more specific so I can file it away for possible use later."

"Oh, I guess it's not BS—that's not fair, that's too harsh. It's just the things you've got to do to keep a relationship going if it's going to work, that's all, like compromise occasionally and ride out the usual peaks and valleys. It's nice to have someone around sometimes, obviously, but to be honest, for most of my life I think I've enjoyed being by myself more, just reading or working in the garden or making preserves in the kitchen with some good jazz on the radio. Does that make me a terrible person?"

"Probably. But since I feel the roughly same way, you've got company, so don't feel too bad."

"Really? You felt the same way? Even when you were with your ex you lived with for so long?"

"At its best, it was more like a very pleasant solitude of two people than a typical relationship with all of the usual—

"BS."

"BS, thank you. But now that I think about it, when it did get hard—for exactly the kinds of reasons you were talking about—

on some level it probably did seem easier to just stop trying because I knew I'd eventually be all right on my own doing all the things I like to do. Maybe not as happily as I might have been doing them with someone else around, but..."

"You would have been okay."

"I would have been okay. Does that make me a horrible person?"

"Oh, definitely. But there's safety in numbers, so relax."

Before I can relax, though, or do anything else, Caroline whips off the blankets down to her waist. "Whew, sorry," she says. "I thought I'd put hot flashes behind me when I went through menopause."

"Are you all right?"

"Do you mean am I going to spontaneously combust? No, you should be okay, there's no imminent danger of fire."

"Good to know."

Her fingers are entwined and resting behind her head now too; both of us are staring at the ceiling.

"How did you end up being a bookseller?" she says.

"I always liked books."

"That sounds a little too simplistic to be true."

"Sorry," I say. "I guess I really am that simple. That's probably something you should know about me."

"Well, I'm sorry, but I'm not buying it."

"What's not to buy? I'm sure I wasn't the first person who liked the idea of being a writer a lot more than actually sitting down and writing something. And although the concept of bantering back and forth about William Blake with my fellow scholars in the faculty lounge and occasionally condescending to address an auditorium full of dazzled undergraduates had its daydreamy appeal, the fact was, I felt happier on the floor of a bookstore than in the front row of a classroom. I guess I'd really rather just be left alone with the illustrious dead than have to share them with backbiting colleagues or apathetic students."

"Okay. I suppose I believe you."

"Why did you become a mailwoman?"

"You're expecting me to say it was because I loved mail?"

"I was thinking more along the lines of job security and a good pension."

"Actually," she says, "it was because I wanted to be a philosopher."

I roll on to my side and prop up my head with the palm of my right hand. "That sounds too complicated to be true."

"When I was in high school growing up in Halifax," she says, "I thought the coolest thing in the world would be to be like Simone de Beauvoir. You know: sit around all day thinking about life and writing big important books, travelling all over the world, having lots of fascinating lovers. But the single philosophy class I took when I got to university was so incredibly boring, I knew I'd never be able to make it through four years of that stuff, let alone endure years and years more of graduate school."

"That's a lot of self-knowledge for a kid. I guess I wasn't precocious like you. You should know that about me."

Caroline play-punches me in the arm and I play along and act like it hurt. She leaves her hand on my biceps.

"At any rate," she says, "then I came across a book called *Philosopher's Holiday* by Irwin Edman. Ever heard of it in your used book travels?"

"Maybe. I don't know. I don't think so."

"He was a Columbia University professor who mainly wrote popular books on philosophy. And one of them was called *Philosopher's Holiday*. It was about all of the everyday people he'd known in his life who one way or another were philosophers.

Just ordinary people who made it a point in their lives to ask themselves why people thought what they thought and did what they did."

"It sounds like I should read it."

"I don't know. I think it might be one of those books you need to discover when you're young."

"Well, that's not going to happen."

"How old are you?"

"Fifty-two."

"I'm fifty-five. So there you go. You're the youngest person in the room."

"I feel spryer already."

Caroline smiles, continues. "In one of the essays in the book he says that the ideal occupation for a true philosopher is a postal carrier. Plenty of exercise to help keep mind and body healthy, no one to fill your head all day with work-talk gobbledygook, plenty of relatively undisturbed time to think."

"That's amazing. You read that when you were a kid and had the foresight to know that that's what you should do with the rest of your life."

"Oh, God, no. I started working for Canada Post because I had an English degree from Dalhousie that wasn't worth the paper it was printed on. It was between them and UPS, and Canada Post had better job security and a good pension. Plus, brown has never been my colour."

"This *is* a complicated story."

"It's not a story, it's my life."

"Aren't they the same thing?" I say.

"Look who's the philosopher now?" Caroline says, sliding over and resting her head on my chest. It's morning, but I have no idea what time it is. What's more, I really don't care.

"I've been trying to give myself a crash course in Western philosophy," I say. Caroline couldn't be more surprised to hear me say it than me.

"Impressive," she says.

"Not compared to someone who devoted herself to the contemplative life when she was a teenager."

"Yeah, well, my aspirations were a lot stronger than my dedication. Besides the occasional nature book or gardening guide, I haven't opened a book that wasn't history or a biography in years. Even then, when I think about all of the books on my shelves that you're just going to have to box up and cart away someday, I feel sort of... I don't know... swinish. Maybe the right thing would have just been to get a library card."

"No," I say. "Keeping your books around you isn't swinish. It's the right thing to do."

"Because otherwise people like you would be out of work?"

"I *am* out of work. That's why my house is full of books, remember? No, I mean... I bet you can tell me where you got every one of them. Your books, I mean. Well, not every one, but most of them. Not only that, but I bet you know how old you were and why you bought each of them and who you were dating at the time and whatever else too."

"So my library isn't just a library, it's also a journal. Like one of those Ginsu knives they used to sell on late-night TV infomercials that not only slices and dices but can also find your car keys and trim your hedges."

"Something like that."

"And that's a good thing?"

"Of course it is. You're not who you say you are or what you post on your Facebook page—you are what you do. And what you spend your money on. And what you choose to surround yourself with. Books matter to you. That's why your home is full of them. For somebody who wanted to be Simone de Beauvoir, though, why mostly biography and history?"

"No idea. I guess I like stories, and a good historian or biographer is a good storyteller. Besides, if you read enough history, you don't have to bother reading the newspaper beyond the headlines or pay much attention to TV or the radio or your phone."

"Because history repeats itself."

"Because it's the same shit, different century. And let's not forget that history is a whole lot easier to read than philosophy. Oh, well. So much for the examined life."

"Why don't you do it with me, then?" I say.

"Do what?"

"Read the same beginner's guide to philosophy stuff I've been doing so we can talk about it. Up to now I've just been making notes in a journal. Having somebody to discuss this stuff with will make it a lot more interesting, I bet. Probably make more sense, too."

"I *was* looking for something new to read next. I just finished an eight-hundred-page book about Albert Speer and whether he did or didn't know about the death camps when he was Hitler's architect. I guess I wouldn't mind something a little less..."

"Nazi-esque?"

"Something like that."

"At least you're still reading new books. All I ever seem to do anymore is pull down old favourites and skim."

"You know what you like—there's nothing wrong with that."

"Yeah, well, until I started this philosophy thing, I was in danger of only liking what I know. That and the occasional, reasonably well-written music biography."

"Are you serious, though? About the philosophy stuff?"

"Sure I'm serious. We can't just have sex all the time. As admittedly mind-blowing as it is. That's not what people who are dating do."

"There's that word again," she says.

"I guess."

Caroline's head is so close to mine, it would be easy to just close my eyes and kiss her. So I do.

•

As undoubtedly some deep thinker I've never heard of said, it's not all beer and skittles, it can't just be sex and philosophy, everybody has to pay some dues sometimes. And if they haven't said it, they should have. Someone other than me, I mean. Wisdom always sounds wiser coming from someone else.

Zoran and Tesla are here, and that's a good thing. Filling the latter's water bowl and listening to the former's take on today's news keeps me from thinking about my comatose website and the time and money I apparently wasted having it built. Keeps me from thinking about it a little less, anyway.

"Phil, I have question of fact for you," Zoran says, meaning he's about to tell me a joke, his customary semi-amused smirk and bushy quotation-mark eyebrows having been replaced by his idea of a winning poker face. Meaning he looks as if he's just learned of a particularly horrific piece of information he hasn't had time to entirely process yet.

"Shoot," I say. Thankfully, there's still plenty more online cataloguing left to do, and because Benjamin is as busy spending time with his new girlfriend as he theoretically is on his online summer class, my finishing up the job works for both of us. He can use the extra time and I can use the saved wages, and having something to do helps keep me busy. *Busy work* is only a bad thing when you don't need to be busy.

"The city of Hamilton," he says. "Its name—its name it gets from First Nation people who lived there—this is where the name comes from, it is their word, you understand?"

"Right. Go ahead." I'm on the couch with the iPad and a stack of books, tapping in information. Zoran's in the middle of the room with his hands locked behind his back and walking a long figure eight. Tesla is lying not far away on the floor, his face impassive but his eyes following Zoran wherever he goes.

"And this word—the word *Hamilton*—do you know what it means, what it originally means?"

"No. What?"

"Let me tell you. It is old First Nation word. It means"—he stops pacing and stands in front me. Tesla and I wait for the inevitable punch line—"Somebody who could not make it in Toronto."

I laugh—as much at Zoran's own deep, rolling laughter as at his joke—and type in the publication particulars of another book. Zoran kneels down and scratches Tesla between the ears, which inspires the dog to flip over onto his back so as to better provide Zoran with the optimum amount of belly-rubbing room. It's difficult to say who's having a better time: Zoran, with a big smile on his face, or Tesla, with eyes closed and four short legs stuck straight up in the air. Maybe I should get a dog. Continual quiet companionship. Somebody always glad to see you when you come home. A four-legged security system. Like taking up yoga or regularly flossing my teeth, however, it's just one more thing that would probably be good for me that I probably won't end up doing.

"So," Zoran says, standing up and leaving Tesla open-eyed and still on his back. "How about these Blue Jays? They have now won three baseball games in a row. That team that is ahead of them in their division, the American League East division, are now only two games ahead of them."

I'd be willing to bet that Zoran has never watched or listened to an entire baseball game in his life, but, like his Hamilton-bashing joke, his knowledge of the Jays' record and their early-season playoff chances is an example of his proud adoption of Toronto as his new home. Once Serbia was back to being a relatively divisive-free democracy and his son moved back to Belgrade, Zoran decided to stay behind. "He said to me," Zoran told me at the time, "'time to go home now, Dad.' I tell him that where you are happy at is home, and I am happy here. What is not to be happy about? Big city with lots of big city things. Lots of different kinds of people with all different colours and languages and foods. No stupid prejudices and hatreds and wars because this people wants to feel better about itself by hating that other people. Besides, I say to him, 'You are proud to be Serbian? I was proud to Yugoslavian. Then politicians come along and—poof—no such thing as Yugoslavia anymore.' I miss long-time friends, yes, but home, home is where you are happy."

"They're on a good roll," I say. "As long as their bullpen holds up, they should be okay."

"Da, da, da," Zoran says, *da* being the Serbian word for *yes*, although I'm sure he has as clear an idea of what a baseball team's bullpen is as I do what a soccer halfback does. That's okay. If he's comfortable with his confusion, why shouldn't I be? Go Jays, O Canada, our home and adopted land.

"Okay, we go now," Zoran says, clapping his hands, and Tesla rises, stretches, shakes his head, is ready for whatever's next. I really should get a dog. I'm sure I could learn a few things.

I see them off at the door where Zoran apologizes for not buying a book, and I tell him it's fine; don't tell him that I'm getting used to no one buying anything. I shut the door and decide that this latest batch of books can be catalogued later. WWTD? What Would Tesla Do? Tesla would take a nap.

Before I head upstairs to my bedroom I remember to shut down my main computer. I press a key and the machine wakes up, and before I can click the shut down icon I see that there have been two abebooks.com orders. For books. My books. The nap can wait. I've got work to do.

•

Here's what happens when you're happy. Here's what's going on when you're as beatific as you can be.

You're not *you*.

You're a book-searching machine, in the basement of your house on your knees with a penlight looking for Randall Jarrell's *Letters*, Houghton Mifflin Company, 1985, 540 pages, Book Condition: Near fine, minor shelf wear, previous owner's signature on ffep, otherwise fine in a like jacket. Looking, looking, looking, no, no, no—it has to be on one of the bottom shelves; crawling on your hands and knees now, penlight clenched between your teeth—looking, looking, looking, no, no, no, YES. Standing up with the book in your hand, dusting off your knees, peeling the cobwebs from your mouth, clicking off the penlight, heading back upstairs with what you came looking for. Step one: complete.

You're a papering, taping, labelling apparatus, *Mr. Thomas J. Noyes, 1342 Hathaway Lane, Wichita, Kansas, 67213, U.S.A.* Put it with the other recently ordered, located, wrapped, and addressed book on the table by the front door for the short trip to the post office later today. Step two: complete.

You're a delivery man, putting the two freshly packaged books in your extra-large, over-the-shoulder mail satchel and waiting your turn in line at the post office and filling out the forms and paying for the postage and getting your receipt and walking home the same way you came. Step three: complete.

And everything you see and hear and will do along the way back is that much better because incessantly tetchy you isn't you. Not for awhile, anyway. Step four: complete.

NINE

A date, a tutorial, a sleepover, whatever. Call it what you want, but it's Friday night and there was another book order waiting for me when I got back from the post office which I happily hurriedly filled so I could get it in the mail before the P.O. closed at 6:00 p.m., followed by a shower and a shave and what do you know, I've got somewhere to be and someone expecting me to be there. What a pleasant change.

I pack a bag with a toothbrush, a bottle of Merlot, and a paperback copy of Frederick Copleston's *A History of Philosophy: Volume 1, Part II*, an identical copy of which I gave to Caroline last week in preparation for our first philosophy one-on-one. Welcome to the wonderful world of middle-aged dating. One thing I don't pack is condoms. There *are* advantages to sex in your fifties. I slip another bottle of wine into the bag and turn off the kitchen light when I hear voices coming from the other room. If it's thieves, boy, will they be disappointed. Not a single shiny item that beeps, rings, or lights up worth stealing.

It's not a burglar, it's Benjamin, as expected, and Cameron's with him. I'd asked him to scout the big Mississauga Value Village for stock, and here he is with the result, a couple of brimming cardboard boxes. "I thought you said you'd be out," he says. "I wouldn't have just come in if I knew you were here. Sorry."

"I said I might be out by the time you got back," I say. "Hi, Cameron." Cameron is busy texting someone, but manages a little half wave back. "It doesn't matter, don't worry about it." He's just my brother's kid, but I kind of like the idea that someone I'm related to by blood has a key to my house. I can't think of a good reason why it makes me feel good, it just does. "I'm heading out now. Just leave the boxes where they are and I'll go through them later."

"We made out okay," Benjamin says. "Nothing special, just like you thought, but some good meat-and-potatoes stuff. Novels mostly, but also a complete hardcover set of Virginia Woolf's letters, without the jackets, unfortunately. That was the real score. I'm going to post a shot of all six of them on the store's Instagram page tonight. Cameron found those."

"I had no idea how pushy people can be at these things," she says. "I had to almost run this one guy over with my chair just to get at them before he did. How about keeping six feet apart, dude?"

"That's nothing," I say. "You should come with us when we hit all of the UofT college sales in the fall. Every bookseller in town and plenty more from everywhere else camps out in line for hours just so they can get first crack at the best stuff. You have to practically wear elbow pads and a helmet once the doors open up and they start letting people in."

"Sounds like fun," she says.

"It is, actually. I've been going to them for twenty-five years and I still get excited. You never know what you're going to find. Every year is different."

Cameron gives me a raised-eyebrows half smile and that's okay. I'm happiest hunting down old books, she's happiest building people virtual businesses. Lucky us whose job descriptions include happiness.

As if she knows what I'm thinking, "How's everything going with the virtual world?" she says.

"Great. In fact, I made my first sales today."

"Sales?" Benjamin says. "As in plural?"

"As in plural, yeah. Don't sound so surprised."

"I'm not—I was just thinking how lucky you are to have such an incredible social media specialist."

Everybody laughs, but who knows? He might be right. And you know what else? That would be okay.

"Where are you off to?" Benjamin says.

I look down at the white cloth bag in my hand. I shift it to the other hand. "Just going to a friend's."

"A friend named Caroline's?" Cameron says, smiling. Benjamin joins her. To people their age, people my age dating must seem impossibly quaint, adorable even, like pictures of monkeys wearing top hats and smoking pipes, who look almost as if they're real people.

"Maybe," I say. "And what are you two up to tonight?"

They look at each other. Benjamin shrugs. Cameron shrugs. Then her phone vibrates and she's gone, lost to the text.

"Dad says I should visit Grandma," Benjamin says.

"You should," I say. "But not on a Friday night."

"What's so special about Friday night?" he says.

"Nothing, it's just that it's... you know, it's Friday night."

Now it's Benjamin's phone's turn to buzz. If you had told me when I was their age that I'd voluntarily carry a telephone around with me wherever I went, that no matter where I was or what I was doing, I'd be a servant to a ring tone, I'd have said that even *1984* wasn't *that* depressing. I wait until he's done thumb-tapping his reply to whatever demanded his immediate attention.

"Here," I say, offering him two twenty-dollar bills from my wallet.

Staring at them, "I owed you hours from last week," he says. "Even after the two hours I put in today I'm still behind."

"This isn't for work."

"What's it for then?"

"Because I had a good day at the office and I can't stand the idea of you and your girlfriend spending the rest of the night waiting for your frigging phones to ring."

"What's going on?" Cameron says, her phone back in the palm of her right hand.

"Here," I say, handing her the money instead. "Go to a movie or get drunk or buy some drugs or *something*."

"Okay," she says, taking the cash. She looks at Benjamin, who just shrugs.

"Don't forget to lock up when you leave," I say. "And don't not do something I wouldn't do."

"What's that supposed to mean?" Benjamin says.

"I'm not sure. But try not to not do it anyway."

•

—And tell me again why it's necessary for you to record us?

—It's not necessary, it's just so that we'll have a record of our talks.

—Now you're making me nervous. A record for what?

—I don't know...just a record. I mean, when I started reading up on this stuff I told you that I kept a kind of journal, right? It was just a way to maybe help make sure I understood it a little bit better. It wasn't like I planned on going back and rereading it.

—So we're recording our conversations on your phone although we're not going to listen to them later.

—Now you've got it.

—I think I understood the Hellenistic Age better.

—What a wonderful segue.

—Nope. That's it, actually.

—Okay, then I'll take the baton. Basically, the Greeks were going through what every big, powerful empire does once it eventually starts running out of gas.

—They decline.

—Exactly.

—Hello to our land-of-the-free, home-of-the-brave neighbours to the south.

—Exactly again.

—And so instead of the pure philosophy of people like Plato, you get—let me get this right, let me check my cheat sheet—oh, yeah: the Cynics and the Stoics and the Epicureans.

—And thank goodness. No more "Does this table exist?" or "Is mathematical knowledge innate?"

—So you're admitting that you're a low-brow philosophy student.

—Absolutely. Maybe these guys were only concerned with what philosophy means in terms of how people actually live because the times they existed in were making them uncertain and unhappy, but at least their idea of philosophy makes sense. Why we're here and what to do once we are. Philosophers or not, that's what most people wonder about.

—So now we're taking our cues from *most people*?

—In this case, yes. In this case, I'm most people.

—All right, then, Mr. Everyman, which one are you: Cynic, Stoic, or Epicurean?

—Why do I have to choose? All of them have their pros and cons.

—You sound like you're trying to decide which car to buy.

—Number one, I don't drive. Number two, if I did, isn't a fleet of different kinds of vehicles better than just one?

—I believe that's called the Smorgasbord School of Philosophy.
—Maybe. But here's why I want a little bit of each on my plate.
—Let me get some more wine first.
—What a typically Epicurean thing to say.
—If I had a nickel for every time I heard that...
—Hey, this wine isn't bad, is it?
—Wine is like sex and music. Even when it's not great, it's still pretty good.
—That sounds... I don't who that sounds like.
—How about me?
—Okay, let's go with that for now. Anyhow, Diogenes is another one of those guys, isn't he? Like Socrates or Jesus, I mean—nothing he wrote survives, so it's mostly by the example of how he lived his life that he did his teaching.
—That's the best kind of teaching.
—Putting your money where your mouth is.
—Not just talking the talk, but walking the walk.
—And I think we've now officially reached our quota of clichés for the evening.
—Okay, well, I like the way that the Cynic believes that virtue equals happiness, and that because the world is mostly a nasty, unvirtuous place, to be happy means staying clear of it as much as possible. No attachments, as few possessions as possible—Diogenes supposedly slept wherever he lay down at night, right?—you get the idea.
—And you don't depend upon anyone or anything else to make you happy.
—True. Except that by throwing out the baby with the bathwater—I know, I know, another cliché. Give me a break. I carried a mailbag for twenty years, not a thesaurus—you're missing out on all sorts

of things that admittedly complicate and even mess up your life, but are kind of the point of being alive, right?

—Like...

—Like other people. Who will undoubtedly make life difficult at times and occasionally drive you crazy and sometimes let you down, but who also have the ability to make you happy in ways you never could be on your own and who will be there for you when you need them. And then there's the way that the Cynic tries to have as little as possible to do with the material world because things go wrong, they don't last, they create all kinds of fresh headaches. It's the same basic idea as Buddhism and I don't buy it.

—Why not?

—Look, there's always something that needs to be dealt with around here, but I *love* my house. When things out there in the big bad world don't make sense or make me angry or are just plain sad, I've always still got my beautiful garden and my little library and my sunroom where I like to sit in the morning when the weather is nice. Even though the raccoons keep eating my vegetables and some of the bookshelves need reinforcing and the mudroom is drafty and needs new windows.

—The world giveth, the world taketh...

—And as long as you remember that that's part of the deal...

—So what do you make of Stoicism?

—Uh-uh. Your turn. I'm going to have a little more of this lovely wine that some silly Cynic would never dare enjoy because it cost money, which would mean the inconvenience of having a job, and which can give you a headache, which means physical pain and all sorts of other terrible, terrible things.

—Okay, well, as far as I can figure it out, Stoicism is Cynicism with one major difference: you still don't want the affairs of the world to distract you from life's purpose, which is to be happy, which means living virtuously, but there's one major difference: virtue means living in accordance with nature or the *logos* that permeates existence.

—Which leads to the obvious question of what the hell *logos* is.

—Exactly. I've always been kind of jealous of animals because they *know* what they're supposed to do and who they're supposed to be, you know? Dogs hate squirrels and don't need someone to write an essay arguing why they should hate them, why it's the logical, correct thing to do. They're born knowing exactly who they are. They're like perfect Stoics because they live according to their undeniable *logos*.

—But no such luck for us.

—It's fine to say that you'll have peace of mind and be happy if you ignore everything but what nature wants you to be, but human beings aren't born with a one-size-fits-all life plan. I mean, my idea of a good time isn't hanging out with a committed, rabble-rousing environmental activist, let alone being one, but obviously the world needs people like that. Every human being should be issued a T-shirt that says LIFE: INSTRUCTIONS NOT INCLUDED.

—I'd buy one of those.

—I'll give you one if you take us to the finish line with the Epicureans.

—Deal.

—Speaking of Epicureanism, let's finish up this bottle.

—Thanks. Cheers.

—Cheers.

—Okay, well, on the one hand, Epicureanism seems pretty straightforward. Pleasure alone is good. What have I highlighted here? Okay. And physical pleasure means avoidance of pain, while mental pleasure means avoidance of fear and anxiety. So the key to a happy life is to overcome our fear of the number-one cause of all our anxiety: death. Which, as everyone knows, is easy peasy, right? Which, as I can personally vouch for, is just a piece of cake.

—You actually do seem pretty….

—Resigned?

—I don't know what the word is. But whatever it is, you seem to be it.

—I've had practice. When I got sick the first time—with the breast cancer, when I had the mastectomy—I'm not embarrassed to say that I fairly flipped out. You never met such a self-pitying, pissed-off person in your life. Somehow—I really don't know why—it doesn't feel as scary this time. Even though this time I know I'm not going to get better.

—You've gotten used to it.

—I don't think anyone ever gets used to being afraid of dying.

—Why do you think, then?

—Maybe I got all my crying out of the way the first time.

—Maybe you just want to be happy.

—Hey, what do you know? It turned out I was an Epicurean all along.

•

Good news I don't want to hear: a voice message from Alex informing me that a mint copy of the Dead's *Europe '72* (including the hard-to-find six-page colour booklet) has landed in his shop and he'll be holding on to it for me until I have a chance to drop by. But I've just filled my first orders in months, and with so little money trickling in, this is definitely not the time for money to be going out on anything other than food or utilities or store-upgrade essentials. I feel bad—I feel guilty—that I'll have to tell Alex thanks but no thanks. Just like the best tippers are waitstaff and bartenders, a second-hand bookseller feels a responsibility to buy something every time they step inside a used bookshop or record store. People tend to talk a good game when it comes to supporting what matters, but get beyond the cultural cheerleading and what you'll likely find is illegally downloaded music and borrowed books. The number-one commandment if you're in the retail game: *Buy from others as you would have them buy from you.*

Alex is busy conferring with a customer at the back of the store so I occupy myself with three rows of new vinyl arrivals. I can't help but eavesdrop, just like I can't help but envy Alex his easy interaction with a real live customer. Cyber business has thankfully picked up, and although it's nice to know that when someone orders a book from the website you're making them happy, it would be even nicer to assist someone with finding what they're looking for and seeing the satisfaction in person, even if both of you were compelled to don surgical masks to make it happen. What most people call reality has never seemed particularly interesting or even real to me—click on the ten o'clock news or flip through a newspaper and tell me I'm wrong—so if, as of right now, 12:13 p.m. today, reality means wearing a mask and keeping six feet part and all the COVID-19 rest of it, sure, fine, whatever, okay. It's probably the same reason I rarely vote, don't march, and make it a point not to chip in and pull my weight and do my societal part. I guess that makes me a Stoic. Or a Cynic. Or an Epicurean. Or something else I should be able to positively identify but clearly can't.

"Right," the woman says. "I was looking for his new book, the one that's about music."

"The book of essays, right," Alex says. "Like I said, I don't carry a lot of books, but he actually lives in the neighbourhood, so I've got a signed copy."

"Oh, great. Thanks."

"You bet."

Alex removes the book from the shelf, rings up the woman's purchase at the counter, puts it in a bag, and ding-a-ling the shop door opens and closes and you'd think I was the one who'd made the sale, I'm so pleased. Misery loves company, but sometimes so does happiness. Alex dips behind the counter only to immediately reemerge with the LP he'd set aside for me. Handing it over, "I knew you'd be pretty psyched to see this," he says.

Psyched isn't the word I would use, but, yeah, it does feel great to hold a fifty-year-old rock-and-roll artifact in your hands, especially one in such excellent condition. It's a triple album, so it's a gatefold plus one more pocket, each of the three sleeves tastefully adorned on the inside with pictures of Jerry and the gang as well as recording and tour details and plenty of other wonderfully superfluous information.

"Check out the booklet," Alex says. "I've never seen one so clean. Even if you find one that's unmarked, one of the corners is usually torn or frayed or *something*. Not this one."

I carefully remove the booklet from the middle sleeve, but only flip and skim, alone and at home with the lights dimmed and headphone-stoned the optimum conditions for properly appreciating this vinyl-and-paper wonder. The gourmand and the record geek have at least this much in common: neither one wants to be watched while they gorge. I just as carefully slide the booklet back inside the sleeve.

"It's great," I say.

"Yeah." Making money selling stuff is good; making money selling good stuff to people who appreciate it is better.

I'm just delaying the inevitable, but, "How much are you asking?" I say.

"If I was putting it out on the floor, forty—I could get fifty, easy, but things are kinda slow right now and I'd want it to move—but give me thirty and we're good."

Alex's generosity only makes me feel worse—thirty dollars for this record in this condition is almost like getting it at cost. I remember something I saw in the new arrivals and turn around and pluck it out. "This is pretty neat," I say, placing it on the counter.

"I know, right? It's from the same collection that I got the Dead record. Everything the guy had was in really good shape, and this one and a few others were still sealed."

It's a still-in-the-cellophane 1978 original pressing of Captain Beefheart's penultimate album, *Shiny Beast (Bat Chain Puller)*. I don't need to hear anymore about the man whose collection it was. Alex's life is filled with widows too.

"Man," he says, "I heard the craziest story last week."

"Oh, yeah?"

"This seller from Windsor, the guy who sold me the Dead and the Beefheart records, told me how before COVID he got a call from a guy who said he had a lot of old records to sell and would he be interested in looking at them? So the guy says sure and gets the address and drives over to this crummy part of Detroit and finally sees the address he's looking for, but it's an old boarded-up strip mall. He parks his car and is sitting there wondering whether or not he should be there, the scene felt so dodgy, when some guy holding up an LP steps outside one of the boarded-up stores, so he figures this must be the place and it's safe to get out."

"Good," I say. "I thought this was going to be an organ-harvesting story."

"Just wait. It's ten times weirder than that."

"I'm not sure I want to hear it. I just had lunch."

"Oh, you're going to want to hear this."

The door dingles and a couple of teenage girls slump inside the store. Twenty years ago vinyl was dead, you couldn't even buy it. Now it's big-time back, in part because of kids like these. The Lord and retail buying habits move in mysterious ways.

"So our guy follows the other guy into the building and boom!"—the teenagers freeze, stop their record flipping and look around the store—"He's in a frigging time machine, it's suddenly forty years ago."

"What do you mean?" The two kids resume their silent perusing.

"I mean, it's a Peaches record store that went bankrupt in 1979 that got shut down and locked up, except that somebody—some accountant or lawyer or whatever—forgot to do the paperwork or something, and the store was pretty much exactly the way it looked the last day it was open, and that's when this guy, the guy our guy was meeting, bought the entire strip mall, all so he could tear it down and build a parking lot."

"Wow."

"I know, right? I mean, not only was every record in the place still sealed with the Peaches price sticker still on it, but all of the promotional stuff that the labels gave the store way back when was still where it was the day the doors closed for good. You know: life-sized cardboard cutouts of the Stones, posters advertising new releases, all of it."

"Man."

"Right? This guy was in a virtual time warp."

"What did he do?"

"You know what he did. He bought up everything in the store. All of the records, all of the promo stuff, even all of the stuff with the Peaches store logo on it. Of course, a lot of the records were junk. Sealed or not, a Captain and Tennille record is still a Captain and Tennille record, but he also got all of the Dylan, all of the Ramones, all of the Miles Davis—you get the idea."

"And all of it was..."

"Perfect, yeah."

I pick up the Beefheart album. "And this is one of those."

"He only had, like, twenty or so of the sealed records left. He'd already resold most of them, and he kept a few for himself."

"I bet."

"But I managed to pry this one and a few others off him because I bought a whole bunch of his other stuff. The only problem is..." Alex takes the album from me.

"You don't want to break the seal," I say.

"You got it. Because once you do—"

"It's not perfect anymore."

"And it's not 1979 anymore either."

We're both looking at the record in Alex's hands.

"Makes it kind of hard to listen to, though, unless you open it," I say.

"There is that."

We don't notice that the teenagers have left until we hear the bell attached to the door ding-a-linging. I take the Beefheart from him and place it on top of *Europe '72*.

"Is sixty bucks okay for both?" I say.

"You got it."

I pull out my wallet and count out my cash. "I'm a little short," I say.

"Don't worry about it, Phil. I know you're good for it. I'm just glad they're both going to a good home."

TEN

On the one hand, getting dizzy when you stand up is obviously concerning. On the other hand, when you're eighty-one years old occasional dizziness might not be the greatest of your physical concerns. On the other hand, when it's your mother who's the one who stood up too quickly during Saturday-night socially-distanced bingo and nearly blacked out and had to be helped back to her room in a wheelchair by an attendant, it's not so easy to be so blasé. On the other hand...

"You know I'm not a complainer, Fred," Mum says. "I never was."

"I know, Mum." And it's true, as true as it is that Fred isn't my name.

"But these doctors they've got here, you tell them what's wrong with you and they still don't know what to do about it. I tell you, I'm at my wits' end."

I switch the phone from one ear to the other. One-on-one Mum talks are best achieved in person—the simple corporal companionship of mother and child, most of what needs to be said accomplished simply by being together in mute physical proximity—but I've got a widow to visit later this afternoon and I'm meeting Caroline for dinner on Roncesvalles at 7:00 p.m., so a telephone tête-a-tête is all that's going to happen today. Besides, she's feeling okay now.

"You know what the person I was speaking to after you weren't feeling well told me, Mum?" I'm mindful not to use the dread word *doctor*.

Cellphone silence. I wait. I continue.

"She said that it's not unusual for people, once they get a little bit older, to feel dizzy sometimes, especially when they stand up too fast, or if they've been sitting or lying down for a long time."

"So everyone who's not a spring chicken anymore is lazy, is that it? That's their answer to everybody's problems."

I won't take the bait. I'm here to help, not to win an argument about client–medical personnel relations.

"She said that a lot of people, when they're not feeling 100 per cent, they just take a little nap, and once they do, they usually wake up feeling better."

"Well, that's wonderful advice if you can afford to just lie around all day, but I've got a family to look after. What am I supposed to say to them when I decide to sleep my life away?"

A broken clock still tells the correct time twice a day, and even though Mum is a little hazy on her familial facts, I understand the underlying point of her petulance. Your entire life has been—and been about—doing things, accomplishing things, looking back at the end of the day and saying, "I had that and that and that to do and I did them all and now I can relax and rest because I know that I did what I had to do." Then you blink and the decades dissolve and everyone who mattered to you is either dead or grown up and gone away or doesn't need you anymore, and all that's left is to be a good girl, now, don't bother yourself with this busy messy living stuff anymore, leave that to someone else, just crawl into bed and close your eyes and count to eternity. The sentiment is well-intended—the old workhorse's work is finally done, it's time for it to dozily chew some grass in the shade and shoo away those pesky flies all day long with its tail—but no one, no matter how elderly or tired, wants to end up seeming obsolete, redundant, forgotten. Might be what they are, but no one wants to hear it.

"I think all she means, Mum, is that it's a good idea—medically speaking—to take it a bit easy sometimes. Just for a little while, until you're feeling better."

"I know what she means. I know perfectly well what she means."

In spite of the air-conditioning, the phone feels squishy against my ear. I switch it to the other one and try to think of a new strategy.

"Remember when Fred or I would get sick," I say, "like with the flu or something, and you'd always set us up in the living room with the bucket right beside the couch?"

"That was in case you had to throw up. Once the flu hits a family, believe you me, everybody eventually gets it. One person in the family gets sick, you can bet your last dollar everybody else in the family is gonna get it too."

"The only good part was that you got to miss school and watch TV all day," I say. "*Let's Make a Deal. The Price Is Right.* The soaps. What was that one that you used to like, Mum? *As the World Turns*?"

"I never watched *As the World Turns* in my life."

"I thought you did."

"Never. I wouldn't even know what it looks like."

"Okay. I guess I—"

"*General Hospital.* That was my show."

"Oh, right."

"Not that I watched it every day."

"No, no, of course not."

"You've got to remember, Phil, I had an entire family to look after, and that's not always easy."

"Geez, no. I only have myself to look after, and sometimes I—"

"I couldn't just stop whatever I was doing and sit in front of the television whenever I felt like it."

"I'm surprised you ever had any time to yourself at all."

"Oh, I managed."

"Still..."

"But I did like *General Hospital*."

"Oh, yeah?"

"It was the only one I really cared for. I liked Dr. Hardy."

"I don't think I remember him."

"He was a nice man. You know, I started watching that show just after your father and I got married, and Dr. Hardy was still on there when your dad passed away."

"Really?"

"That's a very long time."

"It sure is."

Mum yawns. Which makes me yawn. Which makes me laugh.

"Are you getting enough sleep, Phil? That's how people get rundown and get sick, you know."

"Yeah, I just... yeah, I'm okay."

"Why don't you try to have a little nap this afternoon? Your expensive new computer set-up you've got, it'll tell you if you need to do something for work, won't it?"

"Maybe I will, Mum. That's a good idea. I don't want to get rundown."

"That's right. You get rundown and you watch, you'll be sure to get sick."

Mum yawns again, and this time she laughs. "Maybe I'll have one too," she says. Quickly recovering, "You can never be too careful," she says. "Especially if something is going around."

"That's right."

"I know it's right."

"I should probably let you go, Mum."

"Okay, son. I'll talk to you soon."

"I love you, Mum."

"I love you too, son."

"Bye, Mum."

"Bye bye."

•

I know what I'm doing while I'm doing it—not for the first time in my life, but enough of a rarity that the corresponding knowledge that I could also stop what I'm doing and return home is an actual option. I've already invested a TTC fare and thirty minutes on the streetcar spent breathing through an increasingly hot, moist mask, however, so I walk up the sidewalk to Caroline's house and am about to knock on the screen door when I see through to the backyard and her on her knees working in her garden. Surrounding her on the ground are several gardening tools, a grey metal watering can, and a white plastic spray bottle that's most likely some kind of bug spray. She's moving her lips while she works. She's singing to herself.

Dropping by without calling first already felt a bit new-relationship risky—A wonderful surprise? An unwanted intrusion? Something uncomfortably in between?—but continuing to watch Caroline unawares, weeding neat rows of tomato plants, feels almost immoral. She's wearing a floppy yellow hat and a large white men's dress shirt with the sleeves rolled down, but she's not thinking about ultraviolet rays. She's not thinking about anything except for weeds and tomatoes and earth and water and sunshine and insects. I know I should either knock and announce myself or turn around and go home, but I don't do either, just stay where I am watching Caroline working in her garden. And singing.

The car alarm belonging to an SUV parked on the street in front of Caroline's house wails and whoops and wheezes me away from her doorstep and down the sidewalk and back to the streetcar stop where I'd gotten off ten minutes earlier.

It comes, I get on, I'm gone.

•

"Hi."

"Hi."

"What, uh... what are you up to?"

"I just came in from the garden, actually. I was getting ready to jump in the shower."

"Oh, yeah?"

"Yeah."

"You really enjoy gardening, don't you?"

"Well, I like to have at least a few tomatoes left that aren't completely devoured by the aphids when it comes time for preserving."

"It's not time for preserving yet, though, is it?"

"No. But it will be soon enough."

"But it's not for awhile."

"No, it's not for awhile."

"Good."

"Good?"

"We're still on for the dinner at Tristessa's tonight, right?"

"Unless you know something I don't."

"Nothing that I'm aware of."

"Then I guess I'll see you tonight.

"And I guess I'll see you tonight too."

"Phil?"

"Yeah?"

"Is everything all right?"

"Everything is great."

"It is?"

"Trust me. It is."

•

"Hello."

"Hi."

"Please come in."

"Thanks."

And that's it, that's all it takes for someone born when and where I was born to feel good about when and where they live now. Because today's visit was set up entirely online—thanks again, queenwestbooks.ca—when Jean and I agreed upon 2:00 p.m. today for me to look at his recently deceased husband's books, I had little reason to expect widow Jean to be a Black man with a faint French-Canadian accent. Yeah, yeah, everybody knows how you can make a you-know-what out of you-know-who if you *assume*, but in this case the twist is that I'm happy to be made into an ass. I was alive when *fag* was the playground-appropriate nomenclature for anyone you didn't like, for whatever reason, and a young man when homosexuals were expected to stay stuck inside their fairy-filled closets. I detest language-debasing, thought-smothering PC speech almost as much as the careless, casual vitriol that inspired it, and maybe—maybe—the day will come when *gay positive* will metamorphose into *gay indifferent*, but for now I feel lucky to live in a city where a same-sex couple simply isn't a big a deal. Not to me, anyway, and I was brought up to believe it should be. Which makes it feel kind of like a big deal. To me, at least.

The shoes come off ("If you wouldn't mind, thank you"), my mask stays on (taking my cue from him, who greeted me at the door wearing his own), we walk the length of the first floor of the house (shoes, hell: it feels as if I'm intruding upon a glossy home décor magazine shoot—everything ticket-price new and hypoallergenic clean and the most innocuous throw pillow carefully fluffed and positioned at just the correct angle—and that I should have donned a sterilized clear-plastic bodysuit upon entering the front door for fear of grubby bachelor contamination), and the recently buffed wooden basement stairs lead us down into Jean's husband's bibliophilical domain, the not unpleasant sting of Pine-Sol tingling my nose hairs as my eyes grow used to the scalding artificial light.

Once they do, it's my mind's turn to adjust to what it's seeing: row after row of ceiling-high, identical grey metal bookshelves entirely but tidily stacked with books, books, books. There's no washing machine or dryer in the corner, no summer-stranded skis or single bicycle wheel leaning against the walls, no downstairs toilet or wash basin or garden tools anywhere to be found. Just row after row after row of books. I could be in the basement of a university library or an unusually orderly subterranean second-hand bookstore.

"Man..." I say.

"My husband was a collector," Jean says. "He never got rid of anything. Particularly books. I think he kept every one he ever read. And a few he never got around to. More than a few he never got around to."

Jean says this with crossed arms and expressionless eyes, but it's obvious he's nonetheless proud of his partner's collection. I stroll to the end of an aisle; turn the corner and saunter back down another.

"He'd spend hours and hours down here," he says.

"I can understand why."

"To tell you the truth, I think he enjoyed collecting his books as much as he did reading them. Maybe more."

"I see that a lot," I say. "'Beginning my studies the first step pleased me so much,/The mere fact consciousness, these forms, the power of motion,'" I add.

Arms still crossed, Jean raises a single eyebrow.

"Walt Whitman," I say. "'Beginning My Studies.'"

"My husband was the literary one in the family. I'm the visual one."

"Are you an artist?"

The faintest first indication of something approaching a smile. "Not quite. A graphic designer."

"What did your husband do?" I inwardly cringe at my use of the past tense. It's grammatically correct, but to any new widow, it's also wrong.

"He was in finance," he says.

Which could mean he was either a bank teller or a hedge fund analyst, but I don't ask for clarification. I'm here to appraise books, and if I'm going to make my dinner date with Caroline I'd better get started. As if sensing this, "I suppose I should let you get down to work," Jean says.

"Absolutely." I don't move, though; instead, look around the basement. "It almost seems like a shame to have a hand in taking this all apart."

Jean puts his hands in the pockets of his neatly creased cream-coloured khakis and joins me in surveying the room. "I understand what you mean. I actually thought about leaving everything as it is as a sort of... tribute to Edward."

"It would make sense."

"In the end, it wasn't that I needed the space or even so much the money that made me decide to call you."

"No?"

"It was because Edward had been an organ donor. In fact, there's someone walking around right now with a brand-new healthy liver because of him."

"That's fantastic," I say.

"Edward was a fantastic man."

We're just standing there now, us and all of Edward's books.

"I came to the conclusion that he'd want people to have his books too. So other people could enjoy them as much as he did."

Jean opens his mouth like he's going to say something else, but then changes his mind. Eventually, "I'll leave you to it, then," he says, and before I can answer, he's headed for the stairs.

•

Caroline is waiting for me in front of the Revue Cinema. It's a nice summer night and she's wearing a pleasantly faded light yellow sundress and equally well-worn opened-toed leather sandals. Seeing me coming down the sidewalk, "I still don't understand why we're meeting in front of the theatre instead of forty feet down the street at the actual restaurant," she says. Suddenly, Toronto has become a city of socially distanced sidewalk cafés, European life along the boulevard right on the shore of Lake Ontario.

"What if one of us had been unavoidably late and the other one had to sit there alone waiting and looking like they got stood up?"

"I guess it's pretty obvious you haven't hit the DGASA years yet."

"What's that?"

"The don't-give-a-shit-anymore years."

"I'm getting there. Give me time."

We kiss—lightly, briefly, like any other new couple graduating beyond private lust to something else, something public—in front of the old theatre.

Old buildings are better. The Revue Cinema is one hundred and something years old and still occupies the same Edwardian building it did when World War One was only a rumour on the wireless. The original owner operated it until his death in the early 2000s, and when his children decided they'd rather not be in the repertory film business, neighbourhood volunteers raised enough awareness and money for new owners to be located and the building to be leased back to the Save the Revue people and for the admittedly shabby theatre to be cleaned up and buffed up and made operational again. There are a series of black-and-white photographs of the exterior of the Revue through the decades hanging on the walls of the lobby showing horse-drawn buggies passing by in the street, Model Ts parked out front, shaggy hippies loitering outside. It feels good to stand next to something that was around before I was and that'll be around after I'm gone.

"You blew it," Caroline says. "Five more minutes and I might have gotten tired of standing and got us a table and slipped the waiter my credit card and treated you."

"Maybe you still will. Maybe I forgot my wallet at home."

"Let me check," she says, moving closer and hooking a thumb into each of my back jean pockets.

"Okay, you got me," I say. "I'm just cheap. Anything to score a free enchilada and a few margaritas."

Pulling me closer, "Wait a minute, I'm not done looking yet," she says, pushing her pelvis into mine, her open hands palming my ass.

"You're going to get us arrested," I say.

"I don't feel you pulling away."

"If you can't do the time, don't do the crime."

"You think that quoting the theme song to *Baretta* is going to help you get lucky?"

This is why you date people your own age—you don't have to explain crappy seventies TV-show theme-song references. "I don't feel you pulling away either," I say.

We kiss again, this time not lightly or briefly.

"See?" I say. "Aren't you glad we didn't already get a table?"

We kiss again.

"You know," she says, "I don't think I'm as hungry as I thought I was."

"Me neither," I say.

ELEVEN

Knowing each other longer, better, makes it easier to ask. Caroline's very potent pot doesn't hurt, either. Neither does getting my brains fucked out. Getting laid regularly has very effectively helped fill up the hours previously spent getting high by myself. A crystalline Jerry Garcia guitar solo and a nice ripe Indica/Sativa blend can take you to a lot of places, but underneath a sweating, grunting woman grinding her way to sighing satisfaction isn't one of them.

On my back, where she left me after she came and climbed off, arms and legs splayed and head-to-toe dewed in good fresh sex sweat, "Aren't you"—inhale, exhale, catching my breath—"supposed to be sick or something?"

"Or something." She pulls deeply from her joint before offering it over. She's sitting up in bed, naked except for her black bra. Sometimes we do it with her padded bra on, sometimes we do it lingerie-less, with her survivor scars showing. It's always good.

I manage to hold up an I-give-up hand. "Let me catch my breath."

She smiles and shrugs and takes a puff for me. "You'd think you were the one doing all the work."

I take another deep breath and rouse myself to a similar sitting position. "*Work*. That sounds awful grim. I hope it was at least a labour of love."

"A labour of what?"

"A labour of..."

She gets what she wanted—we both laugh—but I was the first one to use the *L*-word and it stays stuck in the air. I attempt to swat it away with a peace sign brought to my lips indicating I'm ready for the joint now, and Caroline passes it over.

"Although," she says, "if we do end up having this amazing love affair, they can call it *Love in the Time of Corona.*"

"That sounds like one of those best-selling Canadian novels people are always trying to unload on me."

"Oh my God, yes, the—what-do-you-call-it?—the Giller book. The Giller-prize book or whatever it's called. Does this make us bad Canadians?"

"You know it. *Bad Canadians*, sub-species *White, Privileged, and Middle-Aged*. I've got news for you: that makes us bad human beings."

"It's not like I read much fiction anyway. Or any, now that I think of it. At least not lately. I don't know why, I really don't. I think the last Canadian novel I actually went out and bought and read when it was first published was *Barney's Version*."

"Which I'm 99.9 percent sure won the Giller."

"Well, there you go."

"There you go, what?"

"They *all* can't be *Love in the Time of Corona*. Maybe it's time to give fiction another shot."

"I used to love Richler."

"You don't like him as much now?"

"It's not that. It's just that I don't read as much as I used to. Or at least as much as I should. But I'll still pick up one of his books, or someone else's books that I love, and just read a few pages—fiction, non-fiction, it doesn't matter. Just to make that connection with another person, with another soul, via little black squiggles on a white piece of paper. And to laugh. He's one of the funniest writers I know. Maybe you're right. After we solve the mysteries of Western philosophy, let's read a novel."

"Maybe they're the same thing. Maybe that's what a soul is. Laughter."

"Christ, this is good pot."

"Right? I wouldn't advise it as a lifestyle choice," she says, taking back the spliff, "but I have to admit, a terminal cancer diagnosis does come with its perks."

"This is very good stuff."

"And all I have to do is ask for it and they give me just as much as I want."

"That sounds like it could be kind of dangerous," I say. "Appealing, but dangerous."

"Speak for yourself. I'm under a doctor's care, remember? This is prescribed medicine." She grins and inhales and passes back the joint.

"I am speaking for myself. I've been trying to cut down on my pot smoking. I *have* been cutting down on my pot smoking."

"Really. Why?"

"I'm not sure." I pass the joint back to Caroline, which she extinguishes in the ashtray. "I got high a lot—probably three or four times a week—but only at home, and only after the workday was done, and usually only late at night when I was listening to music."

"That's a lot of *onlys*. So what was the problem? It sounds like you were a very conscientious stoner."

I wish we were lying in Caroline's bed and not mine: it's easier to think and talk about things you don't want to think or talk about, or things you don't understand, when you're not at home surrounded by your life. Maybe that's why I never take vacations.

"You know how they say you shouldn't mix your drinks?" I say.

"Yeah."

"Well, I rarely got high without listening to the Grateful Dead."

"You were a Deadhead? You were one of those people who followed the band around?"

"In the house of the Dead there are many mansions," I say. "I don't like crowds or the smell of patchouli and I don't wear tie-dye, so, no, that wasn't the kind of Deadhead I was. That I *am*. Whatever. For me, it isn't about anything but the music, particularly the sound of Jerry Garcia's guitar. Whenever I need a transcendental transfusion, all I usually have to do is play some Jerry. No matter what, I know his guitar will hook me up to the infinite and take me for an extraterrestrial joy ride. I need to hear it fairly often or I risk endangering my fragile sense of worldly wonder."

"I get that. If I don't get my hands dirty in the garden on a pretty regular basis, I tend to become a little squirrely. It's the same thing if I'm not in the middle of reading a good, long book and always having somewhere to go that isn't about me or the world I wake up to in the mirror every day. But when it comes to music, I guess I must be the opposite of you. I like the radio because the music never stops and I don't have to choose what gets played and it's a nice surprise when whatever's next comes on. Don't you ever get tired of the Grateful Dead?"

"Sure I do. That's when I know it's time to listen to some solo Jerry Garcia. Although recently even that hasn't done the trick. I have been enjoying lots of early live Allman Brothers and some nice and jammy Traffic and a few other things, but I miss having something surefire to really sink my teeth into, you know?"

"I suppose that's one of the benefits of working from home now. Being your own DJ at work."

"I guess that's true. It has been scientifically proven that all of the most serious listening usually gets done with an air guitar in your hands and no one else around."

"Air guitar. I'm impressed."

"You'd be surprised at how little actual skill is required to play an imaginary instrument."

"I meant I'm impressed that you've already admitted to me that you regularly play air guitar."

"Better you hear about it now than stumbling across me in full rock-god glory later."

"But I still don't understand what the big deal was. What did the Grateful Dead have to do with you smoking too much pot?"

"You're into jazz," I say, "so maybe this will actually make sense."

"I wouldn't say I'm 'into jazz.'"

"I've never heard you listen to anything else."

"Because I like it."

"Yeah, but *why* do you like it?"

"I don't know. I suppose because it sounds sort of like what life feels like most of the time: sort of shapeless, kind of slippery, kind of hard to get your brain around, but underneath it all, holding it all together, even when it seems slipperiest and most fuzzy, is something hard and permanent and beautiful. But that doesn't mean I know much about it or even understand it."

"That's either a very commendable attitude or a very pathetic one."

"Well, either way, it's mine."

I pick up the joint from the ashtray and light it and inhale; I pass it to Caroline.

"You asked me what happens when good weed and good Dead come together. To me, I mean. Actually, it's not even the Dead—like I said, it's mainly Jerry Garcia's guitar. It's like you can crawl inside one of his guitar solos and taste and touch and hear things that there was no way you could experience otherwise. It was like I finally understood that William Blake line about seeing the world in a grain of sand. A ten-minute song feels like an entire lifetime.

I guess the question became, 'How can you get excited about going to a dinner party somebody invited you to when all you need to cruise the cosmos is a nicely rolled fatty and some prime Grateful Dead?'"

"So what you're saying is that you were afraid of becoming a Grateful Dead–obsessed shut-in?"

"Nothing quite so dramatic as that. I just think that there were things in life—other things, other people, maybe, I don't know—that I wasn't... I mean, after my store closed down, I felt sort of like... geez, this really *is* good weed."

Caroline has almost finished the joint; she stubs out what's left. "Why don't you put some Grateful Dead on?"

"Are you serious?"

"I've never turned down a potential cruise on the cosmos before."

"Hold that thought."

Although the turntable and my vinyl collection are downstairs, I keep my compact discs and a small stereo in the bedroom. With a good pair of headphones and both feet up on the windowsill and the big tree in the front yard for company, it's a non-bibliophilic sanctuary and the perfect place to watch the leaves die in the fall and return in the spring and to listen to Jerry try to make sense of it all. At least it used to be before I began bunking down with several cardboard boxes full of store stock.

I pull out *Dick's Picks Volume 11*, 09/27/72, a three-CD set capturing the Grateful Dead at the Stanley Theater in Jersey City, New Jersey, inestimable founding member Pigpen sick at home and dying of alcoholism, but recent addition Keith Godchaux's jazzy piano tinkling and cascading filigrees making for prime GD. I push CD two into the player and out comes a classic '72 "China Rider," the Dead's own "China Cat Sunflower" seamlessly segueing into the old folk tune "I Know You Rider," nearly thirteen minutes of Jerry riding wave after wave of celestial spray and mist. I return to bed and we both lean back and listen.

After the song is over, but before it's Bob Weir's turn to take the wheel with his "Playing in the Band," "This is live, right?" Caroline says.

No one "gets" the Dead on first listen—it's not about liking a particular song or enjoying an overall sound, it's about listening and listening until you finally hear Jerry's guitar siren-songing your name—so I appreciate the no-nonsense question.

"It's from a series called Dick's Picks, various concerts that the group's archivist Dick Latvala dug up from the band's vault and made available to the public in small, limited editions."

"And by the look of your shelves, you've got a lot of them."

"I've got all of them, all thirty-six volumes. And after Dick passed away and Dave Lemieux took over as archivist, every volume of their successor."

"Let me guess: Dave's Picks."

"I only said the music was profound. Some of it, at least. Up to about the end of the seventies."

"You also told me you weren't a collector anymore."

"I'm not. Those books covering that wall are about it. I'd say I've only got a couple hundred of my own books left. And even those aren't particularly valuable. A lot of it is just stuff that was a big deal to me when I was younger that I like to keep around."

"Let me guess again: *On the Road. Tropic of Cancer.* A little Beckett. The poetry of Leonard Cohen. Emily Dickinson. Maybe *Mrs. Dalloway* or *To the Lighthouse* when you were feeling a little artsy. And Richler, of course. Am I getting warm?"

"Warm enough."

"What's that one?"

"Which?'

"The two big black volumes. The ones without jackets. To the left of *The Life of Johnson*. I can't read what's on the spines."

"*Black Lamb and Grey Falcon*. Rebecca West. A two-volume, 1,100-page part-travelogue and part-history of Yugoslavia that was published in 1941 and that I've never read and very likely never will but that I'll also never get rid of."

"How come?"

"I read an interview with her once when I was young and her saying that she knew when she was writing that book that no one was going to read it because it was too long, but unfortunately that's just how long it had to be. From that moment on, that's what a *writer* was to me. Somebody who failed on their own terms. How could I possibly part with a book like that?"

Caroline and I look at the wall of books.

"Even the books I haven't read," I say, "like that one, I can usually remember where I got them. Growing up, there were so many great bookstores in Toronto. *Black Lamb and Grey Falcon* I got from Abbey Books, which always felt like you were stepping into a church, it was always so quiet and cozy and dim. And almost right next door was About Books, which had the same creaky-old-wooden-floor feeling to it, but also the smell of pipe tobacco courtesy of the male half of the store's owners. His wife and daughter were always there and part of what About Books was about too, just like the lazy old yellow Lab who was usually stretched out on the floor. Sometimes he'd be lying directly in front of the section you wanted to get at and you'd have to sort of step around him to find the book you wanted because you knew he wasn't going to move."

"I had the same love affair with John W. Doull Books," Caroline says. "Which, by the way, *is* still here."

"They're still in Halifax? I thought they moved."

"They did. To Dartmouth. I said they're still here, I didn't say it wasn't the 21st-century. Anyhow, there weren't as many bookstores in Halifax—a few, but not as many as here, I'm sure—but it didn't matter because Doull's was so big and had so much great stock. When I moved to Toronto and the movers had left and I found myself confronted by a house full of book-filled boxes, I have to admit, I felt a little foolish, I hadn't read probably a quarter of what was inside them. That's probably why I never visited your store. If I lived to be a hundred, I thought, I knew I still probably wouldn't get through half of them."

"I know what you mean. Like I said, pretty much everything other than what's in this room is just inventory I happen to live with. Which is why where I sleep these days is more like a stockroom than a bedroom. Again—sorry. Sometimes it feels like I'm being driven out of my own house by having to play store twenty-four hours a day. But I used to be a big-time collector, believe me. I don't know many second-hand booksellers who aren't. Or weren't."

"So what happened?"

"Turning fifty and getting lazy and just not reading as much as I used to probably had something to do with it. That and something that was written on the inside cover of a paperback collection of Paul Tillich essays I picked up at the Victoria College book sale once. It had belonged to a recently deceased customer of mine—he'd written his name in it and he'd bought it from me, from my store. And now there it was, along with a bunch of his other books with his name written inside each of them, and all of them scattered across the room to be picked at and flipped through. I couldn't help but think of that old joke—you know, the one about how you don't buy beer, you just rent it? Just like my old customer, I was only renting my books. Dust to dust, and old paperbacks, too, I guess."

"That's interesting, but I wasn't talking about your books when I said you told me you weren't a collector anymore."

We both look at the floor-to-ceiling wall of CDs. "I guess I am sort of still a collector," I say. I'm not sure how I feel about this. What else about myself have I been sure about that plainly isn't true?

"Aside from the actual music," I say, "what's most interesting about all these live Dead shows is that most of them were never even meant to be heard by anyone but the band, they were just soundboard tapes made by the road crew in case the group wanted to check out the show afterward."

"Okay."

"But it's more than that," I say. "It's like . . . what you're listening to was stolen from time."

"I don't follow. And I don't think it's because of the weed."

"I mean, here we are, in Toronto, Ontario, Canada, several decades after the fact, enjoying something very, very special that wasn't even supposed to be heard by anybody outside of the band, if at all. By '72 it'd become more or less routine to just tape the shows, label them, and file them away without even bothering to give them a listen. But think about this: one of my favourite 'Dark Stars'—"

"What's a 'Dark Star'?"

Yes. What *is* a "Dark Star"?

"'Dark Star' is a song by the Dead—a long song, rarely less than twenty minutes and usually a lot longer, that's all about jamming, deep-space jamming. One of the band members, I forget which one, once said that 'Dark Star' never stops, it's always playing somewhere in the universe, it's just that sometimes the Dead tap into it for a little while, for twenty minutes or so on this or that particular night."

"Well, I'm glad we got that cleared up."

"That's not the important part. The important point is that one of my favourite 'Dark Star's is from a 12/20/69 gig at the Fillmore in San Francisco."

"What's 12/20/69?"

"Sorry. Deadspeak for December 20, 1969."

"Okay."

"This 'Dark Star' is twenty-two minutes long and is otherworldly as only something cooked up in the hothouse of planet Earth could be, and no one had heard a second of it since those lucky people who were actually there that night on December 20, 1969, heard it. Right up until 2012 when a woman who used to be married to someone who used to engineer for the Dead found two boxes of reel-to-reel tapes in her attic and returned them to the band. For whatever reason, this guy, who she wasn't married to anymore, had the only band-recorded copies of this concert sitting in his attic for thirty-three years. The music—that 'Dark Star,' that perfect 'Dark Star'—which everybody assumed was lost forever, a moment in time whose time had come and gone and was never going to exist again—is suddenly alive again. It's like, if life is just a bunch of moments, tapes like this one are stolen moments, the good stuff that time tries to cheat us out of that we somehow manage to experience and enjoy again anyway."

"This one sounds pretty good for a soundboard recording," Caroline says.

"They're all just two-track recordings, but, yeah, they're okay. The best tapes are the Betty Boards, the recordings made by Betty Cantor-Jackson. They're two-tracks too, but hers just sparkle."

"Why are hers so special?"

"Don't get me wrong—they're all good. Bear—Owsley Stanley, the Dead's original soundman—he was the first person to record their shows, and his mixes are just fine, if a little lacking in bottom end for my taste, probably because his priority was mixing the band's instruments so they'd sound good onstage. A couple of their roadies picked up the slack later on, and the tapes that they're credited with are really good too. But Betty's tapes, they sound so warm. It's like you're right there, right onstage, forty years later. That's the irony. She claims that her tapes sound the way they do because basically she mixed the band to sound good in her headphones, right there, right then."

Caroline fires up what's left of the joint. "Well, thankfully we've got sufficient quantities of high-quality, medically prescribed pot to honour Saint Betty and all of her illustrious underlings." She sucks, holds it in, passes it over.

"There's no question about the quality," I say, taking it, toking, "But what is it supposed to do?"

Caroline closes her eyes and smiles a deeply grooved stoned smile.

"I'm not *that* fucked up," I say. "It's supposed to make you feel better, I get that. It's just that I don't see..."

"See what?"

"Well, why you need it. I mean, maybe you look a little tired once in awhile, but... who over the age of thirty doesn't?"

Caroline taps the ash of the joint into the ashtray resting on her bare belly before taking another pull. "Okay," she says. "Here's how it is." She offers me what's left of the joint and I shake my head and she gently stubs it. "As you might imagine, this isn't my favourite topic. It's not how I'd prefer to spend my time."

"I get that." I watch the ashtray gently rise and fall with her breathing.

"But since you shared with me the mysteries of Jerry Garcia's guitar, and since we're... whatever it is we are... I guess you need to know what's going on. What's *going* to go on."

"I'm not trying to pry," I say. "I just—"

She puts her finger on my lips. "I know." She pulls the covers up to just below her collarbone. "Right now—tonight—I don't feel too bad. It's kind of like you've got a cold that won't go away and you feel sort of achy all over. That's what the marijuana is supposed to help with. That and my appetite. But it's really not too bad. In fact, the pot you're supposed to use for this sort of thing is mainly CBD-based, but the stuff we've been smoking is mostly TCH."

"I've heard of CBD, but I guess I always thought pot was just pot."

"The CBD relaxes the body and the TCH is what gets you high."

"So... I mean..."

"It's okay." She takes my hand. "What do you want to know?"

"So... why do you need the pot that's supposed to help with the pain? Like I said, you seem to be in pretty good shape—really great shape—for somebody who..."

"Is dying?"

"Is sick."

"You of all people should know better than to judge a book by its cover," she says. She smiles; I don't. "I *am* going to be in a lot of pain, and sooner than later. The kind of pain that no strain of marijuana is going to have the slightest effect on. Around-the-clock-morphine pain. No more sex pain. No more philosophy-talk pain. No more gardening pain. No more anything-good-anymore pain."

I don't do it on purpose, but I squeeze her hand. Instead of squeezing back, Caroline gently but determinedly pulls her fingers away and plucks up the roach out of the ashtray with her thumb and forefinger. She manages to light it, and with a succession of tiny puffs gets it glowing red again.

"Maybe it won't be as bad as you think," I say.

"Phil. *Please*. If there's one thing I don't need to hear it's—"

"Hold on, I'm serious. I mean, obviously I don't know much about any of this, but isn't chemotherapy supposed to really wipe you out? Like I said, you look great."

"That's because the chemo's been over for awhile. And people usually feel as good as they're going to feel once it is."

"But why is it over? Isn't chemotherapy part of what you're supposed to do?"

"It is if you want to spend what little time you've got left puking your guts out and being totally drained and exhausted and feeling like you're already dead."

"I know—I mean, obviously I don't *know*, but I believe you—but it's supposed to help, right?"

"Phil. Sweetie." Caroline called me *sweetie*. She lays her free hand on top of mine. "I have stage-four lung cancer that has spread to my liver and my lymph nodes. I'm taking five different kinds of medication to help slow it down, but there's nothing I can take that's going to stop it."

"Yeah, but—"

"*Nothing*. I could have had more chemo, just like I did when it was breast cancer, but this time all they could promise me was that if it worked I might get another six months, maybe a year. A year of more pain and suffering and slow deterioration. I watched both of my parents slowly die of cancer. No thank you."

I don't say anything. What the hell is there to say?

"So, instead, I choose to spend the time I've got left being myself for as long as possible and doing the things I've always loved doing. Reading. Working in my garden. Drinking good wine. Listening to good music. Spending time with nice people doing nice things." Her hand is back underneath the blankets and doing something very nice to this person. "Things like this."

"But hold on a second," I say.

But she doesn't hold on. Well, she does, but holding on to what she's busy doing it to isn't what I meant.

"You want me to stop?" she says.

"No, but... shouldn't we talk a little more about..."

"About what? About this?" The white duvet is moving up and down faster and faster; it looks like a nervous miniature ghost.

"No, about..."

"About what?"

Even if I could remember what we were talking about, I'm sure she's right, there's really nothing left to say.

•

Before the internet, when you had to physically go looking for the right book to get the right information, procrastination was defensible. Now, when all it takes is to type the desired subject into a search engine, your only excuse is either not caring enough to bother finding out or caring enough that you don't want to know. I punch in *lung cancer stage four liver lymph nodes,* and in .73 seconds there's the inevitable end of Caroline's life in pulsating pixellation. I click and click again and check my website to see if any new orders have come in. They haven't. Then I look up the weather forecast for tomorrow and the day after that and the day after that and learn that they're all going to be pretty much the same as today. I bring up queenwestbooks.ca again, but nothing's changed since I checked it five minutes ago. I clear the screen of everything but the website where I started.

Pain
Delirium
Fatigue
Cough

Constipation
Fever
Shortness of breath
Lack of appetite
Dsyphagia
Depression
Et cetera

Caroline was right—of course she was right, why wouldn't she be right?—the sky is darkening and the temperature is dropping and the air feels different: a storm, definitely, is coming. You can smell it, you can feel it, and when it arrives, the roads will all be washed away and no one will leave their homes and communication will be all but impossible. That's what happens when it storms. That's what storms do. I shut off my computer.

TWELVE

It feels right, it feels wrong, it feels like it usually does when you think you're probably doing the right thing, probably. If your terminally ill girlfriend can out-fuck you, maybe it's time to consider putting down the potato chips and picking up a dumbbell. If, however, you do decide to join the recently reopened local gym, the same gym Debbie used to belong to ($49.99 a month, including optional early-morning Pilates classes and complimentary towel service) and begin to stretch and strain and sweat away all those unwanted pounds, the question has to be asked: Is it right to grow stronger when the person who inspired you to do so is heading, however slowly and relatively inconspicuously, the other way? I don't bother going back over my notes on the pre-Socratics to determine what they've got to say on the matter. Where's a philosopher with all the answers when you really need them?

"Being in shape" wasn't a concept you needed to concern yourself with for the first few decades of your life. Just as an alcoholic calls them "mornings," not "hangovers," youthfulness is synonymous with healthiness. You might not be Calvin Klein–model material, but that's not going to stop you from growing and craving and striving and going and getting and doing all of the things your bursting body and busy brain by their very needy nature conspire together to do. Just like it seems as if it'll never be any different. And why would it? Plenty more sap where that strapping redwood came from. Until one day when the leaves begin to turn and the bark starts to coarsen and it's difficult to deny the possibility that even mighty oaks eventually topple and rot and meet their mulchy end. So off to Scotty's Gym you go, only a five-minute walk from your house, but a whole other world away.

It's a pandemic gym—masks are required at all times when you're not exercising and you need to reserve your machine of choice online for a maximum of thirty minutes—but it's still a gym: rows of treadmills, elliptical trainers, stationary bikes; a room full of free weights, leg-press machines, bench-press machines; floor mats for sit-ups and stretching, ropes and wall-to-wall mirrors for skipping and for keeping an eye on one's form. But it's the people, as usual, who make it more than what it is. The strangest contraption can't compete with its inventors for unadulterated interestingness. I step onto the elliptical trainer, press a couple of buttons on the green-lit keyboard to read MANUAL and START, and move my legs and arms faster and slower, faster and slower, then right in rhythm with how quickly I feel my first-fit-day-of-the-rest-of-my-life body can cope. I'm not moving very fast, and I'm certainly not going anywhere, but I'm moving.

You can get away with staring when you're working out in a gym. Maybe it's bad manners, but it's a lot more fun than looking at your huffing, puffing, perspiring self in the mirror. The rest of the world may very well be composed of little more than billions of other huffers and puffers and perspirers, but they're not you, and for this reason alone they're inherently intriguing. Until you speak to them, of course, and get to know them. But in a gym you don't talk. In a gym you lift and pedal and row and run and look.

Look at big ones waddling on treadmills. At thin ones conquering skyscrapers on Stairmasters. At light bulb–shaped men slamming down barbells when not making eyes at their own rippling reflections. At grunting women leg-pressing their own body weight. At young people plugged in and oblivious. At old people pedalling along to their own thoughts. At white people and brown people and Black people and Asian people and other colours and kinds too. Then the keypad says WORKOUT OVER and you step off and towel down and rehydrate and do what everyone else does, tear off a paper towel and grab the spray bottle of disinfectant and carefully wipe down your piece of equipment like any other responsible gym member.

I walk home and shower and change and am surprised that I feel as good as I do—not sore in the least and even sort of energized. Maybe I'm not in such bad shape after all.

In the morning I'm surprised again. Either someone had surreptitiously taken a meat tenderizer to my legs, back, arms, and abdomen during the night while I was asleep or I'm in much worse shape than I thought.

I groan, I laugh, I can't wait to tell Caroline.

•

"I know. I know. Like I'm supposed to know that, right? Right? So he's, like, 'Just do it when you're done.' And I'm, like, 'I already told you, I don't know when I'm gonna be done.' And he's all, like, 'You said you did.' So I say, 'No I didn't. I said I *might* know, but I might not know either, I don't know.' What? I know. I know. *I know.* And then—wait, hold on—and then—"

And then, blessedly, aisle seven comes to an end and I make a sharp right-hand turn and push my cart straight to the produce section. I buy most of my fruit and vegetables from the open-air markets on Roncesvalles, only shop at Loblaws for things like toilet paper and Corn Flakes and canned soup, but the detour is worth it for not having to listen to, like, another episode of the further fascinating adventures of the woman with the face mask and the phone headset and the shit-coloured fingernail polish and the shopping cart empty but for a single frozen pizza and several cans of cat food. Poor animal. I hope for its sake it's not exclusively an indoor cat.

Now that my ears can breathe again, I'm capable of being a bit more charitable, am able to acknowledge that it's not the woman's fault that she either believes that the world wants to hear every dull detail of her life or, more likely, isn't even aware of the verbal diarrhea she's spraying everywhere. It's not her fault she's young. I feel self-conscious just laying out my groceries in the checkout aisle for the person in line behind me to see. I mean, what if they think I use the toilet paper to wipe my ass? We're wrong, of course, they're wrong, obviously, it's every generation's right to be as foolish in its own inimitable way as the one that came before it. Love my neighbour? Not a chance. Give them some slack, the same slack I'd like them to grant me? Sure. I can at least try.

I push my cart and fill it with what I need and find myself quietly singing along to the music playing in the store. When I was the age of the woman with the headset, grocery-store music was old-people music, not *real* music, and certainly not composed of songs whose every word you knew. Like everybody, I tell myself I'm the exception to the rule, am unusually young at heart, am not old like old people were when I was young. Not *really*. And hey, as far as AM radio top-forty fodder goes, "Spiders and Snakes" is a pretty damn catchy little song. I hum myself to the checkout line and wonder if Jim Stafford is still alive.

I have to walk across a portion of the parking lot to get to the shortcut around back of the grocery store that'll take me home, but that's okay, it's a lovely late-July day—warm, dry, bracingly breezy—the kind of weather that makes you wonder why you feel so good until you realize there's no particular reason at all, you simply do. I even manage to ignore the row of newspaper boxes at the entrance to the store insisting in bold type and big pictures that I concern myself with today's COVID-19 update or the most recent scandal involving our sage federal senate, those ex-professional hockey players and coaches, those sycophantic journalists, those influence-buying businessmen, those sundry lackeys and boot-lickers who comprise our theoretically democratic nation's upper house of Parliament. I haven't encountered any of history's most illustrious political theorists in my saunter through Western philosophy yet, but I remember enough public school science to know not to stare directly at the sun. Just because it exists doesn't mean you have to go blind looking at it.

Then I see something I can't help seeing. Cameron. In the passenger-side seat of a grey Lexus. Leaning across to the driver's side and kissing the woman sitting behind the wheel. Who's kissing Cameron back. Who's kissing her back. There's no misunderstanding, no possibility of misinterpretation, no way not to register precisely what's going on. There's no ambiguity about what the two sets of hands I can't see below the front windshield are probably up to, either. My two cloth bags full of groceries and I do an about-face and scuttle back inside Loblaws.

I manage to kill a few minutes by withdrawing some money from the cash machine located near the stacked cases of pop and bottled water, and a few minutes later I step back outside and peek in the direction of the Lexus like a person without an umbrella checking to see if it's still raining. The car is gone. I can go home now.

•

—Are you going to tell him?

—Of course I'm going to tell him. How could I not? He's my nephew.

—I know, but... I just mean, no matter what happens, he's going to resent you. Not that that's fair...

—I know. Believe me, I know. But if I don't tell him then I'll feel guilty for an entirely different reason.

—A perfect lead-up to today's subject.

—I don't follow.

—You know. Today's topic.

—Right...?

—The rise of Christianity after the decline of the Greeks and the fall of Rome? The domination of the Catholic Church for a thousand years?

—Oh, okay, I get it. Catholicism. Guilt. Gotcha.

—Why don't you kick things off? I think you might need something to keep your mind occupied.

—I'll do it, but only because you started last time and I don't want you to think I didn't do my homework.

—That works too. Go for it.
—There are basically two big periods of Catholic philosophy.
—You say "basically" a lot. Did you know that?
—I do now.
—It's not a problem. I just thought you'd like to know.
—That's very considerate of you. Can I continue?
—Basically, yes.
—I think we need more wine.
—First please explain to me why you don't sound drunk or stoned to yourself when you're drunk or stoned.
—For the same reason other people don't sound drunk or stoned to you when you're drunk or stoned.
—Makes sense, but then I am a little drunk and stoned. I'll get another bottle while you pick up where you left off. Go ahead, I can hear you from the kitchen.
—Before you interrupted me, you mean.
—Sorry, I'm in the kitchen, I can't hear you.
—Anyway, basic—essentially—during this whole period, the entire thousand years or so, most secular philosophy ceases to exist.
—Give me your glass.
—Thanks.
—Now, do I have this part straight? It seems kind of important. In the earlier period, it's Plato who the Catholics use to help construct their theology, but later on it's Aristotle?
—That sounds right.
—So although non-Christian ways of thinking and talking about the world were scarce and even forbidden...
—Like during the Crusades.
—Like during the Crusades, all of the Catholic heavyweights, the so-called Church Fathers—

—Like Augustine and Aquinas.

—like Augustine and Aquinas, they built most of their theology on the back of a bunch of Greek heathens.

—Yep.

—Sounds kind of fishy, doesn't it?

—Hey, my family wasn't religious, but I grew up picturing Jesus as a nice older white guy. Maybe a little on the tan side and with some funny ideas about manly footwear, but looking a lot more like us than the Middle Eastern guy who worked at the 7-Eleven.

—I know, it's weird, right? Plato and Aristotle always seemed more like old Oxford professors to me than hairy Greeks.

—I guess it shouldn't be too surprising. Xenophanes said that people usually imagine gods that look like people. Like themselves, I mean.

—The old man upstairs with the silver beard who punishes people when they're bad and only lets them into heaven if they're good.

—You got it.

—But it's so . . . I don't know, unfair, you know?

—What do you mean?

—Look at Augustine, right? He steals Plato's idea of—what does it say here?—universals and uses it to cook up his own brand of dualism that's the crux of his *City of God*, his magnum opus. Which as far as I can understand means that there are two realities: the world, which is a way station where we're unfortunately obligated to languish for a brief unpleasant instant. And eternity, where we'll justifiably suffer for a few centuries before some of us finally get to float around in unending bliss.

—I'll drink to that. Oh, shit.

—What?

—I think I've been drinking out of your glass. Or you've been drinking out of mine.

—It's okay.
—Yeah, but you shouldn't be... You know, germs.
—I think maybe it's time to admit we're in the same bubble, Phil, and that your germs are my germs and vice versa.
—I guess that's true.
—And from one bubble mate to another, can I ask a favour? I know it's cheating a bit, but can we just skip the rest of this period? It's all just so gloomy.
—You're saying you find the promise of everlasting life and blissful communion with God, your heavenly father, gloomy?
—I'm saying life's too short to spend it in the Middle Ages.
—Hey, cheer up. Next on the agenda is the Renaissance.
—See? Just that word—*Renaissance*—and everything suddenly feels brighter and lighter and better.
—That's easy for you to say. You don't have to inform your nephew that you caught his girlfriend making out with another woman in a grocery-store parking lot.
—If you think it'll help, I'm willing to crack open the books again and see what the Church Fathers have to say on the subject of our truth-sharing responsibility to others.
—I think it's more likely that some more wine will help.
—For now, it might.
—*For now* is about all I want to think about right now.
—Well, there are a lot worse places to be.

•

Procrastination is supposed to be fun. At the very least, you're supposed to feel better than you would have if you were doing the thing you were dutifully avoiding doing. If what you decided to do, however, was drop by a friend's bookstore, better luck next time. Online sales are doing better—I'm almost busy enough—but it's not enough, I still want more, miss actual milling customers and satisfied smiles at checkout and eating a late-lunch takeout falafel behind the counter while the streetcar reliably dings by and the sun slides down the building across the street meaning that another day is done, good job, Phil, good night. If you're not greedy enough, you tend not to get what you want from life. If you're too greedy, you'll never get everything you wanted. Someone with less on their mind—or a better mind—than me could undoubtedly derive a moral from this.

Stephen sees me come in, but is talking to a customer at the cash register, so only waves before returning his attention to the old woman whose book he's processing. I head for the new arrivals section. I've known Stephen since we were twenty-something kids working for minimum wage for a guy named Alan at his Yonge Street bookstore, a shop whose stock tended toward the "tastefully" pornographic and an owner whose devastating halitosis hit you, especially first thing in the morning, like a vaporous smack of wet cardboard. Stephen is one of the good ones—a bookseller who, after being in the business for nearly as long as me, can still occasionally be spotted reading on the job and continues to get excited when he lucks into something really rare or special, and not just because of what he can turn around and resell it for—and we used to see more of each other than we do now.

He and his wife have kids now, that's a big part of it, as is the fact that, when they do get some time for themselves, there's always a show to see at the AGO, an exhibit to check out at the ROM, a dinner party they or someone they know is throwing. They used to invite me sometimes when they were hosting, especially after Debbie and I split up, but even the least inspiring art show or rare artifact exhibit can be survived with a minimum amount of pursed-lip solemnity mixed up with the occasional well-placed *Um*... or *Interesting*..., but dinner parties require not only conversation but active listening, otherwise you won't have a clue what to say when it's your turn to bore other people while they wait their turn to bore you. I preferred to stay home and get high and listen to the Dead.

Stephen's also the competition. Of course, I'm flattering myself—fooling myself is more like it—that we're actually still in the same business, not when he's got a thousand more square feet of prime Queen Street West commercial space than I do (and two rental units upstairs that have to bring him at least four or five thousand a month)—but competitive delusions die hard. I admire his not one, but two, rolling wooden ladders and peruse his newest arrivals and eavesdrop on the conversation at the counter.

"Do you need a bag?'

"Oh, no, I've got my own."

"All right. I'll just slip the receipt inside the book."

"That's fine. And I have to tell you. Until only very recently, I'd never read Muriel Spark before."

"She's great."

"Oh, I *know*. That's what's so surprising. I'd certainly heard of her before, but it wasn't until I was recently hospitalized and someone had left behind a paperback copy of one of her novels in the visitors' waiting room that I actually sat down and read one of them. And she's *wonderful*."

"I get the feeling you've read a few more since then."

"Oh, yes. She's quite addictive. Thankfully, she was also quite prolific."

"She was."

"I've been picking them up here and there, piecemeal, you know, wherever I find them, so I was pleased to find this one here today."

"Well, I'm glad we had it. If you want to leave me your contact information, I can let you know when we get some more of her stuff. It's not common, but it does come in."

"Oh, that would be lovely. But would it be all right if I emailed you instead? That way I could let you know which ones I already have and we wouldn't be wasting each other's time."

"Good idea. Here's our card."

"Lovely. You'll be hearing from me."

"I'm looking forward to it."

"My name is Heather, by the way."

"I'm Stephen. Pleased to meet you, Heather."

"You too, Stephen. I'll speak to you soon."

Stephen waits for the woman to ding the door goodbye before stepping from behind the counter and coming over. We both pull down our masks. "The things we do for a six-dollar sale," he says.

"Plus tax," I say.

"Plus tax, that's true. God knows we need all the receipts we can get. Got to keep Revenue Canada happy."

I pick up an expensive hardback edition of the *Kama Sutra* and flip. "Do you have any other books like this, but where the man gets to lie on his back or to sit in a chair?"

"We're not that old," Stephen says.

"Not yet." He's not the one who had to join a gym because his girlfriend was lapping him in the bedroom.

"You seeing somebody?"

I put back the book. "Nah."

I *could* tell him about Caroline; we *are*, I guess, "seeing each other." But I don't. If I tell him about Caroline and her lovely little library and her big backyard garden and what a good cook she is and how smart and funny she is and how easily we get along and all the nattering, lovey-dovey rest of it, I'll also have to eventually tell him she's going to die. The less you talk about something the less real it is. Mum's the only person I've told about Caroline's cancer, probably because there's a good chance she won't remember it the next time we talk.

"Hey, I checked out your new website," he says. "Pretty spiffy."

"It ought to be. The people who built it charged me enough."

"It was worth it. They did a good job. I've been trying to get mine updated—just freshen it up a bit, you know?—but the company who built the original site aren't in business anymore and I've been having a hell of a time finding somebody I like to do the job. Who did you use?"

"They're called Toronto West Social Media Solutions."

"And you were happy with them?"

"Yeah."

"'Yeah.' That's a hell of an endorsement."

"No, yeah, they were great. They were good. I'm happy."

"What's the name of the person you worked with there? It'd be nice to get someone who has some actual experience with the second-hand book trade."

"Ask for Cameron," I say.

"You liked them?"

"She was good. She's young, but she knows what she's doing."

"And she was okay to get along with? Sometimes some of these tech people..."

"I think she gets what we do," I say, neglecting to add, *Just don't go lurking around any grocery-store parking lots and you'll be fine.* "As much as anybody can who spends half of their life staring at a computer screen or a phone."

"Half? You can tell you don't have kids."

Stephen and his wife have three. And own the building the bookstore is in. And have been married for over fifteen years. In other words, he's exactly the sort of individual I'm predisposed to dislike purely out of personal and professional jealousy. Unfortunately, I have little choice but to be glad I know him.

"I've got a nephew who works for me sometimes," I say. "That's enough."

"I thought you were a one-man operation now."

"I am—basically—but he was helping me out with getting everything online and handling my social media stuff, and if I make a big buy he has a car and helps with the heavy lifting."

"I'm envious. It's so hard to find good help now who are willing to work for what I can afford to pay them. And if you do find somebody who's decent, they never stay. And then the whole thing starts all over again."

"You can't blame them," I say. "To anybody's who's got their act even remotely together, we're just a stop along the way, that's just the nature of the business."

"I know..."

"Hey—we were the same way. Neither one of us wanted to spend the rest of our lives making minimum wage working for Alan. We were the best employees that dump of his ever had, but we didn't give a shit, we both wanted to open our own shop eventually."

"Or at least not have to have Alan breathe on you for eight hours a day."

"There was that too," I say, laughing.

Stephen's phone rings and he pulls it out of his pocket and frowns at the display. "Just give me a second, okay? I've got to take this."

"No problem."

I miss this. I should make an effort to see Stephen more. I miss laughing about crappy things that happened to you a long time ago with the people you endured them with. When Caroline and I tackle the Renaissance next week, maybe we'll get lucky and discover that somebody made a philosophical study of the pivotal role of endured crappiness in human happiness.

"No, my point... no, my point is that you've already started the job and it's too late for me to get someone else to finish it," Stephen says into his phone. "I understand that. I understand that. What I need you to understand is that I've got a tenant upstairs who hasn't had running water now for two days and now you want me to tell her that she's not going to have it for at least one more. No, I—no, I un—no, I understand that. I understand it's an old building. But here's where I've got a problem. You assured me that you were used to taking on jobs in buildings like this one and that it wouldn't be—no, I know there weren't any guarantees, but when you—no, I didn't say that, what I said—" I pat Stephen on the shoulder and give him a goodbye wave. He waves back and mouths a silent *Sorry* before resuming the debate with his plumber.

Outside, on the sidewalk, out of the air-conditioning, it's hot-and-sticky humid, the air feels like a giant sweaty armpit, and I wish that summer was over and the sky was slate grey and the air frosty fresh. If it was winter, though, and I was standing exactly where I am right now, I'd probably be wishing it was summertime and that my shoes weren't salt-stained and my pant cuffs slushy soaked and the sky was blue and bright, like it is today. If I squint, I can see the glowing green cactus that is the Mexican chain restaurant down the street that took over the building next door to where my store used to be.

I don't have to squint to spot the streetcar coming down Queen. If I hurry, there's a good chance I'll make it to the stop before it gets there.

THIRTEEN

Shit shit shit. Times like these, medieval philosophy almost makes sense. What better argument could there be for an all-powerful God with an all-knowing sense of irony than my website not doing what it's supposed to do and me needing to call Cameron? And for her to magnanimously offer to take a look in person because Benjamin forgot his laptop at my house and she was meeting a friend for lunch on Roncesvalles anyway and told him she'd pick it up. A *friend*. And just when I'd begun to master the fine art of doing and saying nothing out of a long-standing conviction in practiced ambivalence. Shit shit shit.

"Yeah, this... right, okay, I gotcha... yeah, okay..." Cameron says, more to queenwestbooks.ca than to me. Occupying my usual spot behind my desk in her wheelchair, she's glaring at the computer screen like the bad cop grilling the suspect while the good cop is out getting coffee. Suddenly, ten flying Cameron fingers and I'm concerned for the safety of my computer keyboard. I'm strictly a two-finger typer with an aversion to computer violence, so I tilt back in my chair that she's pushed off to the side of the desk so that she can do her job unimpeded and watch her pound keys and push around the mouse and deliver a dirty stream of disgusted looks at my website. It doesn't matter what you do—butcher, baker, candlestick maker; bookseller, philosopher, website designer—people who know what they're doing and care about what they do quite often look slightly deranged while doing it.

"Okay," she says, with a final *tap tap tap* to the keyboard before pushing herself away from the desk. "Two very common website problems are broken links and long load times. You had both. Both are now problems no more." She pulls a grey metallic refillable water bottle out of her knapsack hanging from the back of her chair and tilts back her head and glug glug glugs a long drink.

"That's great," I say. "Thanks."

"No problem." She barely looks at me before lifting her water bottle and taking another lengthy pull.

"Is there something I should do in the future so this kind of thing doesn't happen again?" I say. "Or maybe something I shouldn't do?"

"Not really. Your site is still pretty new and these are just the normal kinks that need to get worked out sometimes. Technically speaking, shit happens."

Technically, romantically, metaphysically, et cetera: amen to that, sister. And you don't need to study *Summa Theologica* to know it's true. Cameron returns her bottle to her bag and rests her fingerless-gloved hands on her wheels and looks at me like she's waiting to be excused from the dinner table. I still don't know if I'm going to say anything to her about what I saw at Loblaws—or even if I do, what exactly I'm going to say—but if I keep her here and talking a little bit longer maybe the answers will occur to me. Life is easier without other people in it. Not as interesting, maybe, certainly not as enjoyable, but definitely easier.

"Hey, how's Benjamin?" I say. "I haven't seen him in ages. What's he up to?"

"I thought he said he helped you pack up somebody's library last week."

"Yeah, but once we get packing and hauling boxes, we kind of get into it, there's not much time for chit-chat, you know?"

"He's okay. He finally got into all of the courses for the fall he wanted. That was a major dilemma for awhile. God, I'm so glad I'm not in school anymore."

"He was stressing out?"

"Majorly. I mean, I know it's important to him and everything, but get a grip, dude. It's not like it's real life."

I resist the impulse to point out that, based on my own experience, real life is overrated; say, instead, "That must be a drag for you. Dealing with him stressing out, I mean."

Cameron shrugs.

"It's just that it can be tough on a relationship when one person is going through stuff that the other one isn't," I say.

"Whatever. It's cool. It's not like we're married or anything."

"No, but..."

"But what?" She removes her hands from the wheels of her chair and rests them on her bare knees.

"Well, what would you call what you two are? I mean, if you were going to put a label on it? Which I'm sure neither of you do."

Cameron laughs. "Are you hitting on me, Phil?"

I attempt to illustrate that I find the idea even more ridiculous than she does by laughing twice as loud and as long as her. Which succeeds in making me look as if I'm just the sort of obviously deranged middle-aged man who would actually do such a thing. Cameron appears content to stare at me in mild fascination as I continue to make a fool of myself, so I stop laughing just as suddenly as I began, which, if anything, only makes me seem even more unhinged. In my most measured, most kindly avuncular voice, "No, it's just that he's my nephew, that's all. I just want him to be happy."

"Well," Cameron says, hands back on the wheels of her chair, obviously finished with the topic and ready to roll, "you'd have to ask him about that. That last time I saw him, as far as I could tell, I'd say he looked pretty happy."

"Oh, yeah?"

"Yeah," she says, a quick smirk, not a smile, all the clarification she offers. And all that is needed.

I walk behind her chair all the way to the front door. Once we're there and I open it, "God, I hate it when it's so muggy outside like this," Cameron says. "No matter how many baths you take a day, you never really feel clean." Sunlight has pushed its way inside, revealing gleams of red and gold in her blond hair.

"Maybe it'll rain and get rid of some of the humidity," I say. I open the screen door.

"It doesn't look like it's going to rain," she says.

"No," I say. "It doesn't."

•

I *know* this knock. Soft but insistent, apologetic but self-assured, I've never heard it before, but I know it belongs to someone I know, I just couldn't tell you who. I open the door and, yep, I knew it, even though I didn't.

"Grace. Hi. How are you?"

"I'm sorry to have to bother you at home, Phil. I was going to call first, but I would have had to come around regardless because"—she holds up a large blue plastic Bay Bloor Radio bag—"so, well, I thought I'd just..."

"It's no problem," I say. "Come in."

"I promise I won't take up too much of your time."

"C'mon in, Grace."

I know Grace because I know Howard, her husband, who was a longtime customer. Some people enjoy accumulating signed editions, the author's signature inky proof that you're that much closer to the real thing, the flesh-and-blood author him- or herself, but to every addict his own unique addiction, and Howard liked to collect everything a particular author wrote. *Everything.* Not just books by several of the key figures of early-twentieth-century American literature that he liked to collect and thought were good and worthy of taking down from the shelf again. Not just the books that he knew from reputation weren't really that good and that he'd likely never read even once. Not just books, either—pamphlets or special limited editions were always nice addendums to be added to his collection, as were any contribution said author made to an anthology. It didn't matter that he already possessed the anthologized piece as it later appeared in book form; Howard needed to own it in this format as well. And galleys and advanced review copies, he had to have those too. Howard was a good customer.

For the last few years, though, it's been easier to think of him as his wife's ward. Her elderly, absentminded, frequently incomprehensible ward, the one with perennially watery, bloodshot eyes and a billowing, tobacco-stained white beard. I've only known Grace since Howard was diagnosed with Alzheimer's, when she'd escort him to the store for his book-buying sprees because he couldn't come alone. He *shouldn't* have come alone, but more than once that's what he did, which was when I'd telephone Grace and assure her that I'd keep him around until she showed up to bring him home. I got to know her better when, during the store's final year or so, she would come in on her own to return the more expensive of his book purchases. She'd always let him buy whatever he wanted—the disease might have eventually denied him the ability to read, but he'd been a Queen's University English professor for over thirty years and a respected scholar of early-twentieth-century American literature before they'd moved to Toronto after his retirement, and she wasn't going to allow it to rob him of his dignity—and I'd always refund her Visa card. She's an ex–Queen's English prof. too—specialty Plath, Sexton, Berryman, and the American confessionals—and I'd been happy to sell her several books over the years as well.

"Let's go in the kitchen," I say. "Since my house is now apparently a warehouse, it's the only room where two or more people can actually sit down."

"Oh, no, this is fine, I'm not going to be a minute. I just wanted to let you know that Howard passed away."

I sit down in the room's only chair. When you know someone is going to die—and it was only a matter of time before the Alzheimer's finished what it started—when it finally happens, there's not much you can say that doesn't sound like the most flaccid banality. For better and for worse, though, saying things is what human beings do, so we keep on talking anyway. "That's sad," I say.

"Yes, it is."

"When did..."

"Oh, a few months back. He caught pneumonia and never really woke up."

This time I don't even try to say anything that makes sense. Grace looks at me and smiles. "Like I said, I just wanted to let you know. And to thank you for being so kind to Howard. I know he could be a handful sometimes when he wasn't feeling well."

"It was my pleasure." This is a platitude I can stand behind. Even when, near the end of our retail relationship, he required a shopping chaperone and was nearly catatonic and, once, incontinent, what really mattered were the armful of books he'd pile on the counter. Only the best criticism and scholarly works, even if likely chosen only because of some sort of misty memory or dim association. Somewhere inside of him he was still Howard.

"I want you to have these," she says, holding out the plastic bag in front her. "It's just a little token of my appreciation. Of *our* appreciation. Howard's and mine."

"Really, I don't—"

"Take it," she says. "When I heard about your store closing and you selling your books online now," Grace says, "I thought you could use these. Think of them as a little store-warming gift."

I know better than to refuse the offer—I don't know her that well, but I get the impression that, as composed and considerate as she obviously is, Grace tends to get things done, and this is something she wants to happen—and pull out what are obviously a few hardcover books from inside the bag. It only takes my bookseller's brain a few seconds to begin to bubble with excitement. Mint first editions of E.E. Cummings's *The Enormous Room*, H.D.'s *Palimpsest*, William Carlos Williams's *Spring and All*, Gertrude Stein's *The Autobiography of Alice B. Toklas*: this is one serious store-warming gift. If I can find the right customers, cumulatively I'm looking at least five thousand dollars. But there's no way I can keep...

"Grace, there's no way I can keep—"

Grace holds up her hand. "Our children have taken what they want from Howard's library, and of course much of it is going to stay right where it is, in his study, just like it always has, but these books can help you right now, I know that, and I want you to have them." I look at the quartet of treasures in my hands. "It's what Howard would have wanted, too," she adds.

"I don't know what to say, Grace."

Grace smiles again. "Say you're going to put them to good use."

"I don't think I'll have too much trouble with that."

"And that you're going to keep doing what you're doing. We need people like you."

Now I really don't know what to say.

"Goodbye, Phil," Grace says.

"Goodbye, Grace."

Ten minutes later, I still don't.

•

First, fucking; then, philosophy: as long as I get everything I want, I don't need much. I slide out of Caroline's bed and rest my bare feet on the small throw rug covering the hardwood floor. If Caroline was a prescription drug she'd carry a warning about not operating heavy machinery or driving a motor vehicle immediately after having sex with her. Blood flowing upward again, back to my brain, I stand up and stretch and go to the bathroom and shut the door. We just did all manner of this and that, but we're not yet at the peeing-with-the-door-open stage of our relationship. The oversized clear plastic medication organizer on the sink counter containing every day's unsettlingly large allotment of pills is a reminder that there's no guarantee we're going to get there, either. I urinate and splash some water on my face and use the towel hanging on the back of the door to dry off. It smells like Caroline. Now I do too.

Caroline has woken up and lit up and is sitting up in bed, but with a joint, not her usual post-coitus cigarette. She doesn't offer any details (and I don't press her for any), but she says she's not feeling great. She closes her eyes and inhales. I lie down beside her, but stay on top of the blankets, use one of the pillows to cover my naked crotch. The air-conditioning means it's cool enough for me to get back underneath the sheets, but it's not even dark outside yet, it feels wrong, just like getting high right now would be wrong, like guzzling whisky at a baseball game on a summer afternoon. To every drug there is a season. Besides, after what we've been up-and-down, in-and-out up to, I feel pretty high already. I link my hands behind my head and let go a long exhale.

"Are you sure you don't want some of this?" she says, holding out the joint.

"No, but you go ahead."

"Oh, I plan to," she says.

Caroline's pot is so potent, I'm second-hand high in what seems like seconds. I'm not blaming her—the weed is prescribed medication after all, it has its therapeutic purpose—but now I feel sleepy and sluggish at 6:41 p.m. on a beautiful August evening, and even though there was nothing in particular I planned on doing tonight I resent the fact that it's going to be difficult to do it. Caroline appears content to toke and stare out the window at the big maple tree in her backyard doing a slow belly dance in the warm, early-evening breeze, but unfortunately I'm stoned-stuck with myself and can't help but fixate upon the acrid stink that is an old man's daily decaying body wafting up from underneath the pillow covering my genitals. Pity every middle-aged person's helpless attraction to the smooth-skinned and the sweet-smelling, the bright-eyed and the bushy-tailed. Lechery is just nature's way of saying wouldn't it be nice to be young again.

"Could you please not do that?" Caroline says.

I honestly don't know what she's referring to, but the look of weary imposition on her face makes me wish that I did so that I could be sure to keep on doing it.

"Fanning that pillow up and down," she says. "It's kind of distracting."

Oh, that. Because it takes just the right amount of concentration to stare out the window at a tree.

"Sorry," I say, stopping, and throwing in a turned-head, just-out-of-sight eye-roll free of charge.

"And kind of disgusting, too," she adds.

"Moving a pillow up and down is disgusting?"

"It's not the pillow that's... Just forget it, okay?" She takes an especially long toke and shuts her eyes and leans back against the padded headboard.

And I do forget it. For at least ten seconds.

"It's okay," I say. "Tell me. What's so disgusting about me?"

"I didn't *say* you were disgusting. Geez, relax, okay? You really should have a hit of this. It might help with your paranoia."

"Well, that makes sense. You're the one who's high and I'm the one who's paranoid."

She immediately takes another lengthy toke—out of principled defiance or actual need, I can't be sure—but doesn't close her eyes this time, looks at me with two bloody balls of dilated abhorrence that keep on abhorring me even after I've decided to find the design on the pillow on my lap very, very absorbing.

"So you know more than my doctors do, is that what you're saying?"

"Of course not," I say. "I didn't say that. I just said..." If I said it, why the hell can't I remember what it was? "I just wonder whether or not you're using a little too much medicine, that's all. I mean, it does happen. A person could take too much—I don't know—Aspirin even."

"Aspirin."

"As an example, yeah. It could be anything. People overmedicate, is all I'm saying."

Is that all I'm saying? Or has my mouth turned toxic simply because I'm suddenly in a pissy mood and pissiness is contagious and thrives on a continued stream of abject pissiness? Was it really five minutes ago that life was so undemandingly delicious, straight-up, no conjectural chaser?

Caroline is still looking at me, her face maybe a foot and a half from mine, but the annoyance is gone, and in its place is something much, much worse. For the first time since I've known her, she looks exhausted. Beleaguered. *Sick*. She was up several times in the night for lengthy bathroom visits because, she said, the ricotta she made for dinner was too creamy, but I don't believe her. And today was the day that I just had to point out—only in the spirit of impartial medical concern, of course—that a terminal cancer patient might be smoking a little too much weed. What's worse than *ashamed*? I don't know and it doesn't matter. Being able to articulate precisely what kind of shitty you are doesn't make what you did any less shitty.

"I'm sorry," I say.

Caroline doesn't say anything, only looks down at the ashtray resting on top of the comforter, but at least her eyes are somewhere other than on me. I want to say *sorry* again or put my hand on hers—something—but if you can't do good, at least don't do any harm, so I just sit there continuing to say and do nothing. My copy of the philosophy book we were supposed to discuss later on is in my bag on the floor beside my discarded clothes. I should get up and get dressed. We're not going to need it tonight.

FOURTEEN

Other people are not ordinarily my idea of a good time. A book, a walk, a nap, a bottle of wine and some weed and the Dead, the Jays game on the radio and a glass of iced tea, a few forgetful hours of uninterrupted work: happiness is a dish usually best served solo. Until the shop went virtual, however, I don't think I realized how much other human beings are a part of the overall happiness equation. Customers were to be occasionally bemoaned, certainly. Time wasters, for instance, people who love to ask arcane bibliophilic questions because it's imperative that other people know what undeniable intellectuals and sophisticates they are and who are as keen to deplete your time and patience as they are reluctant to actually buy a book. Or the shoplifters who attempt to sell you books that they stole from the store down the street. Or the junkies who smash your front window in the middle of the night because they think that second-hand booksellers have fat stashes of cash lying around (as good an illustration as any of how hard drugs destroy your mind). Or the people who come in asking for books that have as much in common with literature as Twinkies do with food.

But without human interruptions and irritations and inconveniences, it's difficult to appreciate calmness and quiet and when things do happen to go surprisingly smoothly. You can't be thankful that dawn has finally arrived if you've never prayed for the night to end. I'm alerted when someone purchases a book, I package the book up and mail it to them, and... and then I wait to be alerted when someone else buys a book so I can package the book and mail it to them, and... There's still the occasional actual book-buying expedition, there are still estates to appraise, but I'm past running out of room for more stock and can't afford renting storage space and that's only a once-in-a-while thing anyway. But: every day the door used to open, the door would close, people would come, people would go, people would browse, people would talk, he's got a question, she has a request, cash, debit, or Visa, and thanks for stopping by, see you again. No one said curmudgeons don't get lonely.

Being busy and bothered for eight hours a day has another potential advantage: can assist in helping to avoid being bothered by other things you'd prefer your mind not be busy with. Like my fight with Caroline last night. Which wasn't even a fight—was just me making her feel bad—which serves to make me feel bad today. Today sitting at my desk looking at queenwestbooks.ca and waiting for someone to cyber buy something so I'll have something to do other than sitting here waiting on this damn website. But wait a minute: it was actually Caroline who suggested that, if I really wanted to know what was going in Cameron's love life, I should check out her Instagram page. It's unlikely that she'd post anything directly relationship-incriminating, but if I feel the need to snoop, this is the best way to do it. I tap and click and presto! Cameron Johnson in all of her singular selfhood, public and private.

Only there is no such thing as *private* anymore. Not really. The party pictures I get, I guess. Cameron at somebody's birthday bash. Cameron at a wedding. Cameron holding her baby niece or nephew. But headshots of her just out of the bathtub with a towel wrapped around her head. Pictures of her lunch. A *lot* of pictures of her lunches. And breakfasts and brunches and dinners. A photo of her tucked into bed with her cat lying across her chest. Selfies of her and Benjamin smiling, making faces at the camera, kissing. Of Benjamin stirring a pot on the stove. Of a frowny-face Cameron holding a wine bottle whose cork has broken in half. I know, I know, I'm not a Millennial, I wouldn't understand, I didn't grow up immersed in all of the technology they are, their brains are wired differently from mine. You can even throw in the undeniable fact that no generation completely comprehends any other generation. I get it. I just don't understand what would compel someone to advertise what they had for lunch today or post a shot of their unsuspecting, open-mouthed partner asleep on the couch. If it's about proving to the world that you're living a rich and meaningful life, wouldn't the time be better spent actually living? Who cares whether the world thinks you're happy or not? What did a thumbs-up from the world ever do for anybody?

But at least there aren't any pictures of the woman Cameron was kissing in the car in the Loblaws parking lot. Which is good, I guess. Or is that a bad thing? I wish I had someone my own age to talk to about this. I wish Caroline was here to talk to.

•

"I've been thinking about your problem," Fred says.

Could you be a little more specific? I want to ask.

"From what I understand," he says, "the most substantial outlay you have when you're running an outfit like yours is rent."

"If I was still selling out of an actual store, yeah. But that's not an issue now."

"Oh, for sure. And with the government apparently intent upon shutting down the economy because of a bad case of the flu, I'd have to think that this is definitely not the best time to be in the retail business game no matter what. But I remember you saying before that if you had your druthers you'd be back behind the cash register with actual customers coming and going, right? However few of them there actually are still out there."

"Right. But that's not relevant now. A virtual bookstore is the hand I've been dealt and I'm dealing with it."

"Oh, no doubt, no doubt. But if you *could* afford your own building that you could operate your business out of again, you'd be happier, right? As well as sitting on a nice little piece of equity come retirement time."

"That's never going to happen, Fred. Toronto real estate prices—"

"But if you *could* afford it—just humour me, here, okay?—that's what would be best, correct?"

"Sure, fine, yeah. But why are we talking about this?" I look at the plastic basket of dirty clothes I was in the process of putting together when the phone rang. Five minutes ago you would have had a very hard time convincing me that if only I could be alone with the laundry I'd be a relatively contented man.

"Because maybe I know about a stock that's guaranteed to take off—and I mean take *right* off—that might not allow you to buy a building outright, but would set up you up real nice with a big fat down payment and a very manageable monthly mortgage."

"Fred—"

"Don't worry, I'm not talking insider trading or anything like that. It's all completely above board. I just happen to know that there's going to be a very valuable little technical innovation coming to the oil and gas industry very soon, and that people who are smart enough to get on board as stockholders early on are going to benefit very nicely."

"What kind of innovation?"

"That's not important. What matters is you thinking very seriously about being an investor."

"What kind of innovation?"

"You make it hard to help a guy, you know that? Okay, well, it's an improvement to the liquid injection process that aids in opening up fissures. Aren't you glad I told you?"

"You're talking about fracking."

"Oh, geez, here we go..."

"You're talking about a new and improved method of poisoning the planet." I'm no eco-warrior—don't even always rinse out the peanut butter jar properly before I put it in the recycling bin—but even I have my limits.

"C'mon, Phil, spare me the liberal claptrap—what I'm talking about is getting you back on your feet. Financially. That's all."

"Fred..." I grab a pair of dirty socks from the bedroom floor and drop them into the basket. "I appreciate your thinking of me." And I do. In spite of what he's suggesting, I do. And not just because I would like to have my very own, actual store again. "But I'm good—really—I'm okay with my decision to go online."

"I know you are. And I know you'd make a big success of it. I was just—"

"I know. You were just looking out for me. And I appreciate it."

"If it's about coming up with the investment capital, I'd have absolutely no problem with lending it to you—interest free, naturally—and you could pay it back whenever you—"

"Fred..."

"It's not about the investment capital. I know."

"I've got to throw a load of laundry in the wash," I say.

"I understand."

"No, I really do. I was filling the basket when you called."

"No, I know."

"And I *do* appreciate it. Really."

"I know."

"Good."

"Okay, then, I'll let you go."

"Talk to you later, Fred."

•

No matter whatever else, a book.

A crappy minimum-wage job when you're young, an outrageous, impossible-to-meet rent hike when you're old, a bad day, a long bus ride, a pulled hamstring, a stubborn hangover, a bad week, an ailing mother, a mole that might not have been there before, a foolhardy peek at today's newspaper, a bad month, a good look in the mirror, a brother you rarely talk to, an old friend you never see, plain old self-indulgent if no less unavoidable existential ennui, a spat with Caroline: no matter what, who, or why, always words to welcome you in and keep everything else out and be the body-and-soul existence armour you weren't born with but sure as hell should have been. Just little black squiggles on a white page, but *whoosh*, you missed your subway stop and that isn't all. An old paperback will never let you down.

An old paperback such as F.C. Copleston's *History of Philosophy, Volume Four, Descartes to Leibniz*, which was what I was reading—okay, more skimming than reading, but while making notes in the margins in preparation for my next what's-it-all-about tutorial with Caroline—when my right eyeball blew up. It was as if someone had set off a succession of miniature fireworks inside my eye, a painless explosion of flares and floating dots. I got up from my chair and stood in the middle of the room and closed my left eye and repeatedly blinked the right—slowly, tentatively at first, hopeful for a just-as-sudden return to fireworks-free sight, then increasingly rapidly, so as to dislodge whatever it was that had somehow infiltrated my field of vision. No such luck, multiplied by two.

Thankfully it was a weekday afternoon and I was at home and there's an optometry office on Roncesvalles that I've passed by a couple of thousand times but never stepped inside. I didn't even call ahead and try to finagle an emergency appointment, just showed up and told the receptionist I was afraid I was going blind. She might not have bought my panicky self-diagnosis, but I think she believed that I believed it was possible. I only had to sit in the waiting room resisting the urge to swat away a small but persistent swarm of non-existent mosquitoes for ten minutes before the optometrist called my name.

"Mr. Cooper," she said. "How are you?"

"I'm hoping you can tell me."

When I didn't say anything else, "We'll do our best," she said, and closed the door to her office behind us.

•

"They're called 'floaters,'" she explained, and knowing that there was a name for them and that they weren't uncommon in people over fifty made me feel slightly better, as did being told that, while irritating, they weren't a harbinger of incipient vision loss but merely one more thing to be endured with old age. Still, it kind of felt like I was an actor being informed by his agent that the good news is that he got the lead in the movie, the bad news is that it's a snuff film.

"Believe it or not," the optometrist said, "you'll get used to them. In time, you won't even notice them much anymore."

"You're right. I don't believe it. Not right now I don't." I wondered if Home Hardware sold invisible fly swatters with which to kill make-believe mosquitoes.

"What happens," she said, "is that, over time, the brain learns to not pay attention to them. They're still there, but because it stops registering them, it's almost as if they're not there. Although they are." I was sitting in that same chair that all optometrists have, the one attached to the eye-level device they swing into place through which they ask you to identify when the letter is good, better, best. She could tell I still needed convincing.

"Look at it this way," she said. "Everybody knows they're going to die. But it's not as if everyone sits around thinking about it all day. It's there, but it's not there, if you know what I mean. Does that help?"

I did, and it did—some, which was something—and I said goodbye and paid the receptionist and walked back home.

•

Cogito ergo sum.

Don't look at them. Concentrate on the words. Just don't pay them any attention.

I think therefore I am.

Don't look at them. Concentrate on the words. Just don't pay them any attention.

•

—Can't you just, you know…

—Please don't say "Just don't look at them." *Please.*

—No, I was just going to say…

—What? You were you just going to say what?

—Okay, I *was* going to say "Just don't look at them," but... Hey, you might want to slow down on the wine. We've got a hundred years or so of philosophy to get through here.

—Don't worry about me, I've done my homework. And for your information, I've found that if I drink enough wine I'm somewhat less aware of what I'm trying not to be aware of.

—I'm all for avoiding the issue at hand, believe me, I just don't want your chosen form of self-medication to impair your philosophical performance.

—Don't worry about my performance. You just be concerned with bringing *your* A-game. Prolonged marijuana usage and clear, logical thinking aren't exactly pedagogical peanut butter and jam.

—First we have to deal with Francis Bacon and Thomas Hobbes. The whole time I was reading about this guy I couldn't help thinking about Francis Bacon the painter.

—*This* guy? *This guy*? You mean the man, according to our author, who claimed that neither the Aristotelean nor the Platonic modes of truth determination were capable of delivering truth with a capital *T*?

—That's him.

—You mean the man who proposed, instead, a method of induction from observation?

—That's the one.

—You mean the man who claimed that henceforth truth seekers must accumulate data and interpret it?

—You got it.

—Yeah, I was thinking of the painter too.

—I know, it's weird, right?

—And then there's Hobbes...

—And I'm not thinking of the cartoon.

—Of course you're not. So you can tell us about the philosopher instead.

—As long as I don't have to talk too much about—what's he call it again? Let me check. Oh, yeah—"the science of motion."

—Appetite and aversion, right. And in terms of politics, appetite is the desire for power, and aversion is the fear of...

—Death.

—Right.

—Death. Say it, Phil.

—Death. See? Death, death, death.

—Okay, relax, the Grim Reaper does all right on his own, he doesn't need a cheering section.

—You wanted death, I gave you death. I aim to please.

—If you want to please me, tell me about Hobbes's political philosophy.

—Even though he's also a pioneer in what we'd call analytic philosophy?

—That's the whole "different classes of words" thing?

—How crudely cavalier of you. You mean the whole "different names for bodies, properties, and names" thing, I believe.

—Yeah, that's it. And not to be too—oh, I don't know—crudely cavalier about it, because I know it's important, but I really don't care. My goal when we started this thing was to give myself a gold star for each of the big names of Western philosophy I could cross off the list, and for me to get my Hobbes star all I need to do is understand what he's most famous for.

—Do you know how many copies of Hobbes's *Leviathan* I sold over the years?

—A lot?

—A lot. And not just to undergraduates looking for cheap copies. It must be pretty great to have thought of something over three hundred years ago and have people still talking about it today.

—I guess.

—You guess?

—Well, it doesn't help him much now.

—True. But that's not the point.

—What is?

—I don't know.

—In the meantime, here *we* are, and what does Hobbes have to say about the state?

—You're the one who wants the gold star, you tell me.

—Wait a second, this thing has gone out again. Hold on.

—I'm sure this happens every time people have gotten together to discuss Thomas Hobbes's political philosophy.

—What?

—Oh, you know, someone's joint inevitably goes out and has to be sparked up again.

—There we go.

—Ready to resume now, are we?

—I don't recall seeing your wineglass ever less than half-full tonight.

—Point taken. Now back to Hobbes...?

—Hobbes believed that a state is created when people hand over their power to a ruler. People do this because of their fear of death in a state of nature and general anarchy. Therefore, the only rationalization for government is the safety of the people.

—You're not done yet.

—*And*—I wasn't quite done yet, thank you—*and* the leader must have absolute power so he can protect the people to the best of his ability. Which ignores the fact that people can also fear death from an absolute ruler, but there it is.

—Which also ignores the fact that there might be a compromise between absolute power and anarchy.

—But it's funny, you know? It sounds so antiquated to us—fascism as an essential element of good government.

—It wasn't too antiquated for Germany and Italy eighty years ago or North Korea or China today.

—True, but what I meant was, Hobbes's idea was also pretty radical in its time—progressive, even—because he's essentially claiming that leaders should be sovereign not because of God, but because it's necessary for good government.

—I think I know what you mean. Almost everybody I've read about so far who's had anything interesting to say is a little bit of this and a little bit of that, a little bit this way and a little bit that way, it's never black or white.

—Nothing interesting ever is.

—Then why do we always want things to be that way?

—Simple, you mean?

—Yeah.

—I guess because we're simple.

—So the definition of a good philosopher is someone who doesn't demand that the world seem simple.

—Maybe that's the definition of a good anything.

—*A Good Anything*. That'd make a great title.

—For what?

—For anything.

—Is that wine all for you or can I have some too?

—What goes better with the philosophy of René Descartes than a glass of—what is this?—2007 Château Moulin du Cadet.

Wow. This couldn't have been cheap. Are you sure I should be guzzling this?

—Believe it or not, but I'm not saving my nicest wines for special occasions in the distant future anymore. No, that's not right—whoa, that's enough, I've started these new meds and I'm not really supposed to mix alcohol with them—what I mean is, I've come to discover that *every* occasion is a special occasion.

—Even talking about the distinction between rationalism and empiricism?

—I'm sitting inside my lovely house talking to a lovely person while we drink this lovely wine while there are people just outside that door who are lost and lonely and who've never had the chance to be bored by the distinction between the two major modes of modern philosophic thought. This *is* a special occasion, believe me.

—Given that you've set things up so nicely and you've supplied the wine—which, if you're not supposed to drink, you shouldn't be drinking, by the way—I'll just clarify what we mean by rationalism and empiricism.

—How munificent of you.

—Well, I thought so. Basically, the rationalist argues that knowledge of the world can be achieved solely by pure thinking, divorced from experience.

—While the empiricist...

—While the empiricist believes the complete opposite, that knowledge is derived solely from experience.

—Which makes sense, since Descartes was so interested in mathematics and believed that the world has to be capable of being understood the same way that mathematical truths are understood.

—Right.

—But first he had to find out if any indubitable—his word—truth existed, so he had to doubt everything. And what he found out was that he could doubt the truth of everything except for the fact that he was doubting.

—*Cogito, ergo sum.*

—Better known as "I think, therefore I am."

—Meaning what?

—Meaning that because he can subtract from himself every attribute but thought, he is clearly a being whose essence is to think. To be human is to think.

—And also meaning...

—Give me a hint. Oh, wait: is it that there's mind and there's body and never the twain shall meet?

—I'm pretty sure Descartes never used the term "twain," but, yeah, you get your gold star.

—And in spite of managing to shoehorn God into existence—I'm not really sure how—

—me neither—

—Descartes got himself judged heretical and his books were banned and he was forced to leave France and move to Holland. All because he was using secular means to prove all of the things that the Catholic Church and French society already believed in.

—And didn't the Dutch kick him out too?

—He ended up dying in Sweden.

—You know, I hate to admit it, but I've got to say, since we've been studying together or whatever it is we've been doing—and I honestly don't know how long I would have kept going if it had just been me on my own—I find all of this stuff about these guys' lives generally a lot more interesting than what they said.

—Well, it usually *is* more interesting.

—What does that make me then? A philistine?

—It makes you human.

—When it was just me doing the reading on my own and keeping a journal, it seemed like the ideas were enough, you know?

—People like stories. You and I officially constitute *people*. Your own brain isn't another person.

—I don't know, but this brain is tired. Leibniz and Spinoza are going to have to wait until next time.

—I know he wasn't officially on our list, but can I say something about Pascal?

—As long as it's not that "wager" thing.

—You must be referring to "Pascal's wager."

—I must.

—No, that's not what I wanted to talk about.

—Good.

—I just think it's neat how although this guy was an out-and-out Christian apologist, what's most interesting to most people 250 or so years later is the stuff he wrote that you don't need to believe in God to see the sense of.

—Like....

—Like how... Hold on... Like when he says, "Being unable to cure death, wretchedness and ignorance, men have decided, in order to be happy, not to think about such things" and that... hold on, hold on... And that "the only good thing therefore is to be diverted from thinking of what they are, either by some occupation which takes their mind off it, or by some novel and agreeable passion which keeps them busy, like gambling, hunting, or some absorbing show, in short what is called diversion."

—Like gardening, for instance.

—Like the Grateful Dead. For instance.

—Okay, okay. Anyway: diversions. It makes sense, I guess.

—It's pretty bleak, though, isn't it? "All our life passes in this way: we seek rest by struggling against certain obstacles, and once they are overcome, rest proves intolerable because of the boredom it produces." Makes life seem sort of pointless, doesn't it?

—Not to Pascal. Didn't he also say that if you believed in God you didn't need any diversions. Instant end of pointlessness.

—For Pascal.

—As for us poor, godless, diversion-fixated creatures...

—It does make you think, though, doesn't it?

—It makes me tired, actually.

—But not *that* tired.

—I've had a lot more of this wine than you have. Let's make an appointment for the morning, okay?

—C'mon, aren't you curious to see if we can solve the mind-body problem all by ourselves? It'll also be diverting. I guarantee it'll make you forget all about your floaters.

—I already had. Until now.

—In that case, it'll help make you forget about them all over again.

FIFTEEN

A germ. A goddamn germ. A single goddamn germ. Especially during pandemic time, you cover your mouth and nose when you sneeze, you wash your hands as much as possible, you don't pet stray dogs or talk to strangers or accept any wooden nickels, but, still: sneezing, aching, and a boiling brain screaming with fever. And no in-the-flesh Caroline until I'm all better, either (as well as COVID-19 tested-and-okayed), because her weakened immune system can't risk being exposed to my goddamn germs, run-of-the-mill-virus variety or not. Two days ago I was on the elliptical trainer at the gym. Today I'm on my back on the couch. Goddamn it. Goddamn these germs. Only one thing to do when you're sick and feeling cranky and sorry for yourself.

"Hello?"

"Hi, Mum."

"You're sick."

"Yeah. I'm getting better though."

"Well, you're not better yet, I can hear that."

"No, but I'm getting there."

"Have you been drinking lots of liquids? Are you getting plenty of rest?"

"Yeah."

"Don't give me 'Yeah'—have you?"

"Yeah, I have. I have."

"Were you sleeping without a shirt on? If you sleep without a shirt on with the air-conditioning on as high as you like to put it, that's a good way to get a draft going and to get sick."

It's not that Mum doesn't believe in the pernicious power of germs, it's just that she also believes in the flu-spreading might of drafts, wet hair when you go outside, prolonged constipation, and several other equally insidious illness begetters. To her way of thinking, it's a wonder anyone is ever *not* sick. The way I feel today, it seems like a bit of a miracle to me too.

"How are *you* doing?" I say, although that's not why I called. I don't know why I called. Except that that's what you do when you're sick and feeling cranky and sorry for yourself. You call your mum.

"Oh, I'm fine," she says. And she might very well be, but I'd never know it because one of her babies is sick and her own health is simply not up for conversation because there are other, far more important things to discuss. Like her fifty-two-year-old son's recent bowel movements.

"Have you been going to the bathroom?" she says.

"Yeah, everything is... I've just got a chest cold, Mum. And it's getting better. Yesterday I couldn't even—"

"That's how you get sick in the first place," she says, "that's what you don't understand. If you get all bunged up, all those toxins and all the rest of it don't go away, you know, they stay inside a person's body and that's how they get sick."

As much because I don't want to hear any more feces-based theories on human health as anything else, "When the phlegm turns brown, that's good, right?" I say. "You want it to go from green to brown, don't you?" I'm still gobbing green, but the brown's coming, I can tell, and good news always sounds more convincing coming from someone else. Coming from your mother.

"Of course it is. But you've got to get it all out. Are you taking a good expectorant and not one of those cheap no-name brands? Go get yourself a bottle of Robitussin. We've always been a Robitussin family. That'll help get it all out."

"Yeah, that's a good idea."

"Of course it's a good idea—because it works. And saying it's a good idea isn't going to help you get any better—you have to go to the store and buy it and use it."

"Yeah."

"And take it as often as they say on the bottle to take it. It's usually every four hours and no more than four times a day, but check the instructions when you buy it. This might seem like a joke to you, Phil, but colds can turn into the flu, just like that, if you don't nip them in the bud, believe you me."

I don't feel any better, but I feel better. "Okay, Mum, I better let you go."

"Just go and get that Robitussin and take it and have a nice cup of hot tea and then take a good long nap."

"Okay, Mum, I will."

"I'm not kidding around, Phil."

"I know, Mum. I'll talk to you soon."

"And I want you to call me tomorrow and tell me how you're feeling."

"I will."

"Don't forget."

"I won't."

•

Already half-asleep, "Good night," I answer.

"No—*a* good night," Caroline says. "Tonight *was* a good night."

And so it was: sniffle-free (finally) and one-on-one with Caroline for the first time in a week; Vietnamese takeout in my backyard; a short, after-dinner, hand-holding walk in High Park; reading in bed until we were both tired; other activities in bed that didn't involve books and that made you tired in a different way. And now something else a bed can be used for: sleep. Good? I'll go even further: it doesn't get much better.

"It doesn't get much better," I manage, without rolling over. I like sleeping beside someone else again, but when I do, I also like to sleep on my side facing the wall. Us, yes, but just me also, the social and the solipsistic snugly back to back and nicely tucked in as well. Who says you can't have your couple cake and eat it too?

"Do you really feel that way?" Caroline says.

"Sure I do. Now go to sleep, okay? Part of a good night is wrapping it up with a good night's rest."

"Okay. Good night."

"Good night."

Which it was and is until Caroline says, "Phil?"

New relationship quandary #378: Do I know this person well enough to lie to them? It would be the right kind of lie—I'm tired and talked out and risk getting unnecessarily snippy if I rouse myself to answer—so pretending I'm asleep would actually be an act of kindness, something I'd do not just because it's nearly one thirty in the morning, but also because sometimes you've got to care enough not to tell the truth.

"Phil? Are you asleep?"

Clearly, this isn't a question, it's a command: I need you. I'd like to not talk, I'd like to be asleep, I'd like to point out to Caroline that, whatever's on her mind, it can probably be more sensibly discussed tomorrow morning, but more than any of these likes, I like to be needed. By Caroline. If you stay up too late and are tired the next day, you can always take a nap. You need someone else to need you for someone to need you.

"What's going on?" I say, sitting up. This sounds like a vertical, rather than a horizontal, conversation.

Caroline apparently doesn't concur—stays flat on her back, head still on the pillow. It's too dark to tell if her eyes are open.

"I think I've figured out a way to deal with this," she says.

There's no need to clarify what *this* means. I only wonder if now is when and where everything changes. What if, for instance, out of understandable desperation, Caroline's decided to dedicate the remainder of her short life to, I don't know, a sunflower seed–based cancer-conquering diet she discovered on some well-meaning kook's website? Is this where the manic false hope begins, with the inevitable, depressing collapse to come not long after?

"Okay," I say.

We stay like that—me sitting up, Caroline continuing to lie down—for what seems like a long time. I listen to the air-conditioning purring through the floor vents. You don't know it because you're sleeping, but it comes on and goes off, comes on and goes off, all night long. You're not awake to hear it, but it does.

Finally, "I think the thing to do... is to have one last good night," Caroline says. I wait for her to continue. The air-conditioning goes off. "I think the answer is to sort of eternalize the best moment you can come up with."

I wait a moment of my own before speaking. "Eternalize the best... Sorry?"

"It's like this," Caroline says, sitting up now. "We only exist in the moment, right? I mean, that's our whole world—that moment. We're not in the past and we're not in the future. We just—I don't know—*are*."

"Have you been reading outside the philosophy curriculum without me?" I say. "Or is this something I skimmed that I obviously shouldn't have?"

"I actually got the idea from you. Although our philosophy gabfests might have helped get the ball rolling."

"As much as I like the idea of being your intellectual inspiration, I'm pretty sure I've never said anything about eternalizing anything in my life. That would mean I'd have to understand what that means."

"Do you remember explaining to me your Dick's Picks?"

"My Grateful Dead Dick's Picks?"

"You mean there are others?"

"No, but... I just assumed you were humouring me. In the nicest possible way, of course."

"Well, I was, more or less, but something you said stayed with me. That what we were listening to was something we weren't intended to hear. That although we were listening to it and enjoying it, ordinarily every note the band played on that particular night would have disappeared into the air like smoke if that woman you talked about hadn't been taping the show on her own, just for herself."

"Betty Cantor-Jackson," I say. "The Betty Boards."

"The Betty Boards, right."

"But I don't see what they have to do with... you."

Caroline clicks on the lamp on her side of the bed. Now it's too bright *and* too quiet.

"I wasn't feeling so hot the last couple of weeks. I got it straightened out, it was just these new meds I'm taking that weren't interacting so well with all my other meds. But it got me thinking that there must be a way to do the same thing that Betty did, but with our lives. Maybe the ethereal *can* be forever—well, not really, but sort of—but only if that particular ethereal moment is rescued from all of the other ethereal moments that make up a person's life."

"Rescued how?"

"Like what Betty was up to with those Grateful Dead shows. Capturing a really good night. Commemorating it. Celebrating it. All in spite of the fact that it's not supposed to be that way because days and nights come and go and that's that, it's just one long chain of insignificance. But so were those shows that Betty taped. No one was supposed to know about them ever again, either, right? They were just gigs along the way. It's like they were grabbed out of the air and salvaged from oblivion."

"But you can't tape record your life. And even if you could, after a person is gone, what does it matter? They're still gone."

Caroline gets up from bed and walks naked to the corner of the bedroom where she pulls something out of her bag, her stash, presumably. I already don't understand what she's talking about—worse, I don't think she does either—so I don't believe weed is going to be a useful addition to our discussion. When she gets back underneath the covers, however, I see that I was wrong. She's holding a white plastic bottle in the palm of her right hand.

"It's kind of the opposite of taping a concert," she says, "but it's the same principle. If all we have is each moment, separated from all of the other moments in the past and the future, then this moment, right now, is everything. So why not make one very special moment—a last good night—*be* the last moment? That moment—that happy moment—will be the one that matters most because it'll be *every* moment. Because it's last, it'll kind of be like forever."

"I still don't really follow you, but even if... even if you could manufacture this last good night you're talking about and make it... I don't know... privileged somehow, how can you be sure that it *is* the last one? That's life, isn't it? You never know for sure what's going to happen from one moment to the next."

Caroline opens the hand with bottle in it. "Not if you make sure there aren't any more moments," she says.

We both look at the bottle. "What are they?" I say. "Pills?"

"A liquid. It's a little bitter apparently, so you mix something sweet with it. And there's something else you take beforehand to combat any nausea. But what it really is is just something that will painlessly make sure that I get to experience what I want to experience and nothing more. One last good night. And then..." She shuts her hand and the bottle disappears.

I rest my head back on the pillow. Caroline snuggles down with her cheek resting on my bare chest. "Am I scaring you?" she says.

"No," I say. "A little."

"Phil, I don't want to give this cancer equal billing in my life. And if I can be the one calling the shots, I won't have to. I can't control what happens after the good times are over and this fucking disease gets its hooks into me like I know it will, but I *can* choose what moment is going to be the last one. The one that lasts forever. And it's going to be a damn good one."

The room has become very warm. Why isn't the air-conditioning coming on?

"But you're talking about death. This is about death."

"I'm talking about life. Mine. And it's always been about death. The very first time I invited you over, for dinner—do you remember?"

"Of course."

"That was about death too. Even if I didn't have a wafer-thin immune system because of all the medications I'm taking, inviting a stranger into my house to eat with me and use my bathroom and to share my bed isn't the most reasonable thing to do during a world pandemic. But I did it anyway. Because it was what I wanted. It was what I wanted my life to be."

"I get that, I guess. But this is what you want your death to be."

"This is what I want my life to be."

Caroline's head is still on my chest. I can't see her face, but I can hear every word she says.

"I'd like you to be there with me, Phil. I'd like for you to share a last good night with me. Even though I'll understand if it's something you don't want to do. I will."

"You're asking me to be there when you kill yourself."

"I'd like you to be there when I'm happy one last time. For *all* time. When you were sick last week and we couldn't see each other, I missed you."

"I missed you too," I say.

"And once I got thinking about what I've been thinking about, I realized I wanted you there. Because you help make me happy. Well, most of the time." Caroline laughs; I manage a manufactured a smile. The room is so hot. I can feel the pillow soaking up the sweat dripping off my head.

"What about your other friends?" I say. "Your family?" I know both of Caroline's parents are deceased, but there's a sister and a few nieces and nephews out in Nova Scotia.

"I think it's pretty obvious I'm not exactly what you'd call a people person. At least no more than you are. I suppose I wasn't quite so much of a recluse before I got sick, but knowing you've got a finite amount of time left tends to make you prioritize things a little bit more. And then when the COVID hit, because of my rotten immune system, I had to be so careful about who I saw and how I went about it, after awhile, it just didn't seem worth the hassle most of the time."

"But your sister... I know you said you two aren't close, but..."

"I love my sister—I just don't particularly like her. But that's really not that unusual when it comes to families, is it? When the time comes, she's going to get a long letter I've already written, and there's a little something for her in my will, but the last thing I want when I'm breathing my last breath is her and her four spoiled brats hanging around. Whatever it turns out to be, my last good night does *not* include that, believe me. Does any of this make sense?"

"Yeah, but... I think I need to go to sleep now."

"Okay," Caroline says, and leans over and turns off the light and kisses me on the forehead and almost immediately falls asleep, her head back on my chest. I'm convinced there's no way I'm going to be able to get any sleep tonight, but then the air-conditioning comes back on and the next thing I remember is waking up in the morning, Caroline on her side of the bed with her back to me, me on my side facing the wall.

SIXTEEN

An elliptical trainer won't let you lie. Wishing you'd put in a mile and a half and burned off at least three hundred calories and worked out for thirty minutes doesn't amount to much unless, once you step off the machine, the display panel reads 1.5 MILES and 300 CALORIES and 30 MINUTES. We're not machines, though. We're not science. I can wish that Caroline hadn't decided to kill herself. I can wish that she hadn't told me. I can wish that she didn't want me to be there when it happens. I can also shit in one hand and wish in the other and am reasonably certain which one will fill up first. *That's* science.

I lift up the corner of the towel I use to conceal how long I've been exercising and am surprised that there are less than ten minutes left in my workout. I shouldn't be surprised. In just over a month of coming to Scotty's every other day, time has shrunk, what used to be a fairly agonizing thirty minutes is now a has-it-really-been-half-an-hour-already? In addition to improving my cardiovascular system and aiding in the shedding of a few pounds, the main gain in joining the gym has been being reminded that if you want the minutes to melt away, don't stare at the hands on the clock. There has to be a lesson in this that transcends the most effective way of stepping your way to a slimmer physique, but for now I'll settle for knowing that it's only eight and a half more minutes until a long drink of water and the sweaty satisfaction of another day's corporeal duty done. Wisdom might be rarer and more valuable, but the simple satisfaction of getting the job done isn't the world's worst consolation prize.

Except for the staff, I'm the only one here not wearing earbuds or talking on an invisible headset, but it's not out of principled Ludditism, it's because I've discovered that thinking while you're moving has its advantages. Particularly thinking about things you don't want to think about but which need to be thought. Like whether I'll ever get used to tiny black specks floating in and out of my field of vision. Like the woman who I sleep beside several nights a week ending her own life.

WORKOUT COMPLETE, body and machine wiped down and dried, cold water gulped and black plastic cap screwed back on my complimentary (one per new member, please) metal water bottle, my hand is on the door when I stop and turn around. No one is using my machine yet. Good. Time for one last peek.

1.5 MILES. 302 CALORIES. 30 MINUTES. I don't know yet what I need to know, but 1.5 MILES, 302 CALORIES, 30 MINUTES.

•

Zoran on the sidewalk is like bumping into your grade eight teacher at the grocery store when you're a kid. Of course it makes sense—he lives in Parkdale, and Roncesvalles is only one neighbourhood away—it just doesn't feel right. For one thing, he's not wearing his regular costume and the props are all wrong. Zoran's customary fedora and suit jacket are missing, and in their place are grey track pants and a baggy white T-shirt. And where are my books? Where's Tesla? I don't think I've ever seen Zoran without him. Zoran doesn't seem at all surprised to see me.

After we've shaken hands, "And where's Tesla today?" I say. Zoran shakes his head and stares at the sidewalk like it's done something shameful.

"This is the reason for where I am at this moment," he says, looking up. "This dog of mine, he has not been himself these several days. I take him to dog doctor and they are thinking maybe his bladder is problem and why he is not eating and is not himself. I am just now coming back home from getting the refill of his medicine. The dog doctor in Roncesvalles is much better than one in Parkdale. Rich people, you see, they always get better doctor, even dog doctor."

I know Zoran isn't attempting to make me feel guilty about where I live and where he doesn't, is just saying what he knows to be true—and besides, I'm not rich, unlike some of my more recent neighbours—so we simply continue down the sidewalk on our separate ways, if side-by-side.

"You are taking a pleasure walk?" he says.

"A pleasure walk, yeah."

Zoran nods thoughtfully, as if I've just told him I'm on my way to donate a kidney to a dying man. It's a nice, if a little too hot, August afternoon, and Zoran and I are the two oldest people on the street. When we moved here, Debbie and I were among the neighbourhood's new young people. Every person who walks past Zoran and me today is younger than us. Their phones gripped tightly in their hands, ready for the next life-altering call or text, they seem less like another generation than another species.

Ordinarily, I'd appreciate our shared silence—people don't feel compelled to manufacture small talk with their pets; why do they feel compelled to do so with other human beings?—but if Zoran's not declaiming, not pontificating, he isn't Zoran. We pass by a newspaper box advertising today's half truths and hard sell, and I take my conversational cue from the story on the front page.

"Climate change," I say.

Zoran looks at me, then back at his red running shoes. Zoran shouldn't be wearing running shoes. Zoran wears black dress shoes. Which are always shined. His hands are in his pockets. The pockets of his track pants. Zoran doesn't wear track pants. Pretending that these sort of things matter is part of the job description of being alive.

The sky, all aquamarine blue and fluffy white, makes it a lovely day for a walk, but not so great for contributing to the creation of a couple of illusory black mosquitoes darting in and out of the corner of my right eye. Zoran's eyes, still focused on the sidewalk, don't notice the sky. If a sky is shimmering blue and wafting marshmallow white and Zoran doesn't see it, does it exist? Of course it does. Just not for Zoran, not when he's worried about his sick dog.

"How long were you a waiter at that hotel you worked at in Belgrade?" I say. If world events can't get him talking, maybe everyone's favourite topic—themselves—can.

"Oh, long ago."

"Yeah, but how long?"

"Many years. Many, many years."

Before I can ask how many is many, "This is my house," he says. "I must leave you now, my friend." As often as he's been to both my store on Queen Street and my own house, I've never even seen Zoran's home. Small, tidy, unostentatious: it looks like Zoran.

We shake hands goodbye and I make sure to look him in the eyes as I do so. He explained to me once that a Serbian never makes a toast or shakes anyone's hands without meeting the other person's eyes. That's how friends do it.

•

—I want to confess something, but that thing you're using on your phone to record us...

—"That thing you're using on your phone to record us," what?

—I feel like I'm being interrogated and that everything I say that's not smarty-pants smart can and will be used against me in a court of law.

—Today's your lucky day. You've been granted full smarty-pants immunity by the high court of philosophical truth.

—Oh, well, in that case, my favourite Spinoza quote wasn't by Spinoza but by the guy who wrote the section on him in our book.

—Please cite your sources. For the record.

—I will if you'll please pour us some more wine.

—Oh, the old quid pro quo. You got it.

—Okay. Let me see. Right. Here it is: "Spinoza claimed that his work had no other purpose than to discern how human beings might live happily."

—Makes sense to me. Why the need to confess?

—You know. Because philosophy is supposed to be about right and wrong, what is and isn't beautiful, what we can and can't know. Not cornball stuff like...

—How we can be happy.

—Exactly.

—I get it. I do. When I started doing this—before we started doing it together—I always felt a little guilty when a topic wasn't something I could apply to life.

—Or death.

—

—Or death, I said.

—I heard you the first time.

—Just making sure you're not avoiding the subject.
—Do you really think that's possible?
—Just checking.
—How about we talk about Spinoza?
—I already gave you my favourite quote about him. Let's get your take on something he actually said.
—Fair enough. Well, for a guy whose most famous book is called *Ethics*, there's sure a lot about God in there.
—Because God is all and everything. It's called pantheism, Phil. Get with the program.
—Yeah, I know. And He has an infinite number of modes of being, but human beings can only know two of them.
—Thought and—*cough cough cough*—Sorry. *Cough cough cough.*
—Are you okay? Maybe you should drink some wine. Wait, don't do that—let me get you a glass of water instead. Is there something—a pill or something—I should get you too?
—Phil. Relax. It's just a cough. Even people who aren't dying cough sometimes.
—No, I know. But do you want—
—What I *don't* want is to continue this particular vein of conversation. So. Returning to the topic at hand. As I was saying: thought and extension.
—Right. Thought and extension.
—Very good, Polly. Keep going and I'll give you a cracker.
—Okay, well, Spinoza says we can study ultimate reality the same way, the same way we can study lines and planes.
—So basically Spinoza is the ultimate rationalist because he believes that metaphysics and ethics can be understood just like someone working out a geometry problem.
—And happiness is achieved by...
—Go on.

—No, I'm waiting for you to fill me in on that small point. Math was always my weakest subject in high school.
—My pleasure. Happiness is achieved when you recognize that the world is as it is by logical necessity and that free will is an illusion. So, for example, getting pissed off at the behaviour of other people or the state of the world is illogical. God has created everything exactly as it should be, so just sit back and enjoy the ride as best as you can.
—Or as Tony Soprano would say, "It is what it is."
—Wasn't *The Sopranos* great?
—I was actually just thinking it was about time to watch it again. I don't know why—maybe it's age, it's probably just age—but I don't seem very interested in checking out anything new anymore. Even if I did know what was worth watching. Which I don't.
—I know what you mean. But for me it's also because I don't feel like right now is the ideal moment to park myself on the couch in front of the TV night after night.
—Because it's too nice out to be stuck inside.
—Because in the time I've got left I'd rather be doing something other than watching other people do something.
—Well, for whatever reason, I'm much more inclined to watch something again that I know I love, like *The Sopranos*. I've seen it twice, but I know I'll enjoy it just as much the third time.
—And probably get just as much out of it, too.
—Or more.
—Or more.
—I guess that's the highest compliment you can pay to a television show or a movie. It's like a book: not only can you experience it again, you *want* to experience it again. The number one commandment of any good writer: Thou shalt not bore the reader. Beware of false prophets and dull authors.

—Not that I still don't watch my fair share of crap.
—Oh, god, yes, me too.
—Really? Good. I was worried what you'd think of me if I told you I set aside every Monday night to watch *The Bachelor.*
—People who regularly murder entire evenings slumped in front of YouTube should not cast snobby stones. It's a very sobering experience to come across your search results the next day and wonder how the hell you got from *how to get rid of fruit flies* to *the Facts of Life: where are they now?* with stops along the way at *unknown nazi soldier exhumation* and *the Friendly Giant theme song.*
—We should watch some crap together. Some of mine, some of yours. It'd be fun.
—Maybe next time we have study group we can reward ourselves with some post-philosophy brain candy.
—Sounds good. And speaking of study group, I'll get us some more wine if you can bring us home with Leibniz.
—I think you got the better job.
—Keep talking. I can hear you in here.
—What's there to talk about? Leibniz is Spinoza with a smiley face.
—I like that. A smiley face for eternity.
—There are worse ways to spend it, I guess.
—You know how in *The Sopranos*—or in any mob movie, I guess—when they shoot some guy, execution-style, in the back of the head?
—Right...
—I always imagined that if you really, really hated somebody—if it was personal, I mean, and wasn't just business—you'd tell them they were going to die just before you pulled the trigger.
—You've put some thought into this, I see.
—Well, if you wanted them to suffer, why would you let them off the hook? I mean, the instant before you pulled the trigger they

could be thinking about puppies or sugarplum rainbows or whatever it was that made them happy, and that would be the last conscious thought they'd ever have. Wouldn't you want their final thought to be that they're going to die?

—I think I see your point, and I think I know where you're going with this, but what about Leibniz? And what about that wine?

—Here we go. The best of all possible Super Tuscan—within my price range, of course—a nice Tignanello.

—Well done.

—You haven't even tried it yet.

—I was referring to your clever referencing of Leibniz's famous—or infamous, I guess—declaration that this is the best of all possible worlds.

—Which is clearly untrue because of, just for example, global warming.

—The coronavirus.

—Donald Trump.

—Soft rock.

—On the other hand, this wine... Mmm. Damn, this is good.

—Wow. It is. It really is.

—

—

—Do you know one of the reasons why I like hanging out together? We don't talk about the world.

—We're talking about Leibniz. He's part of the world. The best of all possible worlds, remember?

—*Issues*, I mean. Topics du jour. The pressing concerns of our life and times. That might have actually been the worst thing about the lockdown—no matter what you did or watched or listened to, twenty-four hours a day of non-stop COVID-19 chatter and confusion. Ugh...

—Given that a lifetime of experience would seem to indicate that it's going to do and be pretty much whatever it's going to do and be anyway, the world and I came to a mutually satisfactory agreement a long time ago: beyond basic civility and the elementary obligations of citizenship, I wouldn't give a shit about it and it would continue to not give a shit about me. This undoubtedly makes me a shamefully self-obsessed bourgeois pig, but that's just the way this particular swinish cookie crumbles.

—Except that it's not "bourgeois pig" anymore—it's "entitled" or "privileged." And it's your responsibility to ensure that there are absolutely no nuts or dairy or allergens of any kind in that cookie.

—Which is precisely why I attempt to avoid the news, in whatever form it's packaged, as much as possible. Even though sometimes "as much as possible" isn't enough and I'm consequently compelled to carry around in my head all day a running conversation about, I don't know, some dipshit hockey player who texted his similarly moronic buddy about a teammate's girlfriend's ass being bigger than it used to be, and having his contract voided for his unacceptable misogyny.

—You mean the whole question of what's a private conversation anymore.

—I mean, if they start firing people because they're stupid douchebags, there's going to be a lot of people out of work.

—

—

—This is what I was talking about.

—Sorry?

—A night like this. A moment. A moment like this. A good moment.

—Oh.

—Take it easy. Relax and enjoy your wine. Not this moment. Not this night. But a night like this.

—I think I understand.

—Really?

—A little bit more anyway.

—Well, that's something.

—I mean, I think I do.

—That's a start.

•

I don't need any help—I can't afford any help—but I could use the company, so Benjamin is getting paid to do busywork that I should be doing myself. At least it works. Nothing like being the boss to scrub the brainpan clean.

"Just write it down," I say.

"If you had a rubber stamp or something it would save a lot of time."

"I haven't got around to it yet. You're going to have to write down the store's name and address as the return address on each package."

"They're probably not expensive."

"Probably not. But until then—"

"Write down the store's name and address on each package."

"Thank you."

We're sitting at my kitchen table, and he writes and I do the parcelling, and today, I've decided, is the day I destroy his world. If I was a better uncle I would have done it the day I came home from the grocery store after seeing Cameron and the woman in the car, but it isn't love that makes the world go round, it's cowardice and indecision. At least I'm telling him now. Or I will, just as soon as I can find the right moment. Or a moment that's the least worst.

"So how's it going?" I say.

"What do you mean?"

"I don't mean anything. How are things?"

Benjamin shrugs. "Okay."

How is it that people in their twenties seem to be either perpetually chatting on the phone or texting one another, yet a casual conversation with one of them almost immediately degenerates into a dribble of parched language worthy of a Beckett parody? Well, today he's going to talk. Otherwise I'll have to listen to what's going on in my head, and that's not what I'm paying for. I demand my C-note's worth of diversion. Pascal would be proud.

I try to think of a suitably engaging subject to get the conversation going (Post-structuralism? Eco-feminism? Benjamin's favourite emojis?), but finally give up. Caring about someone other than yourself, I decide, is a lot harder than toking up and putting on a pair of headphones. Eventually, "I guess you and Cameron are getting pretty serious," I say.

My eyes are on the next pile of books to be bundled up, but I can still make out Benjamin's face well enough to register even the faintest reaction. Whenever you're fishing, you've got to keep your eye on your line. I'd have to be a blind man wearing dark sunglasses to miss his energetic eye-roll.

Benjamin shrugs. "We're just friends." He finishes labelling another package and adds it to the completed pile.

I apply a final strip of tape and slide another package across the table, this one containing four fat, out-of-print collections of Pauline Kael's film criticism headed to someone in Moose Jaw, Saskatchewan. I wonder who Tommy Grogan is, if he's just a film junkie in general or if he's recently become addicted to Kael's compulsively readable reviews. I'll never find out, either. Tommy Grogan is just a name on my computer screen, and all I know about him is his name and his mailing address.

"Yeah, but come on," I say, "you've been..."

Benjamin rests his pen on the table and stares at me without so much as a single blink.

"Having sex," I say. "You've been having sex for—what?—two months now."

So far I've been treated to the shrug, the eye-roll, the stare, and, now, the slow headshake. "People our age don't really think like that," he says. "I mean, some people do, but we don't. Cameron and I don't."

"Think like what?"

"Cameron and I are polyamorous."

"Meaning what exactly?"

"Meaning it's okay for us to sleep together if that's what we feel like doing, but that doesn't mean we can't sleep with other people if we feel like doing that too. The main thing is that we're friends. Good friends."

Benjamin's phone rings for only the tenth or twentieth time today, and he stands up from the table while answering. "Hey," he says. "We were just talking about you." He laughs at something the other person—Cameron, presumably—says. He saunters into the living room and I can hear him laugh again.

All this time, all this worry, for nothing. Or something. Or maybe nothing and something. I start wrapping up the last parcel. The sooner I get these orders in the mail, the sooner they'll get there.

SEVENTEEN

I haven't gotten seriously stoned since I came to the conclusion that marijuana and Grateful Dead–abetted mysticism are good for the soul but not so good for some of life's more prosaic pursuits, such as acknowledging the existence of other people and not ecstatically travelling so far up one's cosmic bunghole it becomes difficult to pass back the other way. But if I'm going to go along with Caroline's Last Good Night theory—go along with it until there's nowhere else for us, for her, to go—I'm going to have to put it to the test and try to better understand it, because otherwise I'll have to live the rest of my life knowing that she died alone or in the presence of someone else and that I could have been there and wasn't. And how long after she's gone will *could have* inevitably turn into *should have*?

I'm not sure I understand; I'm not sure I even approve; I'm only sure of this: that I need to come as close as I can to inhabiting what, for me, would be that perfect moment that Caroline's intent upon experiencing one last time, that no-place place where time stops, past and future don't exist, and everything is as everything should be. And for that to happen, I'm not only going to require some vintage Dead, I'm going to have to get very high.

I was saving my last pot cookie for a special occasion. I take it out of the freezer and eat it in two bites. Ordinarily, home—in my chair, in my room upstairs, headphones on and feet on the windowsill—is my preferred place for cosmic lift off, but the last test I took was three and a half decades ago at Etobicoke Collegiate, so I'm a little nervous about this one and don't feel like taking it alone. Thankfully, I know that if I drop by Hidden Rec Room Records later tonight, by the time the cookie has fully crumbled and I'm abundantly baked, Alex will probably be sparking up a much-deserved post-work jay. And if I throw some decent Dead on (I know for a fact that as of a few days ago he had a copy of *Live/Dead* on CD), that should do the trick. And since a few preparatory glasses of wine are part of the equation anyhow—the pump must be carefully primed before the deluge can drown one's consciousness—if I'm going to drink cheap red vino, why not do it at the Lazy Rooster?

Thankfully, it's a Monday night, so other than Angie sitting at her own patio table and turning the pages of today's *Toronto Star*, there are only a few customers and the jukebox is blessedly quiet. I make sure to drop in the only toonie in my pocket and select a few songs before sitting down at the table next to Angie's. She removes her reading glasses, swivels slowly on her seat in my direction.

"Well, well," she says.

"How's it going, Angie?"

A shrug, a half smile/half grimace, and that's that. She stands up and goes inside to get my usual bottle of Zywiec.

"Can I get a glass of red wine instead?" I say.

"Yes. Of course." *Yes. Of course*, but when she comes back with the bottle she's looking at me as much as she does my glass while she pours. I always drink beer at the Rooster, plus it's a sticky-warm night, ideal beer-drinking weather, and we both know that the dusty bottle of budget Portuguese plonk she's pouring from is for Rooster non-regulars not in the know, but I don't bother to explain to her that, as much as any form of alcohol can, red wine is a low-voltage conduit to the numinous. Yes, if you drink enough of it, it'll do what beer or liquor or any other boozy beverage does—relax you, recharge you, buoy you—but red wine does something else too, something that a cold Molson Canadian or a Seagram's Seven can't: connect. You. With something. Not you. Something bigger than you not you. Connect...

Angie brings the bottle of wine back inside, and after cracking the cap off a bottle of Zywiec for an old, white-whiskered Polish man drooping over his drink at the other end of the patio who she doesn't have to ask if he wants another, sits back down at her table and slips on the pair of glasses hanging around her neck and resumes her reading. Traffic's "Dear Mr. Fantasy" might have been too intense a choice for this early in the evening, but Winwood's aching vocals always do the trick, no matter what the mood. I sip, Angie reads, this is the Rooster on a muggy August evening, COVID-19 version.

Metaphors that matter take time. I had to be fifty-two years old and told what Caroline told me before I felt like I knew what death was. What it feels like. What it will feel like for her when she dies the way she wants to die. I drink my wine and listen to the jukebox and remember sitting on the end of a dock as a kid with my feet in the not-quite-warm water and telling myself to just do it already, just fall over into the water and get it over with—once you go in it won't feel so cold or seem so scary and you'll be glad you did it, just tip over into the water, you'll see. And after the endless back and forth—you will, you won't, you will, you won't—when you finally do do it, when you lean forward and the weight of your body pulls you under, it's over in an instant, all you remember afterward is breaking through the surface of the water and the bubbling silence and the instinctive return upward to air and sky and sound. Except this time without returning or remembering.

Angie has discarded the front section of the paper, is on to the local news, and the NEW BILL TO AMEND CRIMINAL CODE FOR MEDICALLY ASSISTED DEATH headline is too apposite a coincidence to pass up. I don't believe in fate or that things happen for a reason, but when something happens that seems like it does, that's good enough for me, plastic karma has its own rewards.

I reach over and grab the newspaper and pretend to be engrossed by something on page 1 all the way through Lucinda Williams's "Drunken Angel," even going so phoney far as cradling my chin in my hand and pursing my lips a couple of oh-so-thoughtful times. When Angie still doesn't take the bait, I bring out the big rod and my best lure.

"Hmm," I say, now rubbing my chin.

"Yes. What is this you read?"

Attempting to appear as startled-back-to-reality as possible, "Oh, no, I was just..." I return the newspaper to her table and pinkie-point out to her the news item in question. I take a sip of wine before elaborating. Now that I've got her on the line, I have to carefully reel her in.

"I was just thinking that I can see both sides of this issue," I say. "I mean, on the one hand, I guess we—society, I mean—have to be concerned about people who are just depressed and might feel different about ending their lives if they got some help. Maybe we have an obligation to stop them for their own good, like the way we make people wear seat belts when they drive."

"You want another, yes?" Angie asks.

"I think I'm okay for now."

Angie nods, looking like she doesn't quite believe me, and returns to her section of the paper.

"On the other hand," I say, "if somebody is terminally ill and eighty-eight years old and in excruciating pain, sure, no question, right? You wouldn't think twice about putting an animal out of its misery, so why should it be any different for a person? And even if somebody isn't going to die right away, and isn't physically suffering too much yet, if they want to end their life, why should somebody else have the right to stop them?"

I lift my glass and have to admit I feel pretty proud of myself. Maybe all of my reading and my discussions with Caroline have made me into a philosopher after all, if only of the barroom variety. More importantly, it's made me feel better about Caroline's Last Good Night theory. What was that line of Spinoza's that Caroline liked so much, the one about his books having no other purpose than figuring out how human beings might live happiest? Thanks, Spinoza. Thanks, clear moral reasoning.

Angie gets up and plugs in the electric kettle occupying an empty table by the Rooster's back door, takes a tea bag out of a small tin box beside it.

"In Poland, this is simple," she says. "Church says suicide is wrong, it is wrong. No debate to have for anyone." She's watching her kettle while she speaks. Even if I did fill her in on what they say in North America about watched pots and boiling, I don't think it would make much of a difference. "But here it is confusing all the ways you think about it, yes?"

"Yeah, but like I said—"

Angie holds up her hand. The jukebox is between songs and we can hear the water in the kettle rolling to a boil.

"Yes, I understand what you say, but this person you speak of who decides to kill themself who is not dying right away but eventually, this is not so simple either. Not because of Church. Maybe person doesn't want to make family go through terribleness of long sickness so they kill themself now to save trouble later."

"Like I said, that's their right, right?"

"Maybe this is their right, but question is when. When they decide to stop living. A person waits too long, sickness will take over and choice maybe not theirs anymore or family must still suffer. Do this thing too soon, even if it is right thing to do, and maybe they miss out on life that could come."

"Willin'" by Little Feat is pushing out of the jukebox speakers, but Angie's kettle screeches like a smart-aleck rooster who's learned to whistle and wants the entire barnyard to know it.

"Chicken," I say.

Angie unplugs the kettle, drops the tea bag in her mug. Slowly steeping it, "I do not understand this 'chicken.'"

"It was this game we played on our bicycles when we were kids. You rode your bike toward another person, and the first person to swerve away or jump off was the chicken, they lost."

Angie sits back down. She blows on her tea, and I watch the steam go up, up, and away, gone.

"If you turned away early," I say, "you lost. But if you waited too long to do it, you might crash into the other person and wreck your bike or get hurt."

"I am sorry. I think I don't understand. We do not have this game in Poland as children."

"You weren't missing anything."

Song over, dead jukebox, my move.

"Angie, can I, uh, get change for, uh, for a five, for the jukebox?"

"Yes. Of course. You want another wine as well?"

Quiver, prickle, sizzle: the drugs are starting to kick in. "I don't think so," I hear myself say. "Maybe. I don't know. Maybe later."

•

Red-wine tipsy, but nowhere near stumbling drunk?

Check.

High high high, but not so high I'm not here?

Check.

Alex perched on his stool behind the Hidden Rec Room Records cash register and ready to roll? Check.

Live/Dead plucked from the used bin and slid without protest into the CD player? Check.

Door locked, lights dimmed, come on, Alex, light that fire and let's hear the opening four-note twin tingle of Phil Lesh's bass and Jerry's guitar heralding *Live/Dead*'s 23:18 version of opening track "Dark Star."

"So I'm screaming 'Asshole! You fucking asshole!' halfway down Roncy. And who do you think looks like the asshole to everybody on the street? Yeah, you're looking at him." Alex still simmering incensed over the shoplifter who earlier today walked away with—or, more accurately, ran away with—a couple of rare original late-sixties British psych records and, while he was at it, three brand-new 180-gram Soft Machine reissues? Also check.

"Well," I say, "at least you know he won't be coming back around here again anytime soon."

The packet of rolling papers is on the counter and the weed in its clear plastic baggie is beside it. Alex, however, is staring over my shoulder at the magic-marker drawn poster he's taped to the wall alerting everyone to the person (male, white, about five feet ten, short brown hair) last seen wearing a black, nearly ankle-length overcoat and stealing from one of Roncesvalles' small businesses. ATTENTION! it screams across the top of the page in Alex's neatest, most strident handwriting. I don't know how efficient the sign has been in getting other people's attention, but it's sure succeeding with Alex.

"You know," he says, "the worst part is not even what he stole—about how much money I'm out—it's more just"—Alex pauses to remove a skin from the package of rolling papers—"more just, what kind of a person steals from a fucking second-hand record store?" He plucks a thumb and forefinger's worth of herb from the bag and sprinkles it the length of the rolling paper. "Does this guy think I'm rich or something?"

"I'm pretty sure he didn't put a lot of thought into it. Or if he did, it was probably along the lines of why I had to deal with shoplifters as long as I had my store on Queen. Outfits like ours are usually one-person operations and when they get busy, store security is pretty much next to nothing."

Alex runs his tongue the length of the paper's gummy seal. "I guess you're right, but—" He applies a second swipe of spit just to make sure it stays glued. "Man, go rob Walmart if you need the money, you know what I mean? Fight the power while you're at it." He sticks the joint in his mouth and reaches into his pocket for his lighter.

"It's a nice thought," I say. "But I'm pretty sure Walmart doesn't stock a wide selection of early-seventies British progressive rock reissues."

Alex extinguishes the flame from his lighter just before it can ignite the joint. "Have I played you any of those new Soft Machine reissues yet? Oh my god, I'm hearing stuff on these things I've never even heard before. It's almost like listening to them for the first time. Want me to put my play copy on?"

Before he can bounce off to the backroom where there's not only his cot and mini-fridge and a couple of garbage bags full of clothes, but also his own personal turntable and a set of headphones and his private stash of LPs, "I *do* want to hear it," I say, "but I'm kind of in a *Live/Dead* mood tonight, you know?"

"Oh, right, the Dead, I forgot." And with that he leans over and pushes play on the stereo and lights the joint and has a pull and hands it to me and we're off.

•

Alec's weed is a nice THC top off, is good.

The "Dark Star" and the "St. Stephen" that flows from it and all of the other ebbing and surging songs that emerge after that are good too.

And after only one more tirade about the shoplifter, about how if he, Alex, was a different kind of person, the kind of person who believed in settling things with his fists (and, I don't add, the kind of person who weighed only slightly more than the sneakers and white T-shirt and blue jeans he's wearing combined), if he ever saw the guy again he'd show him what happens to people who steal from small businesses just trying not to go broke, Alex is good stoner company.

Everything is good.

Just not... *that* good. Not last-night-on-earth good.

Being high listening to the Dead helps. Joyfully existing in the near-mystical moment I understand—intellectually, at least. How if one could feel thoroughly satiated in the moment, that moment could conceivably feel like an eternal moment, the luscious last taste on your tongue before it and every other part of your corporeal being begins its sad, slow decay. But this isn't enough. It wouldn't be for me. And it shouldn't be for Caroline. Better to keep alive, with all of the indignities that will inevitably come with failing health, in the hope that maybe tomorrow or the day after that there'll be another small pocket of pleasure or peace to experience. And when it's undeniable that there simply aren't any more pleasures to be had, no matter how seemingly small, then... Maybe then it's time. For no more time.

"I hate to be a buzz kill, Phil—'buzz kill Phil.' Hey, guess I'm a poet and I didn't even know it—but I've got to, you know... I'm pretty loaded and..."

Oh, yeah: Alex. Being high means not only occasionally blissfully forgetting one's self, but, also, sometimes, your generous host. I should let the poor kid go to bed—another day, another fifty-cents-on-the-dollar-day for him tomorrow—and besides, the next song up is the old Reverend Gary Davis tune "Death Don't Have No Mercy," and that's not a ditty I want rolling around my brain tonight.

Being mutually stoned, there aren't any long goodbyes—well, there might have been, but I'm too stoned to tell—and I'm on the sidewalk and headed for home sweet Golden Avenue where I plan to give Jerry and the gang another shot at celestial success via the mammoth forty-four-minute version of "Playing in the Band" from 06/13/73, Vancouver, when I see a young couple who must be on their way home too, their young child slung over his father's shoulder like a contented sack of flour. We're walking in different directions down the same side of the street, and as they get closer, I see how young they really are, no more than their late twenties. Tired and not talking and not moving very fast, but young and in love and going home. The three of us exchange nothing more than sidewalk-etiquette semi-smiles as we pass each other, but once I feel it's safe to do so I stop and turn around to take one more look. Their child is a boy, probably two or three, and his eyes are closed and his thumb is stuck in his mouth and nothing bad can ever happen to him because his dad will always be there to carry him home and his mum will never not be there in the morning when he wakes up wondering how he ended up in his own bed.

I can't remember the last time I cried. Yes, I can: my father's funeral. But I'm not sad. I'm as far away from sad as any one thing can be from anything else. Then why the hell am I crying? I stand there watching them until they're just another part of the night.

When I get home I take the CD with the epic "Playing in the Band" out of its case, but don't even get as far as turning on the stereo. Instead, I climb on top of the bed without bothering to get undressed and lie on my back on top of the blanket and close my eyes and tell myself to pay attention, that this is important.

Is important.

Is important...

Important...

•

It's good to do things.

I spend the morning processing a couple of orders, getting in my workout at the gym, paying a few bills online, and fairly successfully ignoring the tiny black floating beach balls that periodically pass through my field of vision that are not, apparently, going away anytime soon. *Having* to do things isn't usually as good, but today I don't mind, am appreciative, even. Like a name you can't quite remember but which teases on the tip of your tongue, the answer I owe Caroline hasn't arrived yet. I know what I think, I just don't know how I feel. Which means I don't know what I'm going to say.

"Hello, Phil."

"How are you doing, Edmund?"

"Oh, I'm good. I'm pretty good. My stomach feels a little upset this morning, but I ate three hard-boiled eggs but not with salt and

I feel better now. I don't think it's anything serious. Sometimes my stomach gets upset and I'll eat a hard-boiled egg but without salt on it and I'll feel better. I don't think it's anything serious."

"That's good," I say. "Hey, how about we take a peek at those books you're thinking of letting go? I've got to be somewhere at three and I don't want to have to rush when I look them over." I don't have to be anywhere except Caroline's tonight, but I'd rather spend my time with Edmund figuring out how much money I can give him than discussing his perpetual digestion problems.

"Oh, sure, Phil, come on in. I appreciate you coming by." Edmund is wearing a mask—of course he is—so I take mine out of my back pocket and do the same.

The inside of Edmund's apartment looks a lot like the outside of the apartment building itself: an effectively carved-up former factory of light industry bestowing dignified bohemian squalor upon the occupants of its eight individual units by providing each with twenty-foot-high ceilings and exposed-brick walls and several hundred square feet of cool concrete floors. Edmund's contribution to the shabby-genteel décor is ensuring that every wall and virtually every horizontal surface is covered with books. It's like being in the bowels of the world's largest bookstore where all of the universe's overstock is kept. Only someone's unfortunate decision many years ago to install several rows of fluorescent lighting in the ceiling detracts from the not unpleasing monastic mood. A constant low-level hum from above accompanies you wherever you go.

"Those are not for sale," Edmund says, standing in the middle of the room in his egg-stained T-shirt that used to be white and too-tight blue jean cut-offs and cheap plastic flip-flops, pointing at several rows of brick-and-plywood shelves jammed with books. All of the shelving has been constructed out of brick and plywood, an after-midnight trip to a nearby construction site cheaper than an afternoon at IKEA. "And those are not for sale. And those. And those ones. And those."

"Hey, Edmund? Maybe you can show me the ones you are thinking of selling and we'll go from there? How does that sound?"

"Oh, sure, Phil, no problem. I appreciate your coming by."

Edmund directs me toward the shelf containing the hundred or so volumes he's decided he can live without—Bakhtin, Barthes, Derrida, Lévi-Strauss, each carefully alphabetized in spite of their reluctantly orphaned status, many of which I recognize as having sold to *him*—and I get busy doing my book-buyer's thing. That, and try not to look at the mammoth manuscript resting on the kitchen table (the apartment is essentially one enormous book depository, with the small kitchen and the bare box spring and mattress on the floor and the tiny bathroom the only indications that a person actually lives here—that, and the dirty plates and glasses strewn throughout the room). Which has to be it. *The* book. The unified field theory of all known philosophies and religions that Edmund has been working on for as long as I've known him. Blessedly, he's never discussed its contents with me, would only mention from time to time that this or that title "is just what I need for my book," but when I think of Edmund I think of French Structuralism, questionable hygiene and troubled digestion, and his book.

"Almost done," I say, and Edmund, sitting on one of the kitchen chairs directly in front of a floor fan with his eyes closed, mask on, just nods. It's not too, too hot in here—the high ceiling and the concrete floor help keep it cool—but what's going to happen to Edmund and his manuscript when he's roasting in the assisted-living bachelor apartment he's going to end up being reduced to once his building gets torn down and turned into—what else?—condos? What does he think he's going to do with the thousands of books still left that he's obviously not going to be able to take with him? What's going to happen to Edmund and his hypochondria? If someone was passing the hat to help with his relocation I'd gladly do my small part, but I'm not the type of person to supply the hat or initiate the passing.

"How's the apartment hunting going, Edmund?"

Eyes still shut and the fan blowing straight back what's left of his long, thinning blond hair, "Claire is looking into it for me," he says. "Claire says it's going to be okay and not to worry about it. She's looking into it."

Claire, I know, is one of Edmund's soon-to-be evicted building mates. I've never met her, but "Claire says" is an expression I've gotten accustomed to hearing during Edmund's visits to the shop over the years. I've gotten the impression, though, that Claire is a fair bit older than Edmund, who's around my age, so I'm not sure that not worrying about things like whether or not he can count on having a roof over his head three months from now is such a good idea. If only I was a different person I might be able to do something about it. If only I wasn't me.

"Here's what I'm thinking, Edmund. Does three hundred dollars sound okay to you?"

Edmund opens his eyes. "Oh, you know I trust you, Phil."

"I know you do, but I want you to feel comfortable with—"

"I think I need to eat some toast," Edmund says, continuing to stare straight into the fan, but counter-clockwise rubbing his tummy with his right hand as he does so.

"Okay, but let's—"

"I think I'm going to make some toast now, Phil, so I think you better go now. I think I'll feel better if I have some toast."

"Sure, Edmund. Okay. I'll just leave your money here on the kitchen table. I'll give you a call tomorrow so we can figure out a good time to pick up the books."

I step outside Edmund's building, and the one-two punch of the thick afternoon heat and scalding bright sun make me feel sick to my stomach. Maybe I should go home and make some toast. I've got a better idea. Just thinking about it makes me feel better. A lot better. I pull out my phone.

"Hello?"

"Hey, it's me," I say.

"Hey, you. I wasn't expecting to hear from you until tonight."

"I wanted to tell you something."

"Okay."

"And I didn't want to wait until later."

"You could have just texted me. Oh, wait, no, you couldn't. You don't believe in texting."

"Nothing as principled as that. I *have* to have a cell phone. I *don't* have to text, at least not yet."

"Okay, so anyhow, what was it that couldn't wait for later?"

"I wanted to say yes."

"Come again?"

"Yes."

"Yes?"

"Yes."

"Oh."

"Yeah. I wanted you to know."

"Maybe we should talk about this tonight, Phil."

"We can talk about it. But yes. I wanted you to know yes."

EIGHTEEN

There used to be a video store near the corner of Roncesvalles and Queen that went out of business and became yet another coffee shop that couldn't survive all of the other cloning coffee shops bunging up the street and that then turned into a gourmet cheese shop that's still, the last time I checked at least, a gourmet cheese shop. Which is fortunate for me because I need cheese. Good cheese. I don't know any more about high-end food than I do top-shelf wine except that, if it's expensive, it's more likely to be good. Caroline's coming over this evening—first we tackle the British empiricists, then, if all goes well, each other—and since she's always making me such delicious meals when we're at her house, it's only fair that, in lieu of actually learning how to cook, I supply some super-nice nibbles. Fifty bucks' worth of deliciously stinky cheese and oily olives and a loaf of nice crusty French bread later and I'm all set for tonight, but I turn right toward Queen instead of left toward home. It's not just bad things that can become habit forming—largesse, for instance, can also be contagious, and now that I know where Zoran lives, I decide to pop by and see how he and Tesla are doing.

As soon as I see a stooped-over Zoran in his small front yard wearing a plastic milk bag over his hand like a glove to pick up dog crap I know that Tesla is dead. It's a hot day and he's an old dog, he could be keeping cool inside. He's had health problems recently and he might have had an operation, he could be recuperating at the vet. He could be doing a variety of things and he could be a lot of different places, but I can tell by the determined grimace on Zoran's face as he works to clean up his lawn that Tesla is gone for good. An old man cleaning up his dead dog's shit: this is loneliness. I feel like an intruder. I feel like a fancy fool with my designer paper bag full of expensive food. But Zoran straightens up and sees me and there's no turning back now. Generosity of spirit is so much easier to say than to do. Which probably explains why I'm so seldom generous.

"Phil. Hello."

"Zoran. Hey."

Zoran doesn't look surprised to see me. And if what I think has happened has happened, why would he be? Every day, all day, every night all night: Zoran and Tesla, Tesla and Zoran. Until one terrible day: Zoran. Only Zoran. Now you see someone you love, now you don't. Ever. What can even come close to making someone as surprised as that? A guy you kind of know standing in front of your house? Sure.

Zoran slowly nods a few times even though I haven't asked him anything. He knows what I think I know, which means that I now know for certain. He looks at the hand encased in the plastic bag. "I don't know," he says, just as slowly shaking his head.

I'm not real clear on what it is exactly that Zoran doesn't know, but I know enough not to ask for elucidation. *I don't know* covers a hell of a lot of ground.

"I'm sorry about Tesla," I say. "I haven't been around a lot of dogs in my life, but you could tell right away that he was a good one. I always enjoyed his visits."

Zoran purses his lips and lowers his eyes and nods several times—again, slowly, but vigorously. We both stare at his plastic-bag lobster claw. I shift the paper sack from my right hand to my left. I don't know what I'm supposed to say. Even if I did, I don't know if Zoran would want to hear it. But I have to say something. We can't just stand here gawking at a milk bag flecked with dried-up dog crap.

"Just out of curiosity," I say, "when was the last time you were back in Belgrade?"

Zoran resumes his stooping and searching for Tesla's last remains. "Many, many years ago," he says.

"That's what I thought. Maybe this is a good time for you to pay a visit. Your son and his family live there, don't they? You could see your grandchildren and pay the old hometown a visit while you're at it."

Without looking up from his labours, "Belgrade is not my home," he says.

"I thought you said you lived there for, like, thirty years or something."

"I live there because I work there. Belgrade is place to make money. If you want to make money, you move to Belgrade. My hometown, it is Tršić."

"Is that a city near Belgrade?"

Zoran stands up and looks at me like he's been charged with explaining the alphabet to a slow pre-schooler. "Tršić is not a city. Tršić is a village. On border of Bosnia. Very hilly there. The Bosnian mountains—you see them when you go for walk. Very, very beautiful."

"Maybe you should go for a visit. Do you still have any family or friends there?"

Zoran wiggles his fingers inside the plastic bag. "Tršić is also where Vuk Stefanović Karadžić is born. This is very important man to Serbian people. He is author of first Serbian dictionary in new Serbian language, which he help to reform. He is also collector of many Serbian songs and fairy tales. He also translate the Bible into reformed Serbian language."

"What's the population of the village?"

"But many people, they come to Tršić because of hectares and hectares of trees and streams and forest so they can picnic there and let children play and be outside in nice place in summer time. And all restaurant in Tršić, all of these serve only traditional Serbian food. All grilled, Serbian food. Chicken and fish and pork and vegetables and all outside, on grill outside. In Belgrade, young people, they eat pizza and McDonald's and do not even know what Serbian food is."

"It sounds great," I say. "How far is it from Belgrade?"

Zoran shrugs. "Two hour."

"Well, there you go. Fly to Belgrade and see your son and his family, and when you get tired of that, get him to drive you to . . ." My Serbian pronunciation isn't what it could be.

"Tršić."

"Tršić, and spend some time there too."

"This is not perfect place," Zoran says, as if that's precisely what I've just claimed. "People in Tršić, some of these are very poor. People there work very, very hard and still—" Zoran pulls out the white lining of an empty pant pocket and offers an exaggerated frown. "Young people there, they want to stay and work in place they love, but how? No job. No good job for raising family and having good life."

"Okay, but—"

"And dogs. Dogs without homes."

"You mean stray dogs?"

"Of course. Stray dogs are everywhere. And not just from there, but because place is so beautiful, people from towns and cities who get dog and decide they don't want anymore, they bring them there and leave them, goodbye little dog. Is very, very sad."

"I guess if people have a hard time making a living—"

"Do not believe people do not care," Zoran says, waving a finger on his non-bagged hand at me. "People feed dogs—and cats too, many, many cats—as best as they can. People, they do what they can. A Serbian from where I am from, they have two apricots, they make sure they give one away. You go to Serb's house, and rakia is on the table and everybody drink."

"Rakia—is that like wine?"

Zoran is looking at me like he's contemplating whether or not to spit on my shoes. "Rakia is Serbian drink that is good for everything. You have cold, you drink rakia. Upset stomach, rakia. Tired all the time, have rakia. In Serbia, they say, 'No doctors—just pharmacist and rakia.'"

"So it's like a medicine with alcohol in it for when you're sick."

Zoran takes a big bite from an imaginary lemon. "Rakia is for *all* times. And everyone who make it make it their own way. This person with apricot, this person with plum, this person with cherry."

For fear of appearing even more dim than I already do, and because I'm concerned that my sack full of primo cheese is going to turn into a melted mess, "I better get going, Zoran," I say. Zoran lowers his eyes to his lawn again. He's the man with the plastic mitt, but it looks to me as if his front lawn is finally poop-free. "Think about it," I say. "Sometimes... sometimes when things aren't great, that's a good time to remind yourself of good things. It sounds like your village is one of those things."

Zoran peels off the plastic bag, turns it inside out, and crumples it into a ball in the palm of his hand. He offers me his other hand to shake.

"Take care of yourself, Zoran," I say.

"You take care of you, Phil."

We're looking in each other's eyes as we shake hands goodbye, just like we would do if we'd been toasting each other. We have to. That's the Serbian way.

•

—So that's that. They're polyamorous. As the kids are wont to say, "It's all good."

—Except that I don't think the kids have said *wont* since about the Elizabethan age.

—I've seen the history section of your library, I'll take your word for it.

—So you were worried for nothing.

—Yeah, but that's not... I mean, I'm not opposed to it morally or anything like that, but I just can't get my head around how you can really care about somebody—be really into them, I mean—and still be okay knowing that they're bumping uglies with someone else.

—Well, I think you just answered your own question.

—What do you mean?

—"Bumping uglies." I'm assuming that that's how they view sex. As simply a purely physical act, no different from eating food or eliminating waste.

—You really missed your calling, you know that? You should have quit Canada Post and composed Valentine's Day cards for a living. But look: you can think of sex that way—and I suppose sometimes it *is* like that, and it can be good, too—but it usually

doesn't feel that way, especially when it's the other person doing the bumping with somebody else. It's not that hard to know that it's just good ol' meaningless sex when it comes to you, but when it comes to the other person, your boyfriend or girlfriend or whatever, it's a little bit harder to see it that way.
—They'd probably say that that's just because you're insecure. That if you were confident of what you have with the other person—if it was really, really solid—it wouldn't be that big a deal what someone else does once in a while when you're not around.
—Maybe. But maybe you can be secure about something yet still not want to risk anything or anybody threatening that good thing you're so secure about.
—If the person you were involved with went to the movies with a friend one night when you were busy doing something else, you wouldn't be jealous of that would you?
—Two people sitting beside each other in a movie theatre is a bit different than two people fucking in a bed.
—Some people would say that two people sharing the experience of watching a good film together is a lot more meaningful and intimate than a ten-minute quickie, and that if you were going to be jealous about one of the two things, it would be the first one.
—That's kind of what I mean. I'd be furious if I found out you'd made out with some stranger in the back row of a movie theatre, but I'd be devastated if this supposedly meaningless encounter led to you cancelling tonight so you could go back and do it again.
—It's kind of crazy, isn't it? Relationship problems—you know, the difficulty of meeting the right person, the difficulty of making it work if you do manage to find them, the agony of a broken heart when it doesn't work out—they probably account for 90 per cent of the subject matter of popular music and 75 per cent of the plots of every novel and movie. You'd think if human

beings possessed more than a modicum of common sense they'd realize that love's a losing proposition and refuse to play along.
—And everybody but a complete fool knows that the house always wins, and yet Las Vegas still takes in billions of dollars, year after year.
—I guess we want to believe.
—*Need* to believe.
—But why?
—Isn't that what we're doing? What we're doing tonight?
—You mean eating too much delicious Jersey Blue cheese and getting pleasantly plastered?
—I was actually referring to our joint exploration of life's many mysteries as addressed by the Western world's greatest philosophers.
—Oh, that.
—Do I detect a decided lack of enthusiasm for tonight's subject?
—No, I just—can you please hand me the olives? Am I eating too many? God, they're so good. Thanks—I don't know, I'm still glad we decided to do this, it's just that I thought it would be more...
—Fun?
—More fun. Exactly. I mean, I'm having fun right *now*—eating, drinking, talking to you about the mystery of monogamy. But no, I've got to admit, the prospect of diving into John Locke's *Essay on Human Understanding* doesn't make me giddy with anticipation. I guess I was right all along. I don't think I was cut out for philosophy.
—But when we were talking before about love and all the rest of it, maybe we *were* doing philosophy.
—Not *real* philosophy.
—We were discussing why human beings seem compelled to pair up even though it rarely works out. That sounds pretty damn philosophical to me. And pretty damn important, too.

—I'm not sure John Locke would agree.
—Well, that's just too bad for John Locke then. I think it's an important subject and so do you. All we owe Mr. Locke is a cursory but fair overview of his role as the forerunner of British Empiricism.
—Okay, let's do it, you've inspired me. Besides, I peeked and looked ahead, and after we finish up with these guys and then Kant and Hegel and a bunch of other people that will probably bore me to tears, we get to Nietzsche. I think I've always been a Nietzschean at heart. From what little I know about him, he seems to place a premium on keeping self-delusion and bullshit in general to a minimum. I like that in a person and a philosopher.
—I'll reserve judgment on that matter, madam, until we've had a chance to look at the body of his work in some sort of acceptable depth, thank you very much.
—So the sooner we get through British Empiricism the better.
—I wouldn't put it like that. It doesn't mean we—
—I like it that it took Locke twenty years to finish his magnum opus, the *Essay on Human Understanding.*
—Which has nothing at all to do with what he wrote...
—But if it took him two decades to write it, even if it's not my particular cup of philosophical tea, it means he must have meant everything he said or he wouldn't have bothered to work at it so hard and for so long.
—Meaning...?
—Meaning, if he can spend twenty years of his life writing it, we can spend a couple of minutes sussing it out.
—Suss away.
—Okay. So. I think the easiest way to understand Locke and what he wrote about is to see him as the antithesis of who we were talking about last time, the Rationalists.

—Good point. Rationalists like Spinoza and Leibniz believed that reality could be comprehended purely through the intellect.
—While Locke believed that the world is understood through the senses.
—Meaning that, according to Locke, there can be nothing in our minds that hasn't been provided by experience.
—I liked reading how it wasn't Locke's fairly commonsensical ideas that made him so well-known, but the fact that he gave scientific materialism, which was all the rage, some philosophical legitimacy.
—Which was what partially drove Berkeley to formulate his own ideas. He read *Essay on Human Understanding* as a young man, around the time that Locke died in 1704, and was repulsed by Locke's hard-core materialism and how it seemed so self-evident to most people.
—Well, no one could accuse Berkeley of that.
—He *is* a little out there.
—You think? But the weird thing is, by taking Locke's pretty straightforward idea about how the mind is only conscious of its own ideas, he takes it as far as it can go and turns it into something 180 degrees different.
—Because, according to him, if the mind is only conscious of its own ideas, what need is there for the material world at all?
—But it's okay—it's not as scary as it sounds—because God perceives everything all of the time, so it's not as if objects cease to exist when no one is perceiving them.
—The old "Does a tree fall in the forest if no one hears it?" thing.
—Right.
—Or the contemporary version: "Am I really happy if no one notices how happy I am on Instagram?"
—Okay, but what about writers, Mr. Bookseller? Isn't that what they do too? Isn't that what any artist does?

—I don't follow.

—Well, if people didn't feel the compulsion to share, why would they bother to publish what they write or exhibit what they paint or record what they compose?

—To make a living?

—Not most artists.

—I don't know then. Ask a writer.

—I'm asking someone who makes his living selling what all those writers burn with a desire to have other people read.

—Hey, I thought we were talking about Berkeley.

—*Now* you're suddenly interested in British Empiricism.

—When have I ever not been?

—Sure. Anyway, the bottom line is that because God hears it, the tree is in no danger of not existing.

—Well, that's a relief.

—Speaking of, how about pouring me a little more of that wine? We've still got David Hume to get through and I could use all the help I can get.

—I actually liked Hume. Well, not so much what he said, but the guy himself.

—Thanks. Really? I know he's important, but he seemed sort of... boring.

—Yeah, but boring with style. When he said... hold on, I want to get it right... Here we go: "The life of man is of no greater importance to the universe than that of an oyster," I knew I'd like him.

—He certainly can't be accused of overvaluing what human beings are capable of.

—That's what I like best about him. His skepticism. Essentially, he believes that the human mind is composed of only impressions and ideas.

—Which doesn't sound so bad until he gives you some examples.
—Which is another reason why I liked him. He said that when he got nervous about the pretty severe implications of his epistemology, he'd head for the billiard table and have a few pints with his friends.
—It is a nice change from philosophers who just happened to arrive at conclusions that assure you that all is good and God is in His heaven.
—Yeah. He might be wrong, but it's not because he's twisting the facts to make himself happy or to console himself.
—Is all the cheese really gone? I can't believe we ate all of it.
—There are a few olives and plenty of bread left.
—That's not what I mean. I mean I can't believe we ate it all. Meaning I can't believe I ate most of it. I haven't eaten like this in... I can't remember.
—You didn't. We did. And who cares? I bought it so we could enjoy it.
—Well, mission accomplished then.
—Speaking of, we're not quite done yet.
—But Hume—
—is the last of the Empiricist epistemologists, but there's still John Stuart Mill and his ethical philosophy.
—The "greatest good for the greatest number" guy.
—That's the one.
—So right and wrong are decided upon in terms of the human drives to acquire pleasure and to avoid pain. So something is moral if it tends to increase happiness or decrease pain.
—And if it's a question of societal right and wrong, it's—
—the greatest good for the greatest number. We got it, John Stuart.
—You don't sound like you're buying it.

—No, I do, but . . . look, I think of myself as a team player—I pay my taxes, I recycle, I give to the United Way every year at Christmas—but I can't help but get a little nervous when people start talking about the majority setting the ethical agenda. When you think about it, the only thing the majority really is, is the majority.

—And now we're officially done. What can we say after that that would be even halfway as smart?

—I don't know about how smart it is, but it's about all I've got left in the tank.

—Well, what do you say we shut this down and head upstairs? I can clean up this mess tomorrow. I can think of more important things for us to do right now.

—Maybe we should clean up tonight and save the important things for tomorrow.

—Okay. If that's what you feel like doing.

—Don't read anything into it, okay? Seriously. I'm just really, really tired. Plus, I had enough to eat and drink tonight for ten people, and just the idea of all of it sloshing around in my stomach is enough to make me nauseous.

—You can certainly paint a picture.

—I'm sorry, I just—

—No, it's okay. Really.

—Yeah?

—Yeah. It's even . . . I don't know, kind of nice.

—Nice?

—I don't think we've ever done one of these sessions before and not, you know, gone to bed afterward. I mean, we've gone to bed, but . . .

—I get it. And how exactly is that "nice"?

—I don't know. I guess it's just nice that we don't have to be just one way.

—The other way is a good way.

—And so is this way. I'll grab the plates and all the rest of it if you can handle the wine bottle and the glasses.

—I think I can manage.

—Good. Until next time, then. The march through Western philosophy isn't over yet.

NINETEEN

Even I, who does nothing, can be too busy. This morning, for instance:

1. Another eye appointment, where I learned that I'm wasting my money making eye appointments, that doctors, no matter how professional, considerate, and gently encouraging, can't make everything better simply because I really, really want them to.

2. My apparently unwavering harem of teeny-weeny swarming baby bats and I spending fifteen minutes waiting at the back of the line at the post office—arms loaded up with several parcels of books—until there was finally only one person ahead of me, at which point it was deemed a good idea by staff personnel to make available another employee to customers, and a man, who at just that moment happened to enter the building from the side door nearest to the newly opened spot at the counter, stepping right up and announcing in a loud voice that he wanted to buy a book of stamps. If David Hume could argue the case for the inherent illogicality of the idea of causality, I suppose it wouldn't be that difficult to make a similar claim for the absurdity of having the courtesy to wait in line until it's your fucking turn. All of which

at least lead to the insight that it's much easier to cultivate philosophical detachment when you haven't been standing in line for fifteen minutes with two armfuls of packages.

3. Waiting not in, but on the line for another fifteen minutes, this time on hold with someone with a pronounced East Indian accent from the customer service department of gratefuldead.com, my copy from the latest Dave's Picks series—which, as an annual subscriber, I should have received before it was mailed to the public—long overdue in my mailbox. In spite of the time spent with my phone pressed to my ear, the man couldn't have been more politely helpful and the number of times he put me on hold entirely understandable as he attempted to determine what happened to my copy of Dave's latest offering. The delays I could deal with—the guy was clearly doing his best to get to the bottom of my missing merchandise, and life is no picnic when it's your job to deal with one complaining customer after another—but what did startle and stay with me was the music playing on the other end of the phone while I waited. Pigpen belting out a sweaty, swaggering version of Howlin' Wolf's "Smokestack Lightnin'" (Jerry and the boys, in turn, jamming the hell out of it in odd, angular ways that the Wolf never would have recognized) is a lot of things, but background music while you wait for the customer service representative to come back on the line isn't one of them.

4. A subway trip and a bus ride to visit my mother, during the lengthy course of which it occurs to me—an inveterate observer of public reading habits—that whereas once I would have been pleased to spot a commuter engrossed in a quality book and not some thick piece of shiny trash, now all it takes to put a smile on my face is someone not tapping at their phone like an

overcaffeinated woodpecker or ardently playing video games on the same device. Mere literacy has replaced taste as a barometer of cultural competency.

5. A visit with my mother. Even if I'd somehow forgotten the address or the layout of her retirement home, the onslaught of capri pants and short silver haircuts courtesy of the aged, primarily female population of Edgecroft Retirement Village would confirm that I was in the right place. When my mother greets me with "Where's Fred?" I know this is going to be one of *those* visits.

"It's just me, Mum," I say.

"Well, I can see that. But Fred said he was going to come with you. You didn't forget about him, did you?"

Knowing from experience that attempting to reason with Mum when she's having a bad memory day would not only not get us nowhere, but would likely unnecessarily upset her, I spend the majority of my hour-long visit attempting to interest her in a variety of non-Fred-related topics. Sometimes she goes along with it, sometimes she says things like, "He must be coming on his own. He's only going to be in town for a very short while. He's very busy, your brother, you know." When it's time to go and I hug her and leave her at the door of her room, the last thing she says to me is, "When you see Fred, tell him not to forget to bring lots of pictures of the twins when he comes to visit."

"I will," I say, and wait in the heat for my bus.

•

When I get home I check my phone for messages (unless I'm on a work errand, I try to leave it behind as much as possible) and there's one, from Fred, calling from somewhere on the road to inform me that, because his wife and the twins were visiting her parents in

Vancouver—pandemic travel protocol doesn't, apparently, apply to the nouveau riche—he decided, what the hell, to jump in his new toy, a Nissan Z convertible, and air it out and break it in and drive half way across the country, and that depending on traffic he'd be hitting T.O. in an hour or so and that he had to head back home tomorrow but that he's looking forward to visiting Mum with me. He says he already called her and she seems pleased.

Everything I needed to do today, I got done. The rest of the day is wide open.

•

"Well at least you don't have to go very far if you feel like reading a book."

Fred continues to take in the living room, hands on his plump hips, the Calgary Flames fanny pack wrapped tight around his waist the sole indication that he's on holiday. Otherwise, it's the same short-sleeved sports shirt, baggy tan khakis, and whatever brand of running shoes happen to be most popular—hence most expensive—at the present time. The bald spot on top of his head might be a little bit larger than the last time I saw him, but otherwise it's still my big brother.

"You look like you lost some weight," he says.

I attempt to not appear too pleased with myself and instantly feel bad about noticing his expanding bald spot and his unfortunate habit of tucking his shirt into his pants, thereby emphasizing the substantial roll around his waist that doesn't need emphasizing.

"Maybe a couple of pounds," I say. "I've been going to the gym a little bit lately."

"Well, you shouldn't lose anymore. The first thing I thought of when I saw you was you must have been sick. Are you sure everything's okay? At our age you can't be too careful."

"I'm good," I say. If only I could drop this nasty habit I've acquired of regularly exercising...

"So what's the plan?" Fred says. It's what Fred always says, usually just before he informs you what's going to happen.

"Well, I figured we could take the subway out to Mum's place eventually. But I thought you might want to get a bite to eat or something first. There's that Polish place I took you to before that you seemed to like a lot."

"I've got a car, remember?"

"Right," I say. "Good. You can drive us."

"Let me just give Benny a quick dingle first," Fred says, pulling out his phone. "I told him we'd rendezvous after we finished up at Mum's and he was done with whatever he's tied up with at school today, but if we're all ready to go now, I want to give him the heads-up that we can pick him and his friend up for dinner a little bit earlier. That'll give us a little more visiting time that way. Make sense?"

The question is entirely rhetorical—Fred doesn't wait for me to acknowledge the obvious logic of his airtight argument—but I thought that the allure of a plateful of perogies smothered in fried onions and bacon might have been strong enough to get him briefly ambulatory, if only to Roncesvalles and back. He could use the exercise, and we should probably do something together as siblings while he's here that doesn't revolve around an old age home, but *could* and *should* aren't Fred-friendly words. Fred *does*.

"Benny. It's Dad. I just got in. I'm okay. I pulled over and had a couple of catnaps along the way, I'm fine. What's going on with you? Right. Right. Is there any chance you could switch things around, pal? I'm just thinking that if your uncle Phil and I swung by your place around, oh, I don't know, say three o'clock, that would be better all the way around. We're on our way over there now. Right. No, I understand. You didn't know I'd be showing up out of the blue on your doorstep, you've got your own responsibilities, that's understandable. You'll visit her some other time. Of course. So here's what I'm thinking: she'll have just finished her lunch by the time we get there and we can get in a good visit while she's having her tea. It's a better time to drop by than later, when she'll just be lying down to have her nap."

Now why didn't I think of that? Because I'm a second-hand bookseller sentenced to house arrest and being an abebooks.com factotum, and my brother is a rich petrochemical engineer who's recently moved into a brand-new mini-mansion in a freshly bulldozed Alberta subdivision. I wish I was being entirely ironic.

"Great," Fred says. "I appreciate your moving things around, pal. And if you could do me a favour and be waiting outside your apartment when we come by, that would be great. I tell you, parking in this town is ridiculous. I don't know how people put up with it."

Some people *don't* put up with it, I want to say. Some people take public transportation or ride their bicycles or even—gasp!—walk. I don't say anything, though. I just wait downstairs for Fred to use the bathroom. Whenever he's ready, we'll go.

•

"Here's to Fred, then," Caroline says. Everyone raises their beverage. "To Fred," we all say.

Fred holds up his hands. "It might have been my idea, but here's to my brother for inviting us into his lovely library, I mean home"—everyone laughs—"and for providing an opportunity for all of us to spend some time together. And especially because it gave me a chance to get to know Caroline and Cameron a little bit."

Now it's my turn to be toasted, although what we're really doing is saluting Fred's little speech. That's okay. I'm just glad I was able to talk him out of his original plan. Instead of him attempting to finagle a patio reservation for all of us at some new, very exclusive, very expensive restaurant he read about somewhere, I'd managed to convince him that, all things COVID-19 considered, a couple of gourmet pizzas from Vito's and a trip to the LCBO and my backyard might be the best way to go. Fred's disappointment that I'd capitulated to the government's fear-mongering tactics was thankfully offset by his delight in having something to do while I called Caroline and gave the backyard picnic table a cursory cleaning, and by the time the late-summer sun began to go down, the pizzas were all but gone and everyone had made small chat with everyone else and was pleasantly tipsy, all except for Fred, who stuck to his customary ginger ale.

Fred's speech concluded, with a hand on the small of Caroline's back I manage to migrate us over to the ice-filled cooler that Fred was kind enough to buy for me when he discovered that, incredibly, I didn't own one. So busily chatting away are the others near the picnic table in the middle of my small yard—technically, Fred is busily chatting; Benjamin and Cameron are mostly just listening—Caroline and I aren't missed. We're on the patio where the cooler is. It feels nice to be just the two of us again. I was ready for her to say it was too virus-risky to be around people she didn't know, but after asking, "What step or phase or whatever you call it are we in again?" and neither of us knowing, we'd both laughed and she said as long as it was all outside it was fine, she was looking forward to it.

"Your uncle says you've been a real help with his—what do you call it?—social media stuff," we overhear Fred say.

Benjamin shrugs. "It's no biggie."

"And Benny here tells me you're in the computer game," Fred says.

"I said Cameron builds websites, Dad. Among other things."

"Well," Cameron says, "you can't have a website without a computer, so I guess you could say I'm in computers."

"See, Benny? Your old man isn't so wrong after all. Try not to look so surprised." Fred and Cameron laugh. Benjamin, clutching a can of Heineken, continues to wear the determined smile that I'm guessing he pulls out and pastes on every time he introduces his dad to a new friend.

"Hey, you know what's interesting?" Fred says. "The guy who runs our entire IT department at work—a super-nice guy, by the way, and as sharp as they come—he's in a wheelchair too."

"Dad—"

"Take it easy," Fred says, holding up his hand, "there's no need to report me to the PC police. I was just pointing out that it's a coincidence, that's all."

"It's not a coincidence, it's—"

"Did I say something wrong, Cameron? If I did, I apologize."

"No worries, Fred," Cameron says. "It's all good."

Clearly pleased that there are no worries and that it is, in fact, all good, Fred manages to simultaneously sip his ginger ale and grin a satisfied Fred grin at the same time. It was the same smile he'd flashed me earlier when he'd teased me about the size of my backyard ("I guess you don't need to own a lawnmower to cut a postage stamp"). Fred is exclusively a riding lawnmower man—the proud owner of a brand-new, John Deere, top-of-the-line X394, in fact. I know because he insisted upon showing me a picture of it on his phone.

"Thanks again for doing this," I semi-whisper to Caroline.

"For what?" she whispers back, although there's not much danger of anyone overhearing us. "I'm having a good time."

"For *that*," I say. "For saying you're having a good time." I give her a kiss on the cheek.

Fred sees this, calls out, "This time next year, maybe I'll have to bring a wedding gift with me."

We both flash the embarrassed smiles we're expected to, and Fred returns his attention to Benjamin and Cameron. I rub Caroline's back, which seems thin—thinner, anyway. "Believe it or not, my brother's not trying to be a jerk," I say. "I think he's just happy I've met someone he likes. As I'm sure you've concluded on your own, he can be a bit of a dick, but—and I can't believe I'm going to say this—his heart is in the right place."

"Oh, I know," Caroline says. "I get a kick out of him, actually. He's just one of those people who says what everyone else is thinking but are too polite to say."

"Now *that's* being polite."

"No it's not. It's the truth."

"Actually, I think you are telling the truth. I couldn't believe it when you asked Cameron how she ended up in a wheelchair."

"To be fair, that's not quite what I asked. You walked in at the tail end of the conversation."

"Still..."

"Like you never wondered why she's in a wheelchair."

"I never said that."

"No, because you did wonder. And now you know that she was in a car accident when she was twelve, and only because I asked her."

"Is this an example of the don't-give-a-shit-anymore years you were talking about?"

"I hit that age when I found out I had cancer. That's why I think your brother's just fine. He doesn't need to be dying to know that there's not enough time in life to be too polite."

I haven't told Benjamin or Cameron about Caroline being sick. I still haven't told anyone except Mum. "You're right about that," I say. "I'm pretty sure Benjamin wouldn't use the word 'polite' to describe him."

"Every child is slightly embarrassed by their parents. It comes with having parents."

I open the lid of the cooler and pluck out a can of beer. It's so cold it almost hurts my hand. Whatever else you might say about my brother, he definitely knows his coolers.

Popping the tab on my Heineken, "How come you never had any kids?" I say.

"Who says I didn't?"

"I think I might have spotted a picture or two by now."

"Maybe I did, but I'm just too ashamed to have any photos because the little jerk grew up to be an arsonist or a corporate lawyer or something."

"Every parent is proud of their kids, no matter what losers they turn out to be. It comes with being a parent."

Caroline opens the cooler lid and grabs her own beer. "If you know so much about being a father, why didn't you have any little Phils or Philipas?"

"I could say that it's because I'm an intelligent, far-sighted humanist who didn't want to add to an already appallingly over-populated planet."

"But..."

"But the truth is I just like my life too much. I'd rather read a book or listen to a record than change a diaper."

"People have managed to do both, you know."

"Maybe I never met the right people."

"Maybe you did," Caroline says. "Maybe you met them too late."

We both sip our beers. It's not even eight o'clock yet, but the air is beginning to cool and the sky is starting to dim. You don't need a calendar to know that summer is almost done. Caroline pushes her face into my shoulder.

"What's wrong?" I say.

"Nothing," she says.

When I feel her wiping her cheek on my shirt, I realize she's been crying.

"Hey, hey," I say, taking her hand, gently pulling her around so that she's facing me, her back to the picnic table and the others. "Look: let's just finish these beers and I'll shut this thing down, okay? You've been a good sport and everything, but enough is enough. And I owe you one, believe me."

Caroline lifts her head from my shoulder. Her mascara is running down one of her cheeks. Her eyes are red. She looks so fucking beautiful.

"You get so used to being alive, you know?" she says.

I hug her, the only thing that makes any sense.

"Hey, you two," Fred says, "you've got guests, remember? And there are children present."

"Knock it off, Dad," Benjamin says.

"Meaning, 'Cut that shit out, Dad,'" Cameron says.

Fred laughs, Cameron laughs, even Benjamin laughs. Caroline wipes her face with her beer-can-moistened hand. She tries on a smile and turns around.

"Who needs another beer?" she says.

TWENTY

—How was work today?

—

—What? C'mon, I'm serious. What?

—I'm sorry—for a moment there I thought you said, "How was work today?"

—What if I did?

—Well, to begin with, we're supposed to be talking about Immanuel Kant.

—And we will, we will. Although I hope you were more successful than I was in staying awake preparing for tonight. Geez... what is it about philosophy that brings out the boring in Germans?

—And secondly—and more importantly—have we already reached that point in our relationship?

—What point is that?

—You know: you ask me about my day, I ask you if you got anything interesting in the mail, we start wearing matching robes and slippers while we drink our evening cocoa.

—That doesn't sound like anything to be too concerned about to me.

—It actually sounds pretty good, doesn't it?

—Although I think we should probably pass on the cocoa for now and stick with this wine.

—Agreed. And speaking of...

—Thank you, sir. And hey, by the way: how was work today?

—I'm glad you asked. Work was good. As good as it's going to get.

—Why doesn't that sound like it's good enough?

—It is, I'm not complaining. Well, I am sick of tripping over boxes of books when I get out of bed in the morning. It's just... don't get me wrong, I appreciate the opportunity to still make a living selling books. I do. And working from home has its advantages. As does not having to deal with book thieves, asshole landlords, and having to set an alarm for work in the morning.

—But...?

—But... I have to say, I miss selling books to actual people and not just names and addresses.

—In spite of all the other stuff? And even if you had to wear a mask to work every day and make sure that everybody else is too?

—I think so, yeah.

—I wish I had visited your store.

—I've got pictures.

—It wouldn't be the same. A good bookstore has its own personality.

—That's true. I guess I miss having my own personality.

—Are you sure it's not just a case of missing what you don't have anymore? Like an old flame you dumped, but now that they're with someone else, you're jealous?

—Are you trying to tell me something?

—Only that most people would look at your situation and say you've got a pretty sweet set-up.

—I know I'm lucky. I just...

—Wish you were a bit luckier.

—Isn't that my right as a relatively well-off North American? To take for granted all of the good things in my life and to spend the majority of my time complaining about all of the things I don't have or that aren't perfect?
—That sounds about right. But maybe now that you've got your e-bookstore up and running you're in a better position to have a brick-and-mortar store too. The extra income would help, right?
—It would help, but it wouldn't help enough—not nearly enough. People used to say that Toronto was like New York in the fifties: vibrant and exciting, but not too big and still relatively affordable. Now it seems more like New York in the eighties: still vibrant and exciting, but more and more a have and have-not kind of place. The bookstores of thirty years ago are now the Gaps and McDonald's and American Outfitters of today.
—Doesn't the city seem so much more... I don't know... *intense* now? The people, the traffic—everything?
—It does. And it seems a lot louder too. But I'm also fifty-two years old, so maybe part of the reason is that I'm not as intense and loud as I used to be.
—Maybe. I still think we were lucky to have lived when we did.
—We're still lucky.
—I never took you for the glass-half-full kind of guy.
—I suppose if it's the only glass we've got, all we can control is how we look at it.
—I tend to find that the glass looks a lot fuller the fuller my wine-glass is. Hint, hint.
—Right...
—Just a top off, thanks. Whoa, that's enough—save some for yourself.
—What about you? It's got to be nice not having to deliver the mail through—what is it?—sleet and rain and snow and—

—Stop, please, I get it. Actually, the best part of not punching the clock is not having to pretend to like certain colleagues that you'd much rather prefer to strangle. Back when I first got sick, I was even briefly convinced that my then-supervisor gave me cancer. When I got better, when I felt like a fresh start all around might be a good plan, it helped make the idea of getting a transfer and moving to Toronto just that much more appealing.

—That sounds a little extreme.

—Did I neglect to mention that the aforementioned colleague could be counted on to greet you each and every morning at 7:00 a.m. with "Well, pitter-patter, up and at 'er, folks"?

—No, you did not.

—Or that he could be relied upon at some point every day to announce, "I'm going on a Timmies run, gang, who needs some fresh joe?"

—Again, no, you didn't.

—Or that he had a gift for spraying you with spittle when he got especially carried away while sharing with you one of his many, many quote-unquote jokes?

—Um...

—Such as—

—Okay, I get it.

—Such as—this one was always a guaranteed knee-slapper, I must have been lucky enough to hear it twenty times: A Canadian is walking down the street with a two-four of beer under his arm and his friend stops him and asks, "Whatcha got that case of beer for, eh?" The other guy says, "I got it for my wife." And then his friend says, "Good trade!"

—Okay, I've—

—And do I need to add that he was the laziest, most incompetent person I've ever worked with, but always the first one to complain about being overworked and underappreciated? And that the sole reason that I ever questioned whether the entire labour union movement of the twentieth century might have been a mistake was because without our local he would have been canned in his first week on the job?

—I think I'm starting to feel a little sick myself.

—I rest my case. But, you know, you eventually come to realize that any kind of negativity, whether it's legitimate or not, isn't going to help you, so what's the point?

—Very sensible.

—But I do miss walking my route.

—Even in the rain and sleet and snow and—

—*Especially* then. There was nothing better than being out there breathing in the fresh morning air before the whole city woke up and got busy turning a beautiful, overnight snowfall into a dirty slush pile. It would be so quiet, too, just the sound of your boots all crunchy in the freshly fallen snow. And the world would seem transformed—for a little while, anyway—into something soft and smooth and new.

—Like when you were a kid and you'd wake up in the morning and see that it had snowed all night while you were sleeping.

—Exactly. It's not often you get to feel like you did when you were a kid.

—It's not like you couldn't still go for a walk in the morning.

—I know. Believe me, I know. I guess sometimes you just need to be forced to do the things you want to do. The things that you know are good for you.

—That doesn't make sense, but I know what you mean.

—I didn't create human nature, I'm just describing it.

—But you've still got your garden. That feeling we were talking about—when you were out walking by yourself—that must be sort of what it's like now when you're working in your backyard taking care of your vegetables and flowers.

—The only non-vegetable in my garden is roses.

—Okay, roses, roses are nice, but my point—

—Roses are nice? *Nice*? I bet you didn't know that rose fossils exist that are thirty-two million years old.

—You'd be right. I didn't. And that is pretty amazing. What I was getting at, though, was—

—And that for as long as human beings have been around, roses have meant as many different things as there have been cultures to appreciate them. To the ancient Arabs, the rose was a symbol of masculinity. The Romans were the first culture to associate it with love. The early Christians made the rose the flower of the Virgin Mary. Same flower, different take. The people change, the interpretation changes, the rose stays the same.

—Hey, that sounds a bit like the man of the hour, Mr. Kant, and his "noumenons," the actual thing itself.

—Oh, God, no, don't tell me he's rubbed off on me.

—I said *a bit*. I don't think there's any danger of you writing your own *Critique of Pure Reason*.

—Thank goodness for that.

—All right, it's about time we got down to it. You've obviously got some strong opinions about Immanuel K., so let's hear them.

—That's the problem. I really don't.

—What an oddly non-emotive response to someone who is generally considered the single greatest modern philosopher.

—Cut that shit out. And don't tell me you got all hot and bothered reading about his attempt to synthesize rationalism and empiricism.

—Well, not quite hot and bothered, no, but I have to admit, I was sort of chuffed that I was able to keep his breakdown of the propositions of logic relatively straight. Do you mind if I show off a little?

—Far be it from me to inhibit your chuffness. Please go right ahead.

—The propositions of logic are either analytic or synthetic, and either *a priori* or *a posteriori*.

—So far so good. Now please kindly explain what the hell that means.

—That means...just a second, let me check my...

—I thought you said you had this stuff down.

—Hey, don't look a gift horse bearing explications of Immanuel Kant in the mouth. I just need my cheat sheet, that's all. Okay. An analytic judgment is one whose predicate is contained in its subject, so if you deny it, it's a contradiction. A synthetic judgment on the other hand is one whose predicate is not contained in its subject.

—Very nice. But so what?

—So, an *a priori* judgment is one which is independent of experience, while an *a posteriori* judgment is one which does depend on experience.

—I guess you didn't hear me the first time: but so what?

—Hold on, I'm not done. From these two distinctions, Kant says that there are three possible kinds of judgments.

—Which I bet you've got written down there and are going to tell me.

—Specifically, analytic *a priori*, synthetic *a posteriori*, and synthetic *a priori*.

—Wonderful. Well done. But you still haven't answered my question.

—Which was?

—So what?

—So . . . I've got some more distinctions here to get through first. Impressions and particulars. Categories of thought. Quantity, quality, relation, and modality. There's also—

—If you don't stop, I think I'm going to scream.

—Okay, okay. So, to answer your question of "so what?" Kant comes up with—after setting down the various distinctions detailed previously, such as—

—Scream, I tell you. Literally scream.

—So Kant comes to the conclusion that there are the things we perceive—which he calls "phenomenon"—and there is the actual thing itself, which he calls "noumenon." So all of the big stuff in life—ethics, the soul, God, stuff like that—can never be known as objects of experience, but only through pure reason.

—So his whole "an action is moral if the performer of the action would will it that it should become a moral law" thing—

—The categorical imperative.

—The categorical imperative, it comes from all of that endless category blah blah blah stuff.

—I don't remember coming across the phrase "blah blah blah," but, yeah, it's grounded in the work Kant already did. An action is moral only if the maxim upon which it is based can be made into a universal law without contradiction.

—So it's just a coincidence that the most famous element of his ethical philosophy sounds a whole lot like "Do unto others as you would have them do unto you"?

—Good point. I hadn't thought of that.

—I think that's the biggest problem I have with so much of what we've been reading: your mind is so busy trying to understand what philosopher X has to say, there's no space in your brain or time left over to actually think about what they said.

—I have to admit, I do find that the questions you start out with are usually more interesting than the answers the philosophers arrive at.
—But maybe it's not their fault. I mean, someone like Kant was trying to understand how human beings comprehend reality. He's more like what we would call a scientist today than what most people would think of as a philosopher. I guess I was hoping I'd come across someone who would write something so true, so important, so life-changing, I'd want it tattooed on my body, you know? I mean, if a poem or a song or whatever else means something to you—if it really, really matters—you don't need a cheat sheet to explain it to yourself. You just *know* it, you know?
—We've talked about this more than once.
—What?
—The philosopher not having enough to say about what really matters.
—Life.
—Life.
—
—
—I don't know what you'd call him—not a philosopher; probably just a "writer"—but I read a book about Imperial Rome last summer, and I keep thinking about this line of Seneca's. It's almost like a song you can't get out of your head.
—Without knowing what the line is, that would seem like a pretty good example of what you were talking about before, about what you were wishing for. Of finding something you didn't have to try to remember, of something you *couldn't* forget.
—I guess it is.
—So, what is it? Don't keep me in suspense.

—Maybe it's a little too Zen, I don't know…

—Is there really such a thing as too Zen?

—Okay. Here goes. "A single moment is no different from eternity."

—I'm going to need more wine for this one.

—Really? Doesn't that sound like Betty?

—Betty?

—Betty of the Betty Boards. Remember?

—I know who and what you're talking about, but it's a long way from the Grateful Dead's premier concert taper to a two-thousand-year-old Roman writer.

—But that's just it: it's not. It's the same thing. Two thousand years later and it's still true. It'll *always* be true. I guess that's what I would call philosophy.

—Okay, but what does it mean?

—Really?

—Hey, I didn't get on your case when you couldn't tell me the difference between *a priori* and *a posteriori*.

—But this is important.

—And I'm sure that Kant thought the same thing about what he wrote.

—This is important to *me*.

—What is it again?

—"A single moment is no different from eternity."

—Oh. Okay. I think I get it.

—Right? And if that single moment was a good moment—a really, really good moment—and it was the *only* moment—because maybe it was the *last* moment—it would be…I don't know…a good moment forever. I mean, kind of. It doesn't make sense in a way, I know, but it does, it does make sense.

—I don't know, maybe to you…

—Remember when you were a kid and you tried to think about eternity? About where the universe ends? And you couldn't do it, your mind couldn't do it, it just kept going and going. Maybe that's because the way to get your head around eternity isn't to think about forever, it's to think about a moment. Any moment. Maybe *that's* eternity.

—Okay, but...

—

—

—But what?

—I don't know, I mean...

—

—

—What? You mean what?

—Christ, I don't know what I mean. What about... What about it won't *be* a moment? It can't be. It's not like you're just going to wait around for an especially good feeling to arrive one day and then, you know...

—A good night after a good day. That's what I want. Not a perfect day. There are no perfect days. Or perfect nights. But a day doing what I like to do, doing the things that make me happy—that make me *me*—and a night doing the same thing and feeling the same way. That's what I want.

—I can understand that, I guess.

—I've thought about this a lot, Phil. A *lot*. I thought about it all summer, especially when I worked in my garden. Planting things and helping them grow is a surprisingly conducive way of thinking about eternity. If the goal of life is happiness, and if Seneca is right and a moment *is* an eternity, if your last moment is a happy one, doesn't that mean you'll be happy for eternity?

—That's a lot of *ifs*.

—Eternity is a long time.

—

—

—I just want my eternity to be a good one. Does that make sense?

—I don't know. I mean, it's... I understand why it would seem important. To you, I mean. I mean...

—Relax, okay? Have some more wine.

—I don't want anymore wine.

—Then just relax then. And don't worry. This isn't that night. This isn't that single moment.

—That night *is* going to be this night eventually, though. That moment *is* going to be this moment someday.

—Someday. But not this day.

—I don't think I understand.

—I think you do.

—I think we need some more wine.

—I think that's a very good idea.

TWENTY-ONE

One day you look up and everybody is younger than you. How the hell did *that* happen? When I turned fifty I didn't feel anxious about my mortality or sad about my passing youth, I just felt, sort of... embarrassed. Not like I hadn't accomplished enough in my life up to that point, but more like, *How could I have let something like being fifty years old happen to me?* I had grown a horseshoe moustache at the time and went so far as to purchase a Just for Men moustache-dying kit in an attempt to cosmetically turn back the years. Fortunately, preparing to go from half-a-century grey to young-man medium-brown, I only got as far as opening the package and unpacking its contents before deciding to return it to the store. Not being able to meet your own eyes in the bathroom mirror might not be as reliable a moral indicator as Kant's "categorical imperative," but it got the job done. Along with providing my receipt, I had to fill out a form that, in addition to asking my name, address, and phone number, also required the reason for returning the product in question. *Because I was temporarily a grade-A douchebag* probably wasn't what the woman working the Loblaws customer service desk was looking for, so I entered *wrong colour* instead. I got back my ten dollars and shaved off the moustache.

The gym is a good place to remind yourself that you're not going to live forever. Inside our outside, we're all still nervous the night before the first day of school and still wonder what we're going to do with our lives when we finally grow up; this, in spite of being, outside the inside, a fifty-two-year-old man stepping and sweating his best to something approximating adequate cardiovascular health and a generalized deferral of imminent physical decay. To know that you're really not young anymore, it's helpful to be surrounded by a roomful of young people running treadmills and pumping iron and skipping rope with about as much effort as it takes you to fall asleep in the middle of the day or to have that second piece of pie. Maybe there should be a gym just for over-fifties, with a bouncer at the door and a sign forbidding entry to all persons with flat stomachs, plenty of natural energy, and a clear, sanguine sparkle in their eyes.

Most people when they're working out pretend that other people—young and old, fit or not—don't exist, iPods and earbuds the preferred method of exercise obliviousness. Because my musical tastes aren't of the *unta unta unta* or dunderhead 4/4 rock-and-roll variety, I'm forced to find my entertainment distractions elsewhere, a hypnotic, eleven-minute Jerry Garcia guitar solo not the ideal aural pick-me-up when you're dragging your ass at the halfway point of your workout. Sometimes I bring along an old pair of headphones to plug into the TV screen attached to the elliptical trainer and flip back and forth between its only two stations. There's a business channel, which tends to focus on how to make a fortune by picking this week's stock market winners, and an all-celebrity station that runs features like how Emma Watson's fashion sense has changed—no, not changed: *evolved*—over the course of her career. The former tends to feature pudgy, pallid, middle-aged men discussing stocks and bonds with a disturbing solemnity; the latter to exclusively employ people under the age of twenty-five of every possible ethnic and sexual variety united only by their perfect teeth, trim physiques, and empty eyes. It usually only takes me a few minutes before I'm reminded why I rarely bother to bring my headphones with me to the gym.

Growing up, there was a magnet on the refrigerator at home that said YOU'LL NEVER BE YOUNGER THAN YOU ARE TODAY. My mother's intention in buying it and placing it there was inspirational, I think—a marginally less tiresome version of one of her favourite sayings when Fred and I were kids: Don't put off to tomorrow what you can do today. I wonder what happened to the magnet when we moved Mum into her retirement home and sold the house. One more judicious axiom at the bottom of a landfill somewhere.

Move your legs. Move your arms. Wipe the sweat from your eyes and don't look at the clock. You'll never be younger than you are right now. I mean right now. No—now. Now. *Now.*

•

Cough cough cough.

It's just a cough.

Cough cough cough.

Caroline told me, and she should know: It's just a cough.

"It's just a cough," Caroline says.

"I know," I say. "I didn't say anything."

"You didn't have to. I could tell what you were thinking."

"You're pretty smart, but as far as I can determine you're not clairvoyant."

"I'm also not going to have you watching me all the time wondering if today's the day."

"Today's the day what?"

Of course I know what *what* is, but part of the pact we've never formally agreed to or even discussed is that the coughing-weakening-deteriorating countdown to Caroline's Last Good Night only begins when she—and she alone—decides it does. *So don't look at me like that when I just don't happen to look or feel my best today*, the slight scowl on her face says. She'll know when she knows and then I'll know. In that order.

Ignoring my question, "Is it twelve yet?" Caroline says from her side of my bed.

I look over at the alarm clock on my side table. "Ten more minutes."

The plan had been to go for a walk in High Park before dinner at Kingdom Coming, a new all-vegan restaurant on Roncy, followed by a quiet night of reading in bed until midnight, when an AM radio station somewhere in New York State airs two consecutive hours of old-time radio. Its discovery had been Caroline's, but I was an immediate and enthusiastic convert, lying in the dark while listening to the adventures of Sam Spade and the Shadow, the thrills and chills of the Avenger, a unique opportunity to step out of the twenty-first century for awhile and luxuriate in a time when kindly old doctors still made house calls, the fair coming to town was the social event of the season, and the idea of ordinary citizens not daring to leave home without their telephones or masks would be the very definition of dystopian fantasy.

"I've got time for a cigarette, then," Caroline says, getting out of bed. She's wearing one of my sleeveless white T-shirts over a pair of pale blue underwear that I remember being pleasingly tight but which now seem to sag at the back. Initially, I'd asked her to please smoke in the backyard when we were at my house (although weed was okay) because I thought it might discourage her. Maybe it did, but it doesn't anymore. This is either her second or third cigarette since she got here a little after ten.

"Okay," I say, "but don't blame me if you miss the grand entrance of the Green Hornet."

"I think I'll risk it." She pulls on her shorts and pads downstairs in her bare feet.

She'd called earlier in the evening to say that it was too humid to go for a walk and that she'd had indigestion all day and wasn't up to eating out, but that she'd still be by my place later. I didn't mind her putting the kibosh on the restaurant—for the most part, food is just food to me, and the quarter-chicken dinner to go from Ali Baba's runs about twenty bucks cheaper than what my half of Kingdom Coming's bill would have come to—but I was disappointed we weren't going to High Park. Since I've been working out at the gym I've not only lost weight, I've also gained energy, and exercising these days isn't only something I should do, but quite often something I want to do. More than that: if I don't get my daily dose of getting up and moving around I feel uneasy, the sort of good restlessness that it feels wrong to quell with booze or dope.

Which was partly why I didn't join Caroline when she almost immediately sparked up a joint as soon as she arrived—the other part being that we said we were going to read in bed until our radio program came on, and Hegel, the next big brain on our march through history's foremost frontal lobes, is mystifying enough without adding pot's gently obfuscating charms to the mix. She was temporarily a trifle pouty with my lack of toking participation, but once she got high, seemed content to let me read while she mostly stared at the back jacket of her copy of the same paperback we're using to cram for our next philosophy session. I've got a feeling that I'm going to have to carry the load when we get to the final flowering of German Idealism.

By the time Caroline is back I've got the radio turned on and our station tuned in. It's a little crackly with static, but not enough to interfere with listening, and once she's slipped out of her shorts and is underneath the sheets again I click off my reading lamp and the room is dark except for the green glow of the stereo. That, and the tiny orange light of her freshly fired-up joint. This time she doesn't bother offering me any.

Cough cough cough.

I want to ask her if she'd like a glass of water, if she wants me to turn off the A/C and open a window, something.

Cough cough cough.

"Where is this one supposed to be set?" Caroline says.

"I don't know. I think they said, but..." But I couldn't hear because—

Cough cough cough.

"It doesn't matter," Caroline says.

"They'll probably mention it again."

Cough cough cough.

"It doesn't matter," she says.

•

Every time Caroline coughs a lot I wonder if this is how it'll happen—that the next time I see her she's going to tell me this is it, she's not going to risk getting any sicker and ending up feeling awful and looking like a ghost on a diet, and that tonight is the Last Good Night.

Every time I come home from staying over at her house or she leaves the next morning after sleeping over here, I feel secretly relieved we've survived another evening together.

Every day I remind myself that if you don't talk about something, you tend not to think about it, and if you don't think about it, it's easier to pretend it's not there.

No one has ever had to remind themselves that two plus two equals four.

•

I shouldn't be here. I knew there wasn't any reason to come when I spoke with the man on the phone, whose sister's books he was interested in unloading. Contemporary novels primarily—mostly of the much-praised and award-winning, morally-fibrous and good-for-you variety—the sort of books that are so much in demand last year but are rendered *so what?* twenty-four months later. Political relevance and cultural timeliness plus unanimous critical admiration are usually the highly regarded hallmarks of the most rapidly forgotten books. But here I am on my knees nonetheless, sorting through box after box of yesteryear's absolute must-reads. This is what I get for making a trip across town I had no business—literally—making, all because I didn't want to be at home by myself thinking about Caroline and her cough. No one outsmarts sorrow for long.

I'm attempting to appear as professional as I can—am wearing my mask and uh-huh-ing and hmm-ing as I go through box after cardboard box—but I think that the man suspects I'm underwhelmed, says, "Like I said, every one of them is signed by the author. Karen worked at the Reference Library, and every time somebody came through there promoting their latest book she'd get them to sign it. That makes them more valuable, right?"

"It can," I say, keeping busy with my hands so I'm not tempted to look up and add, *If anyone cared about the authors. In this case...*

At least they're all shorn of one of the banes of the second-hand bookseller's existence, the gratuitous and entirely unwarranted personal inscription of the gift giver to his or her recipient (09 23 98/*To Tom,/I thought of you when I saw this book. May it bring back many pleasant—and stimulating!!!—memories of the summer of '98./Best, Ken*). Although Ken did go to all the trouble of buying a remaindered copy of a discounted book, it's really not his place to sign and date a book whose existence he had absolutely nothing to do with other than possessing the ten dollars and change it cost to purchase it. It's not even the pecuniary matter of decreasing a book's value; it's a matter of sticking your name where it clearly doesn't belong. The writer who writes the book is entitled to inscribe it. The person who buys it is permitted to read it and put it on their shelf or pass it along to someone else to do the same. Karaoke is not an art form.

The man stands nearby, arms crossed, watching me work. If I thought I was going to purchase the collection, or at least a substantial chunk of it, I would have probably learned by now how his sister died and a little bit more about her book-loving life; knowing that I'm just wasting his time and mine, that the entire collection is one big "pass," I don't feel entitled to probe. All I know is all I need to know: she liked books, he clearly couldn't care less, I'm not interested in buying what he's selling. I keep pulling inscribed novels out of boxes, however, keep flipping through them and putting them back and opening new boxes. The man continues to loom above me like a heavy cloud that won't blow away.

Whatever his sister's job was at the library, it's safe to assume that her brother didn't spend a lot of time there, or at any other place where books are kept. He's around my age, but that's about the only thing we seem to have in common. He's wearing the typical office worker's workday uniform—pale blue short-sleeved dress shirt, plastic ID badge hanging around his neck, thick-soled white running shoes—and he must be on his lunch break or have taken a couple of hours off work so as to deal with one more item related to his late sister's estate. He's also wearing a large, and what is presumably a very expensive watch on his right wrist, of which he makes no attempt to disguise his interest. I feel like a fraud, taking up his time like this, and if I had the extra cash and space I'd lowball him an offer on the entire collection just out of courtesy, which I'm sure he'd accept. But I don't, so I can't, so I keep sorting and inspecting and putting books back where I got them.

"And all of them novels or short stories," I say, since someone has to say something, holding one of them up just in case my audience of one needs visual assistance to grasp the profundity of my point.

"She was always a bookworm. Even when we were little. Me and all of our friends would be outside playing in the summertime and Karen would be in the basement of our house with a novel and a can of Coke and a Snickers bar. She wouldn't even come outside and read in the backyard. Used to drive our mother crazy. 'You need vitamin D or you'll get rickets,' she'd say. 'How are you going to get vitamin D if you never get any sunshine? You're more likely to grow mushrooms first.'"

I laugh, although the man doesn't, so I stop. I resume my sham appraisal. The man looks at his watch, then back at me. My only hope is that there are another fifty boxes somewhere else in the house to be evaluated or if I could pull a muscle and be whisked away by an ambulance. Sometimes there are no solutions, only reprieves.

"So what are we looking at here?" the man says. "Ballpark figure."

I finally stand up; rest my hands on my hips. "To be honest"—Why do people always say that? Because the majority of the time they're lying?—"there's really not much I can use. It's not an indictment of your sister's books, it's just that it's not really what I'm looking for."

"Even though they're all signed?"

"I'm afraid so. I mean, I haven't finished going through them all yet, so maybe—"

"How about five hundred bucks for everything?" he says. "I just want to get them out of here. Karen's lease expires at the end of the month and I don't want to be lugging any more boxes than I have to."

"I wish I could. And I'm not trying to haggle. There's also the question of storage space on my end. I'm almost at full capacity now, and—"

The man looks at his watch again. "I've got a meeting at work in forty-five minutes that I *cannot* be late for. Just give me a couple hundred bucks and you can have the whole lot, the entire thing, how does that sound? Otherwise I guess I'm going to have to haul everything to the Salvation Army and I really don't have time for that."

Which is the least worst option? Parting with money I shouldn't part with in exchange for books I don't need, or a lifelong reader's most cherished tomes dumped at the back door of the Sally Ann like a garbage bag full of broken children's toys and moth-nibbled clothes? I can't help but think of Karen with her Coke and her Snickers bar and her paperback novel, the laughter and the squeals of the neighbourhood children a summer-long taunt through the basement window. I pull the roll of bills out of my pocket, peel off two hundred dollars.

"Sure," I say. "I'm sorry I can't give you more."

Taking the money, counting it, "I'm just glad I don't have to put them out on the curb. I'd never hear the end of it from the neighbours."

•

Remember going to the video store and renting a movie? I do. Barely. At one time there were three different rental options within a couple of miles walking radius, and then one, two, three, going out of business, everything including fixtures must go, coming soon: Tim Hortons, Toys"R"Us, another upscale coffee shop. Big deal, Benjamin and Cameron's generation might say—what you can't download off the internet for free you can always stream legally, if only as a last resort. But I liked walking in the door of the Film Buff and being immediately alerted to new releases and all of the long-form cable-television dramas that everyone but me was talking about. I've reached the age when I no longer know what I'm supposed to watch or even the names of all of the new movie stars who have taken the shine off all of the familiar old ones. I feel like seeing a film tonight, though, and I want it to be good, so I'll watch something I've already seen before. I realize that this is a symptom of incipient Geezerism, but to this I answer I don't really give a shit. That not giving a shit is yet another sign of the same, I also acknowledge.

DVDs—plastic, uniform, uninteresting—were never something to collect, but I've got a few old favourites for nights like this. What's a favourite isn't always what's good, and that's okay, that's part of what favourites are. *Reds* is a favourite of mine and that's what I push into the player before I lie back on the bed.

Reds is too long (over three hours) and I adore every minute. Love stories ordinarily bore me, which is precisely what *Reds* doesn't do, this in spite of the fact that the bohemian backdrop of turn-of-the-twentieth-century Greenwich Village and the frothy fervour of the Russian Revolution are merely the places and events that Jack Reed and Louise Bryant inhabit and involve themselves in. I watched it for the first time when I was in high school, and I wanted to be John Reed and to find my own Louise Bryant. I wasn't particularly interested in Communist politics and didn't aspire to be a globe-trotting, muckraking journalist, but I did want to sit up all night in dingy cold-water flats arguing about art and society and life with a bunch of equally passionate and proud middle-class outcasts. Whenever it would play in subsequent years at one of the repertory theatres I'd go and have my faith renewed in the possibility of leading a life that seemed like actually living as opposed to merely existing. I'd walk out of the Bloor Cinema or the Kingsway Theatre believing once again that, appearances to the contrary—crappy job, no Eugene O'Neill or Emma Goldman to call comrades, no Louise Bryant waiting for me at home—there was another way, another life, another me. Hope is more valuable than money when you're young, and it doesn't matter where you happen to find it, just as long as you do.

I never wrote my own *Ten Days That Shook the World*, I never discovered my own Greenwich Village, but the bookstore I eventually opened was High Bohemia enough, allowed me to be daily surrounded by deep thinkers and dark poets and every other sort of intellectual and artist available between two covers. And some of the people who wandered into the store weren't always uninteresting either, this one always on the lookout for Hogarth Press first editions, that one a dedicated collector of books about books, no matter how academically arcane. There were people like Zoran, too, who also, I flattered myself in thinking, enjoyed just being in the pleasant company of the best that has been thought and said. And where the hell is Zoran anyway? Why doesn't he come around and bother me anymore? How boring can life become when there's no one around to bother you.

Sometimes three hours and eighteen minutes is over in an instant, and I put the DVD back in its cheap plastic case and sit on the end of the bed and stare at the dark TV screen. I suppose I should go to sleep. Tomorrow is Monday, tomorrow morning Monday morning, the start of a new work week. Lucky for me all I have to do is bundle up any new orders and take them to the post office. Lucky for me I don't have to set my alarm or pack a lunch or fill a Thermos or flip the sign on the door to the COME IN, WE'RE OPEN side. Lucky me.

TWENTY-TWO

You didn't need a calendar to know that school was about to start: sweat-soaked, sleep-deprived Jerry Lewis on television all weekend raising money for Jerry's Kids meant that Monday was Labour Day and the first day of class was the day after that. How long has Jerry Lewis been dead? *Is* he dead? I think so. I could google it, but what difference does it make? If he isn't gone yet, he will be soon. Live long enough, and every week, it seems, there's someone else who was unavoidably everywhere when you were young who's become erased now that you're old. In time, you go from *I can't believe so-and-so is dead* to *I know that someone famous died recently—who was it?*

Glassy-eyed, tuxedo-tie askew Jerry Lewis might not be around anymore to signify its arrival, but fall is here, there's little doubt about that. If the days are still a trifle globally warmed over, at least the mornings are cooler and even the city feels fresher. I want to call Caroline to ask her if she feels like going for a walk in High Park, but I know she won't, so I save her the trouble of having to come up with an excuse. She and I and Hegel have got a study date for tonight. She'll need all of her energy for that.

When you feel like going somewhere but don't have anywhere to go, it's good to make up a destination, so I leave home on foot for Queen Street and Stephen's shop. By the time I get there I'm sweaty and need to take a piss and want something cold to drink. Everything comes with complications once you're over fifty, even something as theoretically straightforward as a long walk to see an old friend you don't see enough on a nice September afternoon. Five more years and I'll have to pack a compass, a canteen, and a change of clothing every time I leave the house.

Two minutes after I'm in the door, Stephen and I are shooting the shit and bitching and complaining and doing what any two people trying to get by in the same business do: talking shop and trying to figure out how to keep ahead of whatever's next. I still have to pee and I'm thirstier than I was before, but I'm glad I came. Stephen is telling me about one of those rare days that every second-hand seller dreams about, that happens, if you're lucky, only a few times in your career as a picker and a poacher.

"You get the idea," he says. "Every book I snag up off this old lady's lawn is a winner. They're all paperbacks, but we're talking first edition Black Cat Henry Millers, old Canadian firsts of *Green Hills of Africa* and *To Have and Have Not*—Hemingway, Faulkner, you name it. All of them a buck a book."

"You mean those nice little Permabooks that came out of Montreal?"

"Yeah."

"Man, those are sweet little books."

"Tell me about it. And get this: then I spot a copy of Kerouac's *Tristessa*."

"The Avon edition?"

"You got it."

"That's the original first. There was never a hardcover edition."

Stephen just shakes his head, smiles. I do the same except for the smiling part. It's always exciting to hear about someone discovering gold; the only thing better is if you're the one doing the discovering.

"So the old woman"—Stephen is my age, so if he says someone is old, they're *old*—"sees me snapping up practically everything she's got for sale and asks me if I want some plastic bags to carry everything, and I say sure, thanks, and when she comes out of the house with the bags she says I should come inside where she's got a lot more books, she just couldn't manage to get them all out on the lawn by herself. *If* I'm interested."

"Oh, man."

"Right? I'm thinking hard covers of the same quality and vintage. I'm thinking I've discovered freaking Tutankhamen's tomb."

"You bastard. I hope they were all Reader's Digest compendiums and old atlases."

"Nope. Same deal as outside. Then I spot a copy of *The Great Gatsby* that's in pretty good shape, that's still in its jacket, and flip to page 205."

"No."

"Oh, yeah. And there it was."

"No." Any respectable second-hand bookseller knows his or her "points"—book dealer catalogue code for distinguishing rare editions from less valuable ones. In a true first edition of *The Great Gatsby*, a typesetter's mistake on page 205 turned Fitzgerald's "sickantired" into "sick in tired." It can say "First Edition" on the copyright page, but if on page 205 it doesn't read "sick in tired" it's the second issue and not nearly as rare. Or valuable. Stephen's copy has "sick in tired." Depending on its condition, it could be worth as much as five thousand dollars, maybe more.

"And get this," he says. "She says she'll have to charge me two dollars each for these, because they're hardcovers."

"Bastard. Where was this again?"

"Over near Trinity Bellwoods Park. But I'm not done."

"Christ, don't tell me: she had a footlocker full of Hemingway's letters to Fitzgerald. I don't want to hear it."

"Just wait. I'm pulling books off the shelf and piling them on the floor just as quickly as I can in case she changes her mind or someone else comes along and discovers my stash—"

"—Someone like me."

"Right, when I hear this noise coming from the other room, this sort of moaning, almost whimpering, like someone's in pain and wants help but can't speak. Kind of like: *Uhhhh . . . Uhhhh . . . Uhhhh.* Actually, you know what it sounded like? The mummy in those old black-and-white horror films. *Uhhhh . . . Uhhhh . . . Uhhhh.*"

"Christ."

"The old woman sees that I'm a little freaked out by this, so she says, 'Oh, that's just my brother in his bedroom. He's fine, but since his most recent stroke, unfortunately he can't walk or speak. He was a bachelor his whole life, but after this stroke I moved down here from North Bay to take care of him. It took us awhile, but we're doing just fine now, we understand each other and get along just as well as can be expected. These are all his books, actually. I thought it was time we cleared out some of the clutter around here. I'm afraid his reading days are over.'"

"The old man was freaking out because his sister was selling his books," I say.

"Exactly."

"Every book lover's nightmare. A lifetime's worth of collecting sold for pennies on the dollar."

"Exactly."

Stephen is sitting behind the counter; I'm standing on the other side, leaning on it with my elbow. We both look out the window.

"You didn't buy them off her, did you?" I say.

"How could I?"

"Not even the Fitzgerald?"

Stephen doesn't answer. We stare out at Queen Street.

"I told Beth you dropped by the shop after the last time you were here," he says, "and she said to tell you you're supposed to come by for dinner sometime."

"Sounds good."

"She also said you'd probably say something like that, and to let you know that I'm supposed to pester you until it actually happens."

I always liked Beth, Stephen's wife. An orthodontist and the mother of three children and on the boards of the Canadian National Institute for the Blind and the Canadian Opera Company, sometimes it's not a bad thing to be around people who don't give *grown-up* a bad name.

"Hey," he says, standing up, "things are pretty dead around here. Why don't I hang the BE BACK IN TEN MINUTES sign and we can go grab an iced tea or something. You look like you could use it."

I am thirsty and I don't have anywhere to be until tonight, but, "I should get going," I say.

"Yeah," he says. "Things have been pretty slow. My luck, I'll duck out for five minutes and ten people will have come by."

"Probably."

I'd planned to walk home, but only get as far as a couple of streets west when I realize I still have to pee. I put up my hand and a taxi pulls over. I tell the driver where I want to go.

•

—What I'm saying is, once we get through this, we get to the good stuff. The interesting stuff.

—More interesting than Hegel, you mean.

—Nietzsche, for example. You said you were interested in him, right? And then the twentieth century.

—The twentieth century seems like a million years away from where we are right now.

—So pitter-patter, let's get at 'er.

—I'm going to pretend you didn't say that.

—How about "This Hegel isn't going to explicate itself"?

—You know what? That's even worse, if that's possible.

—Hey, here's a thought: Why don't I get us started?

—What a wonderful idea.

—Essentially, Hegel is all about two things.

—

—I said, "Essentially, Hegel is all about two things."

—Keep going.

—Okay, well, thing number one: Separateness is an illusion. The world is not a collection of individual things. It's a complex system—an organism that Hegel called the "Absolute."

—Uh-huh.

—Yes, exactly. Which, of course, means that there's no such thing as time or space as they're traditionally understood, since that would imply separateness. Care to add anything?

—You're doing swell. Please continue.

—But that wouldn't be fair. No one likes it when somebody hogs all the Hegel.

—I—*Cough cough cough.*

—

—*Cough cough cough.* I—

—

—I insist.

—Hey, c'mon, don't do that, okay?

—If anyone ever deserved to get high, it's when they're trying to wrap their head around German Idealism.

—I'll make you a deal. I'll handle the Hegel tonight, and you put out the joint and have some of this very cheap but not too, too bad-tasting Portuguese wine I brought over instead.

—I'm not thirsty.

—It's alcohol—it's got nothing to do with being thirsty.

—I'm fine with—*cough cough cough*—this.

—Yeah, clearly.

—Don't bully me, Phil.

—Christ, you sound like one of these kids today.

—Did you just say "One of these kids today"? You did just say that, right?

—You know what I mean. Anytime they don't feel like doing something or they think it's going to be too difficult, all of a sudden they're "uncomfortable" or don't feel "safe."

—That doesn't sound very inclusive or understanding on your part.

—It's *very* understanding. It means I understand better than a teenager that anything in life that's worth doing or having is probably going to seem pretty damn daunting and difficult at times, and that nothing that's worth it is ever easy. Life is uncomfortable. The human condition is uncomfortable. Get used to it.

—I think we just grew up differently than they did, that's all. Our parents didn't make it as much of a priority to ensure that we were safe and secure twenty-four-seven. I can remember my sister and me riding in the backseat of our grandfather's big old black Buick and there being a leather rope attached to the back of the front seat for us to hold on to. Like that was going to keep us safe if he slammed on the brakes or actually crashed.

—You're kidding. An actual rope?

—Like a rope. I think it was more for helping passengers climb out of the backseat, but people used it to hold on to as well. You don't remember?

—No recollection at all. Zero.

—Well, you're younger than I am.

—Barely.

—Oh, you damn kids and your namby-pamby seat belts. And here's something else wrong with your rant, Grandpa: I'm not a teenager, so leave me out of it.

—Maybe not, but you're acting like one. Doing something that's obviously bad for you because it's the easiest thing to do.

—I can't believe I didn't tell you this already: I'm dying of cancer, not of marijuana.

—I'm not talking about dying—I'm talking about living. And that shit is fucking up your ability to breathe.

—Actually, it's cancer that's fucking up my ability to breathe. This—*cough cough cough*—makes me feel better.

—Obviously.

—Why don't you take care of the Hegel and leave the cancer to me?

—Look, I'm not trying to be difficult. I'm really not. I just don't like to see you suffer when you can do something about it.

—Oh, we're talking about suffering now? Is that what we're doing? Really?

—I just—

—Don't tell me how to live, okay? Or die.

—Like I said, I just—

—And I'm just about finished with this subject. Actually, I'm past finished.

—

—

—What about "dialectic"?

—You're kidding, right?

—Hey, you started this. Finish it. What about Hegel's concept of the "dialectic"?

—It's...

—What? It's what? C'mon.

—Hopelessly confusing. That's what it is.

—I could be wrong, but I think that's what Hegel means in German: *hopelessly confusing.*

—That's pretty good. Did you just make that up?

—Maybe.

—That's almost as creative as Hegel's theory of the dialectic process.

—Which—*cough cough cough*—is?

—

—Which is?

—Thesis. Antithesis. Synthesis.

—That actually kind of makes sense.

—You almost sound like you're not kidding.

—I'm not. Not entirely. I mean, how can you understand something unless you've experienced it every step of its evolution?

—Like cancer, you mean.

—Among other things.

—I don't think that's what Hegel was talking about.

—Are you sure?

—No, but that's mostly because I don't think Hegel knew what he was talking about either.

—Who does? About anything. Completely, I mean.

—That's kind of a depressing thought.

—Are you uncomfortable? Do you feel unsafe? I haven't triggered you in any way, have I?

—No. But you did make me smile.

—Well, that's something.

—It's not philosophy, though, is it?

—Who says?

•

Today isn't a gym day—isn't even daytime, is nearly ten o'clock at night—but an endorphin high is better than no high at all, and I need to manufacture a mood change, pronto. Watching Caroline chimney herself into a hacking mess, the desire to light up alone and get down with the Dead is minimal. But I need a holiday, however brief, from the guilt I feel for being irritated with her yesterday, and the day before that, for coughing me awake most of the night. She's the one suffering—*cough cough cough, cough cough cough*, disappear into the bathroom at something-a.m. for ten minutes, come back to bed, *cough cough cough, cough cough cough,* back to the bathroom—but my powers of compassion have been significantly undermined by both a lack of shut-eye and an inability to not be a bit of a jerk. I haven't said anything to her, of course, but words are only one way of communicating, and sometimes an exasperated *Pardon?* at bleary breakfast or what you thought was a surreptitious eye-roll in the middle of the night speak a whole lot louder. I also feel guilty because, even feeling as cruddy as she does, she saw how frazzled I am and insisted I stay at home tonight and get caught up on my own sleep. When I volleyed back the expected response—that it was okay, that I hadn't been that bothered, that if I feel tired in the day I can always take a nap—she said that her bothering me bothered her, too, made her feel bad keeping me awake all night, and that it would actually be better for her if she slept alone. The only thing worse than doing someone you care about wrong is them turning right around and being nice to you.

A good, nerve-soothing workout, a long, hot shower, a cup of steaming chamomile tea, and I'm under the sheets by midnight, goodbye me, hello oblivion. Except: I can't sleep. I turn on the light and read and wait for my eyelids to dissolve into saggy sandbags. No such luck. I try something I saw on television once: close my eyes and starting at my toes mentally massage each successive body part until I'm rubbery-relaxed enough to drift off. Nice try. And when books and mental relaxation techniques don't get the job done, there's always everybody's time-tested favourite, excessive carb-loading. A couple of pieces of toast and two hard-boiled eggs dosed with Tabasco sauce later and I'm back in the sack and bloated and gassy but not any more tired. After several minutes of tossing and turning and pillow-flipping, I've only got one more soporific trick up my sleeve. I pull back the covers and do what I haven't had to do for a long time, since I met Caroline.

Between my imagination and my right hand, I'm feeling better already, and it isn't long after I've started that I've decided that, whether it helps me sleep or not, whenever in doubt about what to do next, a wank is never a bad idea. I'm almost there, almost there, when it begins: a curious tingling; a not entirely unpleasant, slowly spreading warmth; hot hot hot, what the hell? just don't stop, don't stop; Jesus Christ: my cock is on fire.

After another shower—this one decidedly cooler than the first—and a gentle drying pat-down of the affected area, I return to bed. I console myself with the knowledge that I now know something I never knew before: masturbation and Tabasco sauce do not mix, at least not without washing your hands first. I must have read something by somebody this summer about the difficulty of acquiring wisdom without paying for it with sacrifice and suffering, but I doubt that this was what they had in mind. Too bad. Philosophy would make a lot more sense if there was less chatter about things like Hegel's theory of the dialectic process and more attention paid to singed genitals and human folly.

•

The last time I looked at the clock before I finally fell asleep it was just after three. The last thing I remember thinking was that I wished I was at Caroline's place. That I *should* have been at Caroline's place. Why wasn't I at Caroline's place?

I wake up around eight the next morning and am relieved that I feel terrible. Tonight, I'm going to camp out on the couch in Caroline's living room. It's far enough away from the bedroom that I'll be able to get some sleep, but it's close enough that if she needs me, I'll be right there.

TWENTY-THREE

"Phil. Geez. You look like shit."

You should see the other guy. The other person. Caroline. Shut up, Phil.

"Just tired," I say.

"Everybody needs their Zs," Alex says. "Just can't sleep, or what?"

I hadn't planned on stopping in at the Hidden Rec Room—was on my way to the post office with a couple canvas bags full of orders when Alex spotted me passing by and waved me in—and now that I'm here, I'm not about to go into the reason why I haven't been getting my beauty rest. "Yeah," I say, and thankfully the all-purpose affirmation is explanation enough. The store is empty except for us and the Laura Veirs record playing on the stereo. Alex is on his stool behind the counter. I'm standing just inside the doorway, a heavy bag hanging from each hand.

"I think it's time to admit defeat," he says, motioning my way with his chin.

I look down at myself and don't have a clue what he's talking about. I wonder if this is how Alzheimer's begins: you remember to bring your wallet with you when you set out for the grocery store, you just forget to wear shoes and are carrying a bucket and a mop. Alex recognizes my honest cluelessness.

"You might be able to get away with shorts and a T-shirt for a few more days," he says, "but it's going down to, like, ten by the weekend."

Celsius will always be the numerical new guy, will always be a math translation away from informing me what the temperature really is (double it and add thirty), but once I do a quick Fahrenheit conversion I get the point. The end of summer. The beginning of fall. The first hint of winter. Time to start thinking about coats and gloves and scarves.

"I guess you're right," I say. "I guess I hadn't noticed."

"Crept up on you, huh?"

I nod and look out the large display window at the people walking by. I'm the only one not wearing pants or a jacket. That's how it happens: whatever is, *is*, right up until the moment it isn't anymore.

"Maybe you need to get away for awhile," he says. "I bet you haven't been anywhere in ages. Man, if I could afford the time off, I'd do it in a minute. It'd be good for you—clear your head. Might even straighten out your sleep."

"Yeah, well, no rest for the wicked," I say, bouncing each bag a couple of times. "Maybe some other time."

"Well, just don't wait too long. Not if you're thinking about going anywhere around here. They say it's going to be a wicked winter. The ice caps are melting and the polar bears are drowning, and we're supposed to get killer blizzards all season. Strange times, man. Strange times."

We say our *See you later*s and I've transferred both bags to my left hand and am working on the door handle with my right when Alex says, "Hey, I meant to tell you: we finally caught him."

"Caught who?" Or is it *whom*? Who or whom gives a shit.

"The shoplifter," he says. "Check it out."

I hadn't noticed the sign that Alex had taped to the wall a couple of weeks back, which has now been amended with a big black *X* running from corner to corner. "You know She Said Boom! on College? The owner caught the guy red-handed with a bunch of books and locked the door and kept him there until the cops arrived. Let me tell you, that takes a lot of guts. As pissed off as I was, I don't know if I could have done it. But he did, and the shoplifter guy got charged and everything. Turned out he was wanted for a bunch of other stuff too, like child support back payments or something. Figures, right?"

"Figures," I say, and we say goodbye one more time.

Back on the sidewalk, it *is* cool—cooler than I'd realized—but the sun drenches everything and everyone on Roncesvalles Avenue, and it feels pleasantly warm on my face. It doesn't take a philosopher to recognize that you can't have the one without the other.

•

When Caroline picks me up in her car and is wearing makeup, I wonder if we're doing the right thing. As long as I've known her, anyway, cosmetics have never been a part of who she is—nothing more than a little lipstick that I can remember—and I can't help but worry that the rouge and the eyeliner are there to cover up what she doesn't want me to see: paleness, exhaustion, illness. But she's smiling when I get in the car and put my bag on the backseat and there's busily tinkling jazz on the radio and it's a cool but clear fall day, perfect weather for getting out of town. She leans over and kisses me and puts her VW into gear and off we go. The guy I rented the cottage from said that we could be there in less than two and a half hours.

When a hiking buddy of Debbie's offered to rent us her cottage near Parry Sound for a weekend, I think Debbie was surprised I was so enthusiastic to accept, but a little less concrete and a few fewer sirens and car alarms sounded like it might be nice. It might also, I thought, be a pleasant change from a too-steady diet of Dead and dope. We went, I liked it—I liked the stars in my eyes and the silence in my ears and the fresh air in my nostrils—and we talked about maybe getting a summer place of our own. A hot shower in the morning and my own reading material on the back of the toilet and my own breakfast cereal in the kitchen cupboard—a rural getaway without having to leave home. Maybe that was what I'd been missing.

Not unlike alcohol and nighttime swimming, however, red wine and real estate websites are a dangerous combination. After enough of the former, it seems entirely rational to conclude that, on the one hand, yes, the property you discovered online *is* in Nova Scotia, but, on the other hand, it's only sixty-five thousand dollars and is a hundred years old and has a wraparound porch that overlooks the bay. Another glass of Merlot and you've convinced yourself that commuting to the other side of the country to enjoy your summer house would have its undeniable challenges but is definitely doable. Definitely. And in the morning you wash the dirty wineglass and pledge once again not to pilot the information superhighway pie-eyed. Eventually, though, we did find a place that seemed to check all of our boxes. It was within a three-hour drive of Toronto, it was on a clean, quiet river, it was within our price range. It was even located on Mark Twain Road. What more could a used bookseller ask for? But it wasn't nearly enough nature for Debbie; the guy across the river cutting his lawn, who waved when he saw us checking the place out, put a permanent end to our cottage hunting.

"Don't take this the wrong way, but are you sure you know where we're going?"

"Just keep your eyes on the road," I say. "I'll know when we're there when we get there."

"That's reassuring."

"See, that's what happens when you get mixed up with somebody else. You're something else now, too—you're a team, with collective strengths and weaknesses and all the rest of it."

"So that's what we are: a team. I was wondering."

"I told you this weekend was going to be illuminating."

What I actually said when I phoned Caroline was that I'd found a cottage for rent north of Toronto and that it was cheap because it was so late in the season and that it would be great for us to get away for awhile and it would be nice to look at the stars in the sky and to have a fire outside at night and to breathe some clean country air. I knew she might say no because of how she'd been feeling lately, but I also knew that she might say yes for the same reason. How she responded was going to answer a lot more than just whether or not she wanted to go away for the weekend. And she said yes. Immediately. Enthusiastically. I put down the phone thinking that, even if the stars stayed behind the clouds and we couldn't have a campfire because it rained every night and a nearby tire fire made gas masks compulsory, it would be worth it just to hear how excited she was about going. And she's still excited. Laughing, actually.

"What's so funny?" I say.

The car is moving, if only barely—it's always rush hour in Toronto now—but we're going slow enough that Caroline can afford to look at me. I like her with makeup. I like her without makeup. I like Caroline.

"Nothing," she says. "I was just thinking how I had to drive around to three different grocery stores before I could find one that sold coloured marshmallows."

"Coloured marshmallows. You went all-out."

"I haven't been camping in—I don't know how long. Thirty-five years?"

"Considering that you bought coloured marshmallows and everything, I don't want to disappoint you, but we're not actually going camping. We do have a roof over our heads and indoor plumbing and heating."

"That's okay," she says, the long snake of traffic ahead of us slithering closer to the speed limit. "This is probably one of those cases where the reality of something wouldn't measure up to the memory."

"You can't go home again."

"You can't go camping again."

"Something like that."

"Something like that."

For the first hour you wonder why you bothered. Malls and sprawl and factories and warehouses and shiny new corporate headquarters and, where there presently exists fields and trees and a big blue sky with big white clouds squatting protectively on top, a large sign that shouts 40 ACRES FOR SALE—PRIME DEVELOPMENT LOCATION! Human beings are like a guest who the earth can't wait to go. We're only here for a little while, but the mess and destruction that comes with being us will take centuries to clean up. This is one of the reasons I live in the city—so I don't have to have my nose rubbed in society's industrial and commercial runoff—but here I am traveling further and further into the ugliness. Then, just after you pass Newmarket, something happens. Brown and green and rocks and water and cows and horses and the sky again, it's okay to look up now. You wonder why you live in the city.

"It's pretty great, isn't it?" Caroline says.

"It really is. We should do this again. We *have* to do this again. I bet it would be even nicer in the summertime."

I wish I could punch myself in the face without Caroline noticing. Because I can't, I immediately attempt to change the subject. "The fall has its advantages, though," I say. "No mosquitoes."

"Just the ones only you can see."

"The ones only... Oh, yeah, right. My floaters."

"You don't mention them much anymore."

"They're still there. I guess I just have other things to think about. Like why coloured marshmallows? What's wrong with white ones?"

"Coloured marshmallows are what we had when I was a kid. I don't know why. It was just what my mum always bought. Even at home for when we had hot chocolate, which sounds kind of gross, I know, but it wasn't. For some reason my sister wouldn't eat the strawberry ones, so those became my favourite."

More fields and farms and forests and little lakes and the first signs of the Canadian Shield, but no cracks from Caroline about how she probably isn't going to be here come summertime, how if I want to make a return visit north next year I'll have to pass a driver's test. She looks better, she sounds better—not a single cough so far, although not having a joint or a cigarette stuck in her mouth undoubtedly helps with that—and she's okay with us avoiding a subject she's never allowed me to avoid before. If we got four flat tires and had to be towed home right now, the trip would still be a success.

•

A couple of hours later, "This is Kinmount coming up," I say. "Just go right through town—it'll only take about a minute, I'm not kidding—and there should be a sign for the 503. That's where we want to get to. It's only about five minutes after that."

"Somebody knows how to use their Google Maps."

"I actually sort of remember this from last time."

"You've stayed up here before?"

"Not stayed. But my ex and I came up here once to check out a place we were sort of thinking about buying. It was near the end of the relationship. That's what usually happens, isn't it? Couples who are drifting apart decide to either have a kid or renovate the house or buy something new they can fix up and sell."

"Your ex. I think I'm starting to see what's going on now. Once you decide to get rid of them, you get your significant other to drive you to a secluded spot so you can easily dispose of their body in the woods. Diabolical *and* lazy."

"You know, that's the second time you quote-unquote joked about me doing away with you."

"Is it? I hadn't noticed. So what happened with the cottage? Problem with the owner?"

"Problem with the buyers," I say. "They decided to break up instead. Hey, quick, check out the town."

The laundromat, the LCBO, the perfunctory post office, the little grocery store, the shabby diner with two bearded, pot-bellied men sitting out front smoking, and that's it, say goodbye, folks, we're already on the other side of Kinmount, Ontario, population can't-be-more-than-your-average-Toronto-subway-car.

"It's like it's from a different decade," Caroline says, making the left turn to get us on the highway. "A different century."

"I know. It's great, isn't it?"

"We should come for lunch tomorrow."

"That's a great idea."

"I think I'll order something deep-fried and absolutely terrible for me."

"I'm sure that's their specialty."

Even the highway is beautiful. Not the blacktop and the yellow line down the middle, but the scenery on either side of the road: boggy, mossy, the leaves on the trees tiny explosions of red and orange and yellow.

"Looks like fall has already gotten here," Caroline says.

"It doesn't feel like autumn until the leaves start to change colours."

"Most of the leaves in the city are still green. I guess they didn't hear about global warming up here."

"They will. Hey, slow down, that's our turnoff: Montgomery Trail."

A dirt road with trees on one side and a river on the other takes us to where we're staying, a tin-roofed, single-level building painted entirely red that belies the term *cottage*—it's more like a funky cantina that flunked geography and ended up in the Haliburton Highlands. There's a canoe on the shore, a hundred feet of riverfront and a wooden dock, and trees so tall you need to look up, way up, to see their tops. We park and get out and stretch, each of us making middle-aged, groaning-after-sitting-for-too-long sounds. Caroline laughs.

"We sound like a couple of old farts," she says.

"I've got news for you. We don't *sound* like old farts. We *are* old farts."

She pops the trunk and between the two of us we manage to grab everything. Because I paid for the cottage, Caroline insisted on supplying the food and bottled water and wine and everything else we'll need for the weekend. I add my bag sitting on the backseat to our load and we walk from the car to the house, but not too quickly, in spite of our mutual pack-mule status.

What's that sound? Silence. What's that smell? Fresh air. Who's that? No one. I feel a little drunk, and when all Caroline says is "Wow," I know she feels the same way. The house key is on top of the hydro meter, just where it's supposed to be, and I grab it and insert it in the door handle and we step inside and set our bags down on the parquet floor. It smells like...a cottage. There's nothing else in the world it could smell like.

"If only they could bottle this smell," I say.

"Memories of the Haliburton Highlands?"

"Whatever they called it, I'd buy a case."

The drapes have been pulled back, and sunshine soaks everything inside, there's no need to turn on a light. It's chillier inside than it is outside, though, so I walk over to the living room, which consists of a couple of cat-scratched old chairs and a couch, a TV and a VHS player and a few cardboard boxes filled with tapes, and a fireplace. I bend down on one knee and open the fireplace door.

"I think you need to put wood inside it for it to work," Caroline says.

"You do have camping experience, don't you?"

"How about if I put everything away and you get this place warmed up?"

"Sounds like a plan."

It takes awhile, but by the time Caroline has stored away the food and hung out fresh towels for us in the bathroom and popped open a bottle of champagne (and not sparkling wine, either, but Cristal Brut, the real thing) and poured some into two

Canada '67 Centennial glasses taken down from the cupboard, a flicker of old-newspaper-abetted flame has turned into a steadily burning fire.

"I'll be honest," she says, handing me my glass, "I wasn't real hopeful you were going to pull it off."

"To be honest, I wasn't so sure either."

"To pleasant surprises," she says, clinking her glass with mine.

We sip and *mmmm* and look out the living room window. The cottage is warming up and the champers is wet and dry and refreshing and here we are at last, snug as a couple of Cristal-drinking bugs, but the sun is dappling dancing on the river and the wind is gently shoving the trees around and we should be outside kicking leaves or going for a canoe ride or something, anything, just as long as it's outside.

"How about a little nap?" Caroline says.

"Good idea," I say.

The bedroom is just a bedroom, but there's a bed in it. Later, afterward, just before I fall asleep, "You smell like when I first met you," Caroline says. When we wake up, it's dark.

•

"It's almost enough, you know?" I say.

Caroline is stretched out on the couch in front of the fire; I'm slumping in the chair as much as is possible without being entirely horizontal.

"Yeah," she says.

"You know what I mean?"

"Yeah."

"Yeah."

It's a *yeah* kind of evening. We hadn't woken up from our nap in time to go for a walk, but making dinner and cleaning up and collecting more wood from the shed and keeping the fire going keeps us busy. Plus, every time I step outside to pee I get smacked in the face with a billion burning stars. The first night of a light-pollution-free vacation isn't the time to contemplate any major life changes, but I can't imagine ever getting used to *that*. Instant ego shrinkage with a simultaneous amplification of worldly wonderment every time you need to take a leak at night: now I finally get why real estate agents talk about *location, location, location*. I feel sorry for Caroline for having to use the heated washroom inside the cottage.

"Should we open another bottle?" she says.

"What time is it?"

"I don't know."

Firelight and no phones or clocks or TV time display, it could be anytime. No—it could only be right now. Aside from a handful of times in my life when I was either high or listening to music or fucking, I don't think I've ever been here before. Right *now*, right *here*: what an oddly pleasant place to be.

"*I don't know* sounds like as good a time as any to open another bottle," I say, getting up. "Keep an eye on the fire while I'm gone."

"Why? It's not going anywhere."

I grab a bottle of wine from the cardboard box on the floor by the kitchen table, and when I return to the living room, she's right, the fire is still there, but Caroline is watching it as if it might actually disappear. I fill her empty glass, then mine, then sit back down and join her. For what feels like several minutes, neither of us says anything—just sip and continue to enjoy the lazily dancing flames.

"It's like you're stoned," I say. "All you want to do is stare."

"I know. It's great, isn't it?"

Sip, look, look, "Yeah," I say, "it is."

Caroline looks at the fire. Caroline sips. I do what Caroline does.

"It's too bad you can't take this feeling with you," I say. "When you get back to the city, I mean."

"You can, if you remember it."

"Yeah, but it's just a memory."

"Everything is just a memory. Well, almost everything. Did you ever notice that?"

"That sounds very Proustian."

"I've never read Proust."

"Me neither. I tried to, a long time ago, but the sentences were too long. By the time I got to the end of most of them, I forgot what he was talking about."

The fire pops. We wait for it to pop again. It doesn't.

"We were talking about memories," Caroline says. "Memories of moments. Good ones, like this one. Doesn't everything end up being memories eventually anyway? When it's all over, if you could look back on it, isn't your life just a bunch of memories? Isn't that what life is? Why should one moment take precedence over another one just because it's more recent, because it happened two minutes ago instead of two years ago?"

The fireplace slowly darkens, the wood begins to smoke, the only light in the room is a few glowing orange coals. "I'll do it," I say, and get down on my knees on the tiled hearth and rearrange the wood that's left unburned and add a couple more small logs and put my face almost inside the fireplace and inhale and blow, inhale and blow, until the flames are crackling again. I pick up my glass and sit back down.

"Why, do you think?" I say. "Why do you think it's so... soothing, or whatever it is. Fire, I mean. It's just a bunch of burning wood."

"Probably something primordial, real caveman stuff. Some people get the same buzz looking at a river or watching waves crash on a beach."

"I get it, but..."

"But what?"

"But why?"

"But why ask why? You could just as easily ask *how*? Like, how can I get more of this into my life?"

Because of the way the chair and the couch are set up, I can look at Caroline, or at least at her profile, without her noticing. Her face is softened, shorn up by shadow, and the worry lines etched into her forehead and the weight she's recently lost are hardly noticeable. I think I'll spend the rest of my life alternating between ogling Caroline and staring transfixed at fire. I'm sure there are more fruitful ways to spend one's time on earth, although at the moment I can't think of any.

"Is that what you were looking for when your ex and you were thinking of buying a place up here?" she says.

"I don't know. I guess I just kind of felt like something was missing. Although if I'd never experienced it before, I guess it doesn't make much sense that I was looking for it, does it?"

"Sure it does. Like I said, it's probably something primal. You didn't know what you were missing—you just knew you were missing *something*. How come it's okay to trust our brains but not our bodies? Sounds like your body was trying to tell you something."

"Too bad I didn't listen better," I say.

"Well, you're listening now. Better late than never."

"Find solace in a cliché, in other words."

"Just because it's a cliché," Caroline says, "doesn't mean it's not true."

•

I wake up wondering where I am, a not entirely unpleasant sensation. Apparently, dozing off in your chair in front of the fireplace is yet another of country life's many charms. A streak of moonlight through the living room window is the room's only illumination, and it takes my eyes a few moments to adjust to the almost complete darkness. Once they do, I see that the fire has gone out and Caroline isn't on the couch. Then I hear her—hear what sounds like her vomiting—and rush to the washroom, in the process smacking my shin on the coffee table. "Fuck," I yell, hopping on one leg in the direction of the noise.

"Are you okay?" I say, standing outside the washroom door, rubbing my shin.

The puking sound has stopped, but there's no response to my question. "Caroline. Are you okay?"

"Can you please not stand right outside the bathroom door?" she says. "I just need a little space, all right?"

"Sorry," I say, but before I can clear out, the painfully guttural sound of deep retching again.

"Caroline, open the door," I say.

"Please go away."

"No, I'm not going to go away. Open the door."

"I'm being sick, Phil."

"Yeah, I know, that's why I want you to open the door."

"Will you please just give me some fucking privacy?"

In spite of what my head says is right, I'm on the verge of doing what she asks for when another blast of hard heaving puts my hand on the bathroom door handle. "I'm coming in," I say, expecting the door to be locked and her to lob back another loud admonition to leave her alone. But the door handle turns easily to the left and the only sound she makes is that of more vomiting. She's on her knees, both hands clinging to the puke-sprayed toilet bowel like a petrified driver clutching the steering wheel of an out-of-control automobile. She coughs a couple of times and wipes her mouth with the back of her hand.

"Are you okay?" I say.

Eventually, "I'm okay," she says.

She's not okay—she's definitely not okay—but "Okay," I say. She doesn't look up and I don't move.

"I think I have to go home," she says.

"That's not a problem."

"In the morning. We don't have to go now. We can wait until morning."

"Whatever you need."

She still hasn't moved and I'm still standing there.

"Let me get cleaned up," she says.

"I'll see you in the bedroom."

I close the bathroom door behind me and turn on the kitchen light so I can get us a couple of bottles of Perrier. The bottled water is in the same plastic sack as the marshmallows. *Four Fun Fruit Flavours*, it says on the bag.

TWENTY-FOUR

I told my mother I'd drop by for a visit sometime mid-week, but coming home a couple days early from up north, I've got time on my hands I'd rather not be at home feeling responsible for filling, so here I am in Etobicoke, the COVID-19 test I did before Caroline and I left for the cottage good enough to get me through the door of Mum's residence on short notice. When it's impossible to be happy oneself, making somebody else feel a little less unhappy can sometimes be the next best thing.

When we returned to the city yesterday Caroline insisted on being alone, said she was feeling better but wanted to take a long hot bath and sleep in her own bed. She didn't get sick again or even cough much on the ride home, and beyond a couple of sincere but likely no less annoying *Are you sures?*, I didn't push. I checked in with her last night before I went to sleep, and even though I worried a bit when the call went straight to voice mail, she eventually phoned back to say she felt okay and thanks for making sure she was doing all right and that she was looking forward to our next scheduled philosophy rap session. "Really?" I said. "Really," she said. She figured that, compared to German idealism, Schopenhauer sounded like light reading.

Out of the cancer-coping frying pan and into the retirement-home fire: halfway down the hall to Mum's room I hear voices. Silence or the assault of a television are acceptable Edgecroft Retirement Village noises, but unidentified people talking in your mother's room isn't the hello you're expecting. Or want to hear. I pick up the pace and don't knock, and there's Mum in her chair by the window and Benjamin sitting beside her and Cameron in her wheelchair beside him, all three of them masked up and surprised to see me. Edgecroft has only recently started to allow more than one visitor per resident at one time, but that's not why I'm surprised to see them. They stop talking as I step into the room. I feel like an interloper.

"Well, speak of the devil," Mum says.

"What have these two been telling you about me?" I say. I don't know what's more surprising: Benjamin and Cameron being here, or me being the topic of conversation.

"I thought you weren't getting back until tomorrow," Benjamin says.

"Miss the pollution and the concrete?" Cameron adds.

"Caroline wasn't feeling great, so we decided to cut it short."

"Is she okay?" Cameron says.

"Oh, yeah, she's fine. I think it was just one of those twenty-four-hour things."

"Who's Caroline?" Mum says.

"Uncle Phil's girlfriend, Grandma," Benjamin says.

"You better not let Debbie find out you've got a girlfriend," Mum says.

"Who's Debbie?" Cameron says.

Before anyone can ask *Who's on first?*, "So what's all this 'speak of the devil?' stuff?" I say.

Cameron looks at Benjamin, who then looks at me, who then looks at his grandmother, who has apparently found something engrossing to look at in the tree outside the window. "I was just saying that Dad wants Cameron and me to come out West for Christmas."

"Oh?" Oh, I get it—Mum thought I was Fred. Until she thought I was cheating on my ex-girlfriend. "Oh, okay."

"Why don't we give you a few minutes alone with your mother, Phil? We were just getting ready to leave anyway. You can meet up with us in the lobby when you're ready, if you want."

"Sure," I say. "If you two don't mind waiting."

"No worries," Benjamin says, getting up from his chair. "We've been here for awhile. We set aside the afternoon to come and see Grams. Bye, Grandma."

"It was very nice to meet you, Helen," Cameron says, and that's that, they're gone. Since when does my snotty nephew relinquish his Saturday afternoon to voluntarily visit his grandmother? Did I really just hear Cameron call my mother *Helen*?

As soon as Benjamin and Cameron have gone, the room becomes too quiet, so I don't have any choice but to try and fill it with small talk. Chit-chat isn't one of my strengths, but my mother put my lousy drawings up on the fridge when I was a kid and my whole life has told me I'm handsome, so I owe her. Humour unto your aging parents as they humored unto you when you were young.

"That was nice of Benjamin and Cameron to come and visit you," I say.

"Benjamin's friend is a cripple."

"Her name is Cameron, Mum, and she's a very talented website designer. Remember the new website for my store that I showed you on the computer in the library? She built that for me."

"Do you remember Donny Smith, the boy who had that disease who played hockey with you boys?"

"Donny Smith. Man. I'd totally forgotten about him. I think he had muscular dystrophy, didn't he?" Or was it cerebral palsy?

"He was a cripple too."

"I think they're called differently-abled now, Mum."

"He could walk, though, Donny. He had those metal things strapped to his legs to keep him from falling over, he didn't need a wheelchair."

I almost correct her again, but *those metal things* are about as good as I can come up with as well to describe the steel walking supports he used to help himself get around. "You're right, he always used to play road hockey with us," I say. "He'd take those metal things off and play defence, on his knees. He wasn't bad, actually. He kind of perfected his own version of the poke check. He'd sweep his stick back and forth like a pendulum. I don't think he ever scored a goal, but he broke up a lot of rushes."

Mum's attention has returned to the tree outside. Its leaves are almost all gone, there aren't any birds perched on its branches, but she seems satisfied to stare, so what's wrong with that? Cats and dogs and the mentally diminished are honest empiricists, looking around at stuff until they're tired, then going to sleep. The rest of us are much too intelligent and complex for that, so we talk and talk as if it matters, as if someone was actually paying attention. Then we go to sleep.

"Caroline—you remember her, don't you, Mum? I told you about her—she's sick. She's really sick. And there's nothing anybody can do about it. There might have been once, but... There's nothing anybody can do about it now."

I join Mum in looking at the tree. I keep hoping something will happen—a bird, a squirrel, a lightning bolt—but it's just a tree without leaves.

"I'm going to miss her, Mum. I'm going to miss her a lot. I know that's not what I should be thinking about—I know I should be feeling bad for her, and I do, I do—but I can't help it. I like my life with her in it. I like my life the way it is now."

"Donny Smith became an accountant," Mum says.

"He did? He's an accountant?"

"Oh, he passed away a long time ago. He was a cripple, you know. But he went to school and got his diploma and worked in an office in Toronto. His mother, she's long gone too. I don't know about the husband. Your father would know. He used to talk to him all the time. You'd have to ask him."

•

—Orange juice? I thought we were on a strict red wine diet tonight.

—We are. I just wanted something sweet to drink. Okay. I'm ready. Let's talk Schopenhauer.

—Are you sure you're up for this?

—For the last time, Phil, yes. Yes, yes, yes. Yes.

—I mean, we can just keep hanging out. We don't have to tackle Schopenhauer tonight.

—I finally get a philosopher who sort of makes sense, who I almost enjoy reading, and you want to put the kibosh on him.

—Okay, well, it's your call. Let's hear what you've got to say about Arthur Schopenhauer, born 1788, died 1860.

—Well, for one thing, he's funny. He's *German* and he's funny. Talk about an oxymoron.

—I don't know if I'd call him funny...

—Witty, then.

—I'll buy that. He doesn't suffer fools, that's for sure.

—He's the first one we've read who sounds like an actual person who's actually speaking directly to the reader. I want that in an author. I *need* that. And it doesn't matter if he's a philosopher or a historian or a novelist.

—He writes well.

—He writes well.

—So he can put together a nice sentence—agreed. What about what he actually has to say?

—What about a little grade-A medical marijuana first?

—I've already had—we've already had—quite a bit of grade-A red wine already.

—And your point is?

—That if we combine the two, we might miss Schopenhauer's point.

—You leave the Schopenhauer to me and light this up while I fetch us another bottle.

—It's your house, so your rules, I guess.

—What?

—I said, "Your house, your rules." Hey, what's that on the kitchen table?

—I finished my preserving.

—When did you do that?

—Today.

—You were supposed to be taking it easy.

—I was. I am. It was such a beautiful day for it. Open-up-all-the-windows-and-let-in-the-fresh-air weather. I finished reading the Schopenhauer in the backyard before it got too cool. And I've got to say: all in all, I'm pretty pleased with how my preserving turned out. I set aside a couple of jars of beets on the counter for you to take home with you, so don't forget. How's that spliff?

—First class, as usual. Here.

—Promise you won't panic if I cough?

—Puff and cough away. Here, let me open that bottle.

—Just a splash for me—I want to be able to appreciate this bud.

—Smart move. So. Fully fortified with artificial stimulants, where were we? Oh, yeah: you were about to explain Arthur Schopenhauer to me.

—It's all about the world as your representation, Phil.

—I get the reference—very clever—but you're going to have to do better than that.

—Okay, well, like Kant—

—Nice allusion, by the way.

—Thank you. Like Kant, Schopenhauer argued that the phenomenal world isn't really what it seems, but is actually what we create with our minds.

—I'm not saying it's your explanation, but it made a bit more sense when the book said he was sort of a German Buddhist.

—Right. The world is illusion and the key to being free from this illusion is to cease striving and wanting.

—But what fun is that? We've already talked about this. So you don't desire anymore—no more illusions, but no more learning or lusting or trying.

—But art though....

—Music in particular...

—Music for Schopenhauer is the greatest of all art forms. When we're inside it, it's like we almost stand outside desire and striving. I think that's what he means.

—I think Nietzsche said it better: "Without music life would be a mistake."

—Hey, no fair, no skipping ahead.

—I wasn't. Everybody knows that one.

—Yeah.

—Yeah.

—

—

—This is good pot.

—It is. It is good pot.

—*Cough cough cough.*

—

—Thank you for not asking me if I was okay.

—No, but…

—

—I think I was right about the, uh…I mean, I don't think it's such a good idea to mix philosophy and marijuana.

—We're done with Schopenhauer anyway.

—We are?

—Well, *I'm* done with him.

—You don't think we…you don't think we skimped a bit on our discussion?

—We can still discuss—it doesn't have to be about Schopenhauer. Do you remember when you first asked me if I wanted to do this philosophy thing with you?

—Sure.

—Did you really think it was because I was eager to spend what time I had left boning up on a couple of centuries of Western philosophy? I mainly did it so we could spend time together in an interesting way.

—But you always did the reading. You've enjoyed it.

—Of course I have. It was like when I was—*cough cough cough*—when I was twelve and I joined the Girl Guides because I wanted to wear nylons. Once I became a Guide, though, I got into collecting the badges.

—Wait a minute: which one am I? The nylons or the badges?

—At last we've unearthed the definitive philosophical question: Who am I? Nylons or badges?

—Either way, I've enjoyed it. All of it.

—Me too. It's been good. *This* is good.

—Yeah, it is.

—

—

—Hey, where are you going?

—I'm going to put the kitchen radio on. I want to hear some music.

—I still can't believe you don't have any CDs or an iPod or even any stuff downloaded to your laptop.

—I like it this way. You turn on the station and you don't know what you're going to get. It could be bebop, it could be solo piano, it could be a torch ballad.

—It could also be a commercial or the weather or, even worse, the news.

—It could be. Sometimes it will be. But then it's music again, and I like being surprised.

—Whatever works for you, I guess. Hey, what was that for?

—It wasn't for anything. I just felt like kissing you.

—That's a good enough reason for me.

—

—

—Wasn't dinner good tonight?

—If you're looking for compliments, you've come to the right place. Dinner was delicious. I still can't believe those carrots came from your garden. They were so sweet. They were like candy.

—That's where carrots come from—the ground.

—Yeah, I know, but it was *your* ground, *your* garden.

—You did your part too. I never knew just how perfectly coloured marshmallows completed a meal.
—You thought I'd forgotten about them, didn't you?
—*I'd* forgotten about them.
—You said you'd looked all over town for them. I wasn't going to let all that hard work be in vain.
—Tonight was fun, wasn't it? Our walk in the park, dinner, this—all of it was good, wasn't it?

—

—You mean it wasn't?

—

—Phil?

—

—

—Is what's happening...Is what's happening what I think is happening?
—Was tonight good or not?
—It was good. And tomorrow night could be good too. And the night after that, and the night after that. Remember your radio station? You might be surprised. But you have to turn it on and listen to find out.
—Phil.
—What?
—Stop. Please. Please stop.
—Stop what? You know, I was thinking we should go straight to Nietzsche next. What do you say? You said you were looking forward to reading him, right? I can't claim to know very much about him, but you said you liked the sound of him so I peeked ahead a bit, I admit, and I've got a feeling he's the real deal, you were right, we might actually enjoy reading him. Imagine that: reading a philosopher and enjoying it.

—Hold my hand.

—Don't worry, I didn't actually get into any of his ideas—not really—I was just mainly skimming through what they said about his life. Like how he broke down in the street embracing a horse that was being beaten by a coachman, and that that was basically it, he never recovered, spent the last eleven years of his life as a vegetable. Not *vegetable*... what's the right word for "vegetable"? I'm not being a dick, I honestly don't know. "Comatose," maybe? Does comatose sound right?

—Hold my other hand.

—It was weird, though—don't you think it's weird?—that for a guy who's the godfather of death-of-God theology and every strain of contemporary nihilism and relativism and existentialism, he also believed in this idea of eternal recurrence.

—Mhmm.

—I mean, it seems like he actually believed that with an infinite amount of time and a finite number of events, everything was fated to happen all over again, he actually thought it was logically inevitable.

—

—

—I suppose it *is* logically possible, but so are an infinite number of monkeys and an infinite number of typewriters writing Shakespeare's plays, right? It might be possible, but it's so entirely unlikely, why bother thinking about it? Right?

—Right.

—

—

—This is hard.

—I know.

—

—

—Hey, I almost forgot. There was something I wanted to tell you about Betty. About one of my favourite Betty Boards. After the Dead came back to the U.S. from doing a few shows in Egypt in the fall of '78, they sounded better than they had in a long time. Refreshed. Rejuvenated. The second half of 1979 is when I get off the bus—it's a not-so slow descent into arena-rock Dead from that point on—but whether it was because they'd been off the road for a month and were well-rested and horny to play again or because their first gigs once they returned stateside were at home, in San Francisco, those five shows they did at Winterland in October of '78 were crackling with energy, just crackling. And there's an especially hot "Stella Blue" from the second-to-last night that contains one of *those* Grateful Dead moments, the ones you wait for and hope for but that don't always materialize, at least not every night.

—

—

—At one point during Jerry's solo it sounds like his soul is crying, like his very fucking soul is crying—just *wailing*. And it's crying for all of us, for everybody listening, even if none of us, including Jerry, have a clue why it's all so terribly sad and yet so incredibly fucking beautiful.

—

—

—But at around the seven-minute mark, still during Garcia's solo—you can really hear it if you're wearing headphones—the sound quality suddenly sucks, either because of a bad tape change or the machine stopped working or somebody screwed up somehow, and the producers of the CD use an audience tape to patch up the two or three minutes when the soundboard drops out. This thing—this beautiful, beautiful thing—is still there, but just barely, only faintly, like it's floating around in your headphones in the hissy mist of oblivion that's really just somebody's crappy-sounding audience tape from nearly forty-five years ago. You're pissed off and disappointed because of what you're not hearing, but still grateful and blessed because of what you are. And somehow it's even more beautiful because of it. Because it's almost not there, but it is, it is still there. Somewhere.

—

—

—What do you want me to do?

—Nothing. Just.... just be here with me.

—Yeah, but...

—But what?

—Jesus Christ, Caroline, this is difficult enough...

—What do you want to know?

—I don't know. How about—I can't believe I'm actually saying this—how about what I'm supposed to... What am I supposed to do?

—When it's over?

—Yeah.

—I'm going to go to sleep, that's all. Don't worry, I won't be in any pain. I'm going to go—*cough cough cough*—I'm going to go to sleep, that's all. Except I won't wake up. Then I want you to go home.

—But—

—But nothing, Phil. I've taken care of everything. The organization I bought the medicine from has done this before, believe me. And they don't just hand it out like Halloween candy. The proper steps have been taken. Arrangements have been made. Everything has been looked after.

—But what about... I don't know...

—Everything's been taken care of.

—

—Okay?

—

—Okay?

—Okay.

—

—

—Would you turn the radio up a little louder?

—The radio?

—The radio in the kitchen.

—I know where it is... The radio. Right. Okay.

—

—Do you need anything while I'm in here.

—Just for you to come back after you've turned it up.

—

—

—Now what?

—Now sit back down beside me.

—Okay.

—

—Do you want some more water?

—No. Hold my hands harder. I want to feel you.

—Christ, Caroline...

—I thought you were an agnostic.

—Don't make me laugh.

—It was just a... just a simple question.

—I'm serious, don't make me laugh.

—They say it's... they say it's the best medicine.

—

—

—You know what I just remembered? We never watched *The Bachelor.* We were going to watch some crap together some night, remember? Some of yours, some of mine. After we were done with our philosophy some night. We still haven't watched *The Bachelor.*

—Mhmm...

—

—

—When do you take... when do you take, you know, the pills...

—It's a liquid. That you take with something sweet. I already have.

—

—

—How long before it...

—Tighter. Hold my hands tighter.

—Is that too tight?

—No. That's nice. That's good.

—

—

—Are you awake?

—Uhm hhm.

—Open your eyes and look at me, okay?

—I'm awake.

—Just for a moment, okay? This old customer of mine—actually, he's a friend, his name is Zoran—he's Serbian, and they have this tradition over there when they're shaking hands or drinking a toast, you have to look the other person in the eyes while you're doing it in order for them to know that you really mean it. It's considered bad form and bad luck if you don't.

—That's nice. That's... that's really nice.

—So do it, okay?

—Okay.

—

—

—Caroline, you've got to open your eyes. Just for a second. C'mon.

—Your eyes.

—My eyes are already open. Now open yours. I know you're tired, but just try, okay? Just for a moment.

—Okay.

—

—

—Caroline.

—

—*Caroline.*

—

—*Caroline?*

TWENTY-FIVE

"Just put it anywhere over there. I'll sort out what to do with it later."

Another box, another something to deal with some other time, another day of who-knows-where-the-time-goes. But it goes. No matter how early I come into the store in the morning, it's usually dark outside before I'm through with what I set out to do. It stays light out later and later every day, though, which is always good for business. I'm a long way from being done setting everything up the way I want it, but while it's an in-progress mess, Parkdale Books is open for physically distanced, no-more-than-three-customers-at-a-time business. Owning your own building helps, but a second-hand bookseller can't afford to turn customers away.

Caroline left me her house. Her sister got everything else, I got the house. The only condition was that I sell her place and use the money to buy a building that would become my new bookstore. There wasn't anyone around for me to say *It's too much* or *No, I couldn't* to, so seven months later Parkdale Books exists. The foot traffic won't be as good as it was near the old store, but Parkdale real estate is cheaper, and not having to write a landlord a cheque the first of every month will definitely make up for diminished business. Also on the plus side, I can walk to work now, so if I happen to miss a day at the gym because I'm busy with the store I can still manage to get in a decent bit of exercise. *Healthy body, healthy mind*, someone long dead said, I forget who. And knowing who did wouldn't make it any more true.

"Okay, that's the last of them," Benjamin says. "Anything else before I go?"

"No, that's good. Thanks."

"Are you heading out too?"

"Nah. There are still those shelves along the back wall left to paint. And if I do manage to get that done tonight, I really need to start processing these books. Where are you off to?"

"Cameron's. We're going to get some takeout from this new vegan comfort food place on College."

"Have fun. I almost forgot, we're supposed to talk tomorrow morning about tweaking the website. I better write myself a note."

"All right, I'll leave you to it. See you later."

"See you later."

And there's another note I need to make: Benjamin will be starting graduate school soon—something theory-based, something interdisciplinary, something so crushingly boring-sounding I forget exactly what it is—and scored a teaching assistantship, so I'll need to hire some part-time help come September. When the leaves are just starting to appear on the trees again it seems impossible that one day they're going to fall off, but they haven't not yet, and I don't suppose this year will be any different. Of course, there's no guarantee that I'll be around to notice it when the time comes, but that's never been any different either. You make a note to yourself, you stick it on the wall, you hope you'll be alive to read it. Repeat.

I should get the painting out of the way, but I'd rather catalogue books, and who's going to complain if I do? I slip Dave's

Picks # 23, 01/22/78 disc number three, into the CD player behind the counter and turn it up, the Dead almost past their creative peak by this point, but with still a few aural surprises and pleasures left to offer. And no matter the period, there's always something worth paying attention to if you listen closely enough. "Terrapin Station" into "Drums" into "The Other One" into "Space" into "St. Stephen" into "Not Fade Away" into "Around and Around" is worth it.

In spite of the joyful wail of Jerry's guitar, I resist the desire to spark up a spliff—I also inherited Caroline's substantial stash—will save it for later, when I'm at home and the day is done, while listening to *In a Silent Way* and putting up some new shelves for my expanding jazz CD collection. I've been listening to a lot of Miles Davis lately, particularly the jazz-rock and jazz-funk stuff from the late sixties and early seventies. I've got a fair bit of it now, but there's almost as much that I don't. I'm going to need a lot of shelves. And now that my bedroom is my bedroom again and is filled with only my books, and not the store's, I've got room.

Just as the band is snaking their way out of "Space" and into "St. Stephen"—on a good night, which McArthur Court, University of Oregon, 01/22/78, is, the transition from one song to the next is simultaneously inevitable and unpredictable and not to be neglected—the bell attached to the door tinkles. Just when I was finally making some headway on the books. Man, I missed the sound of that bell.

"Well, well. So this is the new thing with you. This is something I did not foresee as happening."

Zoran stands in the middle of the store, carefully looking left, looking right, even making a point of giving the ceiling a good going-over as part of his scrupulous inspection process. He's attired in his customary grey fedora and blue suit jacket, but the dog at the end of the leash in his right hand isn't Tesla, isn't a pug, is an undersized German shepherd. He sees me looking at the dog.

"Dragan, down," he says, and the dog immediately drops to the floor, head between his two front paws.

"Dragon?" I say.

"Dragan. Is very popular Serbian name. Is name of old friend of mine when I was young man. This man, he is no longer alive now."

"Oh, right. You were going to go back to Serbia—to your village—for a visit. How was it?"

"You were one who said I should go for visit, not me. Instead I go to City of Toronto Humane Society and get Dragan. Very abused, this dog. In crate all day. Starved. Abused by very bad people."

All of which might be true, but today, anyway, Dragan looks well-fed and canine content and is out making the neighbourhood rounds on a cool spring night with his devoted human companion. "He looks pretty happy now," I say.

"Oh, yes, he is happy boy now. Dragan, sit." Dragan shoots up and plunks his back end on the floor. "These type of dog, they need constant stimulation and discipline. He was wild animal when I get him. *Wild.* Bark all the time, jump up on person, afraid of even going for walk, this dog. Imagine this: young dog who is locked in crate all the time does not want to go outside for walk because is afraid of being brought back to place like he was at before."

"That must have been rough," I say. "For you, I mean."

"Rough for me, yes—I have been very, very busy training him, and this is not easy thing to do with abused dog who does not trust any person—but is worse for him. Much worse. This dog, for long time, he does not know how to play, to show affection, he even does not wag his tail for long time. Is that not right, Dragan?" Zoran says, to which Dragan answers with a few powerful wags of his bushy black and tan tail.

"It's good to see you, Zoran," I say.

"It is good to see you as well, Phil. This place—this is your store now, yes?"

"It's mine."

"This makes me happy. I miss store. Was nice to browse at your house where you live, but a bookstore, this is as it should be, yes?"

"Yeah. I feel the same way."

"Look at us, Phil. Me with German shepherd and you with new store. Everything turns out just the way it wasn't supposed to, yes?"

"Feel free to look around, Zoran. Not everything is in order, and not everything is here yet, but... you know."

"Yes, yes, of course. Dragan, come."

Zoran and Dragan proceed to browse the half-empty shelves, and I go back to working through the stack of uncatalogued books piled on the counter. It's a nice collection—lots of first editions with plenty of biography, poetry, essays, and history. Especially history. I purchased the entire collection from a well-read ex-postal worker. I'll do my best to help find her books good homes. They deserve it.

MAY 15

—Nietzsche was born in 1844 and brought up to be a Lutheran minister, studied to be a classical philologist, ended up as an academic outcast and itinerant philosopher/poet.

—Many people believe that Nietzsche was the first modern philosopher, that all subsequent philosophy is a footnote to his ideas; Nietzsche argued that all supposed "truths," except for scientific truths, are illusions, and that all religious, metaphysical, and moral beliefs are relative.

—Scientific truths are undeniably factually true, but can't supply human beings with values, can't give meaning to life.

—In Thus Spake Zarathustra *Nietzsche wrote of the three metamorphoses of the spirit: of how the spirit becomes a camel who takes on the burden of acknowledging sometimes painful realities, of how the camel becomes a lion that destroys false beliefs, of how the lion becomes a child who creates new values.*

—The camel caries the load, the lion demolishes the bogus, but only the child can give human existence meaning. "The child is innocence and forgetting," he wrote, "a new beginning, a game, a self-propelled wheel, a first movement, a sacred 'Yes.'"

—Yes *is a good place to stop.*